Wild Swans of Innisfree

(first mystery in the Pia Jo Borg series)

by Lorie Odegaard

Order this book online at www.trafford.com
or email orders@trafford.com

Most Trafford titles are also available at major online book retailers.

Printed in Victoria, BC, Canada.

ISBN: 978-1-4269-2513-9 (sc)

Library of Congress Control Number: 2009913769

*Our mission is to efficiently provide the world's finest, most comprehensive book publishing
service, enabling every author to experience success. To find out how to publish your book, your
way, and have it available worldwide, visit us online at www.trafford.com*

Trafford rev. 1/05/2010

www.trafford.com

North America & international
toll-free: 1 888 232 4444 (USA & Canada)
phone: 250 383 6864 ♦ fax: 812 355 4082

For Belle Kerman, because of her infectious enthusiasm

ACKNOWLEDGEMENTS

Since a mystery writer cannot hope to achieve a measure of authenticity without the help of interested and knowledgeable people in the field of Criminal Investigation and elsewhere, my heartfelt thanks and appreciation go to the following sources of much-needed information:

Clifford W. Van Meter, Director of the Police Training Institute of the University of Illinois; Ernest L. Neumann, Deputy Director of the Illinois State Police Academy, Springfield, Illinois; Dirck Harris, printing specialist, Bureau of Alcohol, Tobacco & Firearms, Department of the Treasury, Washington, DC; Diane R. Williams, Administrative Assistant, Galena Area Chamber of Commerce, Galena, Illinois; Brian R. Melton, Chief Deputy, Jo Daviess County Sheriff's Office, Galena, Illinois; Steve Endress ("Dewey"), Correctional Officer (and tour guide), Jo Daviess County Sheriff's Office, Galena, Illinois; Sergeant Thomas Contre of the Crystal Lake, Illinois Police Department; and the Reference Librarians at the Crystal Lake, Illinois Public Library. The technical help given me by my son-in-law, Jack Kovachy, has also been invaluable.

I am deeply grateful, too, to literary and artistic greats whose varied genius has provided me with allusions that distinguish ordinary circumstances.

Lead Mines, Prairie du Loup, and other locales featured in *Wild Swans of Innisfree* are largely fictional, as are the characters and events. But since all worthwhile fiction springs, not from a vacuum, but from real life, I have tried to give them an aura of verisimilitude.

I will arise and go now, and go to Innisfree,
And a small cabin build there, of clay and wattles made;
Nine bean-rows will I have there, a hive for the honey-bee,
And live alone in the bee-loud glade."

William Butler Yeats (1865-1939)

Excerpt from *Wild Swans of Innisfree*

The residents of Cranshaw had obviously become aware that a chase was in progress, for some of them laughed and clapped their hands, some screamed, and some hooted as Ox-Eye clamped the sombrero on his head and shouted "Olé" and Pia Jo guided the Jeep through the Fair. But the chase did not abate, and soon a tempestuous wind dislodged a dancing, hot-purple balloon in the shape and size of a man from its moorings and attached it to the Caddy's antenna, where it whipped and gyrated in eccentric synch with Cranshaw's rock 'n' roll band.

- 1 -

Lit by a new moon with minimal power to illumine the dark places where the thickest shadows fell, and deserted by all but a family of raccoons and a Great Horned Owl, the cemetery beckoned eerily. Standing by the undistinguished Le Car that she and Reo had purchased together, Pia Jo stared into the darkness and shivered in her thin nightgown. Aware that the chill she felt was not entirely the result of the upper Midwest late-May climate, she reached into the car for a sweater, a small torch, and a sheaf of mixed lavender and white lilacs; slipping into the sweater and shrugging off the fear that was threatening to immobilize her, she mounted a small hill and followed the beam of light along a path to her mother's grave.

Vexed by the intrusion, the owl let out five penetrating hoots, while the eyes of the silent raccoons shone like beacons from the nearby bushes. Determined not to be faint-hearted, Pia Jo continued to circle the old-fashioned headstones, her thoughts on Reo and their perplexing relationship. She needed to talk to someone who would understand her scattered emotions. While Uncle Sven and his partner/wife Thelma were empathetic souls, their feelings for one another were settled and uncomplicated.

Reaching the resting place, she flashed her torch on its simple headstone, which had been placed, mysteriously and anonymously, on the grave early in May, and read again the inscription that had puzzled them all so much:

Emeline Tillotson Borg—1930-1994
Oh, there will pass with your great passing
Little of beauty not your own,
Only the light from common water,
Only the grace from simple stone.

Pia Jo's mother, Emeline, had died unexpectedly two weeks before Christmas the previous year, and Pia Jo hadn't discovered the headstone until she and Reo visited the cemetery after they arrived at Innisfree in late May, and after spending an hour searching for the poem in Uncle Sven's books at Scandia (her own books were in the apartment in Chicago), she'd identified it as "Elegy Before Death" by Edna St. Vincent Millay. When she'd questioned siblings and friends, none of them had a clue as to the identity of the donor. A few years after her husband, Gustav Borg, had disappeared, Emeline had obtained the title to their farm; and she hadn't married again; nor had she had any lovers that they knew of. They'd all concluded that she hadn't told them all her secrets.

Placing the fragrant flowers on the grave, she conjured up an image of the living, breathing Emeline, her arms full of mixed flowers from her spectacular garden at Rendezvous of the Four Winds on the outskirts of Prairie du Loup. She'd been ill all the previous fall, but no one had expected her to die, at least not until that final week.

Slipping into the sweater and seating herself on the edge of the grave, Pia Jo surveyed the burial plot critically and mentally saluted her brother Gunter and her Uncle Sven, who had planted flowering trees, a crabapple and a cherry, a few yards from the grave to give it shade; and Aunt Thelma, who'd planted a mock orange bush nearby. Characteristically, Soren and Lena, who were takers, not givers, hadn't bothered to remember. A large pot containing a white rosebush stood to one side, no doubt from Elise and Arturo, pristinely suggesting ethereal beauty. Pia Jo had called her sister earlier in the week and had asked her to visit Emeline's grave with her, but Elise had said she'd send a plant— as usual, Arturo took up most of her time. Now Pia Jo was glad she'd come alone. Elise hadn't even wanted to meet Reo so could offer no much-needed advice.

"I miss you, Emeline! I wanted to spend my December break with you, but Reo was eager to finish the paintings for his exhibit, and he didn't tell me that Gunter had called and urged me to come." Tears began to gather and slip down her cheeks. "And now I need your advice desperately. My love for Reo is blinding me, I guess, and I'm hurting because he seems to be tiring of me after our three years together."

She paused to search for a tissue in her sweater pocket, and after dabbing at her tears and blowing her nose vigorously, she continued her reminiscing, "I know you weren't keen on Reo—his tastes in art are so ultra mod, and he didn't hesitate to let you know that he thought the garden art you cherished was commonplace, dated, and effete. And he didn't really need me to be on hand when he painted the final pieces for his exhibit—you needed me much more!"

Her tears were flowing again, but she went on in spite of them. "We've argued about his failure to tell me you were so ill, and I've threatened to leave; but a beauty named Tabitha is waiting around for me to do just that, and I'm not sure I can let him go. I guess I shouldn't blame Elise for being Arturo's slave—I gave Reo every bit of time I could spare from my classes and the play I was directing, and all because of Tabbie Tabor. She's so sexy, and she really likes Fauve art while I only pretend I do. And now you're gone and I can't make it up to you. I can't forgive myself and I can't forgive Reo. What shall I do, Mom?"

She sat for a while, thinking about Reo, who'd been so negatively articulate about her mother's taste in Art, her love for Nature, and her refusal to sell any of Rendezvous' sixty acres. Emeline had been civil to him—that was her way. She hadn't denounced him in return, but neither had she expressed a syllable of approval.

Sensing a presence, she looked up suddenly, and her eyes grew big and round; Emeline was there, her worry lines erased, her smile reassuring. In an instant the impression fled, but it was so strong that Pia Jo remained where she was and basked in the afterglow. Pondering the tiny mystical experience, she said, "I love you, Mom," and returned to the car, her problem with Reo unresolved.

Back at Cabin 6, she parked the car in its customary place and went inside as quietly as she could; but when she closed the door, the sound prompted a call from the bedroom where Reo'd been sleeping. "Peejay, is that you? Where've you been?" His tone strongly suggested that he wasn't pleased.

"Yeah, hon—it's me. I couldn't sleep so I drove around a while." She kicked off her slip-ons, shrugged out of her sweater, and crawled in beside him, hoping her face wasn't still wet from her tears.

It was. "You've been grieving for your mother again! Peejay, it's been six months. Come here, bambina—I'll cheer you up."

She didn't object to his passionate embrace, of course, but she couldn't stop her thoughts. "Bambina! I'm thirty-two, I have a Master's degree in the Fine Arts, and I'm State Certified in Criminal Investigation. And he treats me like a teenager who can be pacified by sex."

While Reo worked on another wildly-colorful painting for his summer exhibit the next morning, Pia Jo donned khaki shorts and an olive T-shirt and drove to Herman's Food Mart, the one grocery store in the area. While there, she swung around to the Sheriff's Headquarters to say "Hi" to her brother Gunter, who was serving his second term as Sheriff of Berger County and had his quarters in a sprawling brick building not far from Herman's on the edge of Lead Mines.

Before Gunter's time, the Offices of Public Safety, thus dubbed by some dedicated bureaucrat, had been an integral part of the Berger County Courthouse, a National Historic Site on Court Street that had been erected in the 1800's; but the ancient building had been so cold and gloomy that a prisoner, a Viet Nam veteran who'd been accused of bombing a warehouse and had finally been freed for lack of evidence, had rigged up a humongous bomb and had blasted the Offices of Public Safety right off the courthouse's historically valuable but readily erodible rear. The vet must have felt some sympathy for the other prisoners, for he'd warned the dispatcher anonymously that he'd planted the bomb and that it was set to go off in two hours. His thoughtful warning had given the officers enough time to evacuate the building.

When Pia Jo had asked Gunter how the former sheriff had known who'd planted the bomb, he'd assured her that disgruntled bomb experts were scarce in Berger County and any idiot could have figured out who the guilty party was. But he added that the veteran had done him a good turn because an office in the former Public Safety Building would not have been a comfortable place in which to conduct the county's criminal affairs. Since the ancient courthouse had been cramped between two other National Historic Sites on a hillside that was the delight of children on sleds but a perpetual trial to busy crime fighters, the County Board had approved a handier site for the new Offices of Public Safety, which were now simply labeled "Sheriff's Headquarters"; and with an eye on the convenient transport of prisoners from the detention areas to the courtroom, the Board had also purchased the adjacent land to erect a new courthouse when the County could afford to do so.

When Pia Jo had parked the tiny Le Car in the ample parking space, she hurried into the large dispatching area, where some of the officers had gathered to discuss their assignments. "Hi, lil sis!" The heavyset man leaning against the dispatcher's desk greeted her with the informally affectionate tone he reserved for her.

She glared a response. "Will you please tell me, Gunter, why people treat me like a child? Reo calls me 'bambina,' Britt calls me 'sweetheart,' and you call me 'lil sis.' Blue, please tell Sheriff Borg that I'm a grown woman."

Chief Deputy Blue Feather's white teeth flashed mischievously in his nut brown face. "Don't pay any attention to lovers or brothers, *little bird*. I'll take care of you." Working on papers at another desk, Blue's younger brother Windy, in training as a deputy and now Jack of all jobs, guffawed.

Melissa Austin, the daytime dispatch sergeant, turned from the map she was mounting on a wall and defended Pia Jo stoutly. "She can out-think and out-draw you, Windy, so show her some respect."

Seeing that the conversation was going nowhere, Pia Jo said "Thanks, Lissy," and abruptly changed the subject. "That's a map of Apple Mountain, isn't it? This is Martin Diver's valley farm? And here's Casper Antonin's horse ranch near the top?" She touched the colored thumbtacks as she scanned the crude map.

"You're right, Pia Jo! Windy thought it was a sketch of Eagle Cliff." Melissa, a lively redhead with a smile that could freeze water or melt ice, laughed maliciously. "Why would we have a map of a mountainous area in another county?" Her laugh became a groan. "We have seventeen districts to cover, and those two wild men are about to shoot one another over some dead sheep."

"Where were you last night, trinket?" Gunter interrupted. "Your heartthrob called me in the middle of the night—wanted to know if you'd gone to Rendezvous."

"I took some lilacs out to Mom's grave, *little boy blue*."

"In the middle of the night?"

"Yes, in the middle of the night! I needed someone understanding to talk to—Melissa needed to sleep and the rest of you are about as sympathetic as vultures circling a corpse."

Since they all knew that Pia Jo had been especially close to her mother, the atmosphere of the office suddenly sobered. Remembering his own double grief, the sheriff cleared his throat, shook his head, and said, "You gotta pull yourself together, Peejay. Mom's been gone for six months an' grievin' won't bring her back. An' now that you're State Certified, I'll be needin' your help this summer."

Pia Jo looked her skepticism. "Doing what? This is a low-population area, and you already have a chief deputy, five sergeants, and eight road deputies, not to mention your correctional officer and your detectives. With a staff like that, you should be able to cover every unincorporated village in the state of Illinois. I'm thinking of taking my expertise elsewhere—I'll die of boredom here."

Gunter eyed her speculatively, as though seeing her for the first time. "Low-population maybe, but we got two long shifts and a lotta miles to cover. Besides, I now have only four sergeants—two road, one records, an' one dispatch," he finally rebutted. "My investigations sergeant had a heart attack and has been advised t' quit the Force. I need you t' stop scoffin' and do some official detectin'."

Pia Jo's eyes came alive. "Really? Who'd I report to if you don't have a chief detective?"

"You'd report to me, that's who. Or to Blue if I'm not around. As Liz said, we've got a caseload that would choke a hippo, an' I can't spare anyone—in fact, I need t' hire a couple o' brainy dicks."

"That's not fair!" Windy protested loudly. "I applied to be a detective long before she came, and you're training me for everything except detecting. Anyway, she hasn't had a training period, so she's not qualified—."

Sheriff Borg gave him such a scorching look that he stopped in mid-sentence. "Not qualified? She aced most of her courses, both at the U an' at th' Police Academy. She's helped me out on her vacations ever since I became sheriff. An' as an actor and a Theatre teacher, she knows how to write focused reports an' act out dozens of roles. Besides, she's got me to advice her—how damn qualified does she need to be?"

Pia Jo was deep in thought. "I'll have to talk this over with Reo—he's getting ready for his summer exhibit, and he needs me—."

"Whadda you mean he needs you? Why does that twit need you to help him daub his God-awful paint combos on his canvasses? Sure, Lu's a heck of a nice girl, but her brother's got a bad case of self-o-mania."

His sister's temper flared, perhaps because, deep down, she knew he was right. "Must you be so contemptuous of Reo?" she demanded. "You know very well *Les Fauves Nouvelles* exhibits are well attended. All the *fauves* loved color, and some of them are still very much in demand—for example, Matisse."

"There ain't nothin' wrong with color—I like it myself. But I can't say I much favor yellow squirrels and red owls. You ever seen a red owl, Blue?"

Chief Deputy Wovoka's full name was Blue Feather Wovoka; Blue Feather was his Winnebagan Thunder clan name, while his grandfather had added the name "Wovoka" to honor the Paiute self-styled messiah who had originated the famous Ghost Dance. Now he chuckled and said, "I saw one on a store sign once. I remember asking my mom if they sold red owls there." He waited for Melissa to respond to a call, then said, "It's Martin Diver, isn't it?"

"Mmmm. He wants to know when you're going to stop dragging your feet and find the dogs or wolves that ripped his sheep open."

"Tell 'im I'm takin' this case myself," Gunter said testily. "I gotta do some serious crime prevention or we'll have a double homicide on our hands. Windy, stop grumblin' about paper work or I'll put you on kitchen duty—and pray you won't poison our prisoners. Melissa, talk some sense into Pia Jo." A hands-on sheriff, Gunter abhorred paper work and often assigned it to the communal secretary or anyone who wasn't busy with something more important. Now he rose, gulped the remains of his cold coffee, and reached for his hat. At the door he turned back to address his sister. "You want t' do some pokin' for me or don'tcha?"

She'd been pondering his offer, and now she nodded. "Why not? I can't keep my mind on anything else. But it had better be more challenging than the pre-certification assignments you gave me—this time I want credentials and I want to dig up the evidence myself. Who's been murdered?"

"Nobody—at least not yet. I want you to find out who stole the Roshnikov emeralds, that's all."

She stared at him, dumbfounded. "But that wasn't a Berger County crime—that's for the Lead Mines Police Department to solve."

"Not any longer. They've had six months, an' the Roshnikovs are gettin' ready to sue the Lead Mines Police Department for draggin' their feet, ignorin' citizens' rights, an' a host of other malfeasances. They raised such a stink that Jack Gramm asked me if I had a Sam Spade I could lend him for a coupla weeks."

"Chief Gramm asked you for help? How come?"

"Because he's short-handed, that's why. He recently had to fire his chief detective and two officers. Look, are you interested or not?"

"Of course I'm interested, but that case is colder'n the Iditarod Trail in January." The theft of the famous diamond and emerald necklace had been the talk of Lead Mines when she and Reo had driven up from Chicago for her mother's funeral in mid-December, but her grief had prevented the chatter from penetrating far into her brain. Since Lead Mines was the jurisdiction of the police department, Gunter, too, had virtually ignored the theft. And now the trail was probably so faint that even Natty Bumppo couldn't pick up the scent.

Gunter shrugged and hitched up his gun belt. "It's your decision. If you don't need the $10,000 the Roshnikovs are offerin' for the return of the Emerald necklace, I'll put you on somethin' easier."

"Ten thousand dollars? Okay, I'll do it!" But disappointment soon dimmed her enthusiasm. "As a sheriff's or police detective, I couldn't accept prize money for solving a case, Gunter—some legal beagle would be bound to object. I'd have to work for less'n ten bucks an hour."

"Yeah, you're right," Gunter agreed reluctantly. "Helen's ambulance chaser would relish shootin' you down as much as he's relishin' tryin' to take Ulf away from me, an' he can make a case outta a scratch on a paper doll. But you can go talk to the Roshnikovs an' get 'em to hire you privately. Their reward is for returnin' the necklace, not for exposin' the thief. If you happen to find out who did it, you can allus pass the information on to Chief Gramm or me."

She didn't take much time to think it over. She needed a challenging occupation desperately; and since Reo's paintings didn't bring in big money, her wages as a part-time teacher were minuscule, and they rarely had enough for entertainment, he probably wouldn't object. "Did Chief Gramm give you the files on the case? If I can have access to them, I'll go see the Roshnikovs."

Gunter considered her request gravely for a short space. "Since Jack removed Brenda White from the case, you might's well have her notes. They won't tell you nothin' you can't find out by doin' a little legwork or by askin' the Roshnikovs, but they might save you a little time." He turned to leave, turned back to say, "Go ask Hooray for the files—tell 'im I sent you," and exited quickly, slapping a period on the conversation by firmly closing the door.

- 2 -

Jorge Cruz, the records sergeant, was a tiny Latino who loved to talk and who had been chastised more than once for giving out confidential information. The chastisement had obviously done little good, for he was not only willing to give Pia Jo the Roshnikov files; he was also eager to tell her everything he knew about Brenda White, the police detective who'd been fired for conduct unbecoming an officer.

"She got bumped when an under-cover officer squealed on her for entertaining some fellow officers at a marijuana and group sex party," Jorge said importantly. "Two of the officers got bumped, too, and now the police department is short-staffed. That's the real reason you're getting this case."

"Group sex! Are you supposed to be telling me this, Georgie?" Pia Jo asked as she accepted the files and waited for him to explode over her nickname for him. "Isn't gossiping also unbecoming an officer?"

"I'm not gossiping—I'm giving you valuable information. You might even call me your informer. And you know very well my name's pronounced *Horhay*, Pyuh Jo."

"And you know mine's pronounced *Peuh Jo*, Georgie. Just be glad I don't call you 'Hooray' like Gunter does. Thanks for the files and the informative gossip."

All the way back to Innisfree in the old Le Car, Pia Jo's mind tossed the theft about, glad to have something concrete to play mental ball with, anything that would make life bearable again. She and Reo had occupied Cabin 6, the one Aunt Thelma had done in Native American decor, since her classes had let out in mid-May; now late May was painting the Fine Arts Colony the colors of early summer—grass green, sky blue, lilac lavender, and daisy yellow—and all she'd been able to do was plant Mexican jumping beans beneath a vine trellis that Bold Bear had woven for her to the rear of the cabin and paint a picture of Clover and Bear Cub with their ponies and goats. She was, she realized, not a painter of Reo's caliber, and her talents fell far short of his sister Luisa's; even so, the Whitewaters had praised the painting's earthy effect, and Sven and Thelma had thought it perfect for the focal point above the mantel.

"It's okay for a beginner," Reo had said when he'd first viewed the painting, "but it's too drab for my taste. And it's old hat to paint Indians in buckskin. Let me do my version."

He hadn't asked Clover and Bear Cub to pose; instead, he'd based his painting on hers; but he'd dressed Clover in bright purple and Bear Cub in chartreuse; his ponies were yellow and the goats were pink. "How's that?" he'd asked after he'd hung her painting in the spare bedroom and had proudly placed his in the coveted spot.

"Your technique is better than mine," she'd admitted without hesitation, "but your version clashes with the cabin's decor."

He'd hooted derisively at this response. "You really must widen your artistic horizons, bambina! Some Native American painters now use more color than the Fauves. When I get time, I'll jazz up some of these pots for you."

She'd shuddered but hadn't argued the point; if she wanted to be Reo's significant other, she must accept him as he was. But in a moment of anger, she'd remarked to Gunter that she was Reo's "insignificant echo," a remark she'd later rued since the incident had enhanced Gunter's contempt for him, already radical because Reo had said "he'd forgotten" about Gunter's important phone call when her mother died.

Seeing her despondency, Uncle Sven had said that keeping busy was the key to survival. "Concentrate on your own interests, Pia Jo. Your plays are well worth publishing! I want you to send copies to Tremaine Classics in Milwaukee. Rex Tremaine is not only my publisher—he's my close friend and a very discerning man." She'd posted her plays to Milwaukee soon after she'd arrived at Innisfree, but only because Uncle

Sven had insisted that she do so; and she was still questioning his advice to keep busy.

After all, hadn't she been much too busy and too concerned about her own interests during the last several years? Busy getting her Master's degree in the Fine Arts from a Chicago University and her State Certification from the Police Academy at Springfield, busy teaching Theatre part time at Halcyon College and being Reo's paramour and sidekick—too busy and too concerned about his paintings to visit her mother more than a few times during her last months of life and not at all during that last week. If only Reo had told her that Gunter had called!

Turning the battered, robin's egg blue vehicle in at the approach that wound between birches, maples, and cottonwoods and led to the Fine Arts Colony that her Uncle Sven, a Yeats scholar, had named Innisfree, she waved to Thelma, who was busy planting *praktmalla* by Scandia, the house she and Sven had patterned after Carl Larsson's famous *Solsidan* (House in the Sun) in Sundborn village in Dalecarlia following a month's stay in Sweden the previous summer.

What a charming mix of cultures, Pia Jo thought as she parked by Cabin 6, reached for her canvas bag of groceries, and hurried to the door! A Native American trading post, a rustic lodge, and six cabins, each decorated in a United Nations vein—it seemed odd that Sven should have given such a conglomeration an Irish name. And yet Innisfree could symbolize any place where people kept the noiseless tenor of their way; and Thelma had done her creative best to keep it uncommercial. The only sign announcing its existence was a piece of barn board with a natural pointer and the words "To Innisfree" painted in brown on its rough surface.

Reo was in the living area, a roomy place with polished barn board paneling and shelves, a huge stone fireplace, and large windows that invited the sunshine in. It had been the perfect backdrop for her Native American collection of traditional pottery, Kachina dolls, beadwork, and Winnebago baskets (the latter the work of Clover Whitewater and her mother, Maize, who had filled some of the emptiness after Emeline's death). At the Trading Post, where Clover worked with her father, Bold Bear, she'd purchased authentic blankets and rugs and had even found some dishes for the kitchen shelves.

"What took you so long?" Reo demanded impatiently. "You know I can't paint well unless I'm wearing a nicotine shroud."

"Sorry, *sposo*—I stopped to talk to Gunter. Here they are." Delving into a bag, she came up with a carton of Marlboros. "I do wish you wouldn't joke about shrouds." She called him *sposo* even though marriage was not on his mind; artists, he insisted, need to be free, and when she'd remarked that to the early Winnebagos living together constituted marriage, he'd grunted that it was good they weren't Winnebagos then. "Do I get a kiss for getting them?"

His dark face relaxed in a smile, the smile that made her sure she loved him. The kiss was long and satisfying, but as soon as it was over, he pushed her away. "Now get lost, *zucchero*! I need to get this done when the light is right."

He was painting a *fauve* paradise, one wherein a chartreuse lion with olive markings stood beneath a bare purple tree, a pair of red peacocks mounted on its back. She'd never really cared for *fauve* art, not even when they'd met three years previously; but she'd taken acting lessons in college, and she'd become skilled at dissembling. She'd even encouraged him to mount the loud *Landscape near Chatou* by Maurice de Vlaminck and Matisse's pink-toned *View of Collioure* in their living room-cum-den in Chicago, and had done her best not to shudder whenever she looked at them. And to please him, she'd read articles on the movement, which, she learned, had originated at the turn of the century and had included such artists as Derain, Brasque, Friesz, and Matisse, "all young, all virile, all enthusiastic and all a little mad." These young men had favored "the uninhibited use of raw color, the art whose practitioners were called *les fauves* (wild beasts)."

"I'll get lost as soon as I've put these groceries away," she tossed back as she carried her bag into the kitchen and cautiously closed the door. When he was creating, Reo liked to listen to hard rock, and she had to close the door to turn it down. After disposing of the groceries, she poured herself a cup of coffee, ate a bun thinly smeared with peanut butter, then hurried down the path that led from their cabin to Wild Swans' Lake, the Roshnikov files under her arm. But seated on a favorite rock beneath a willow tree whose leaves lightly brushed her hair, she did not turn directly to the case. Instead she paused to marvel at the celestial blue of the heavens, artfully contrasted by a line of low-lying clouds white as an Afro's teeth, and to admire the vibrant, darkening foliage of the thickly-clustered trees that lifted mighty arms in unspoken longing for the tranquil sky.

Across the lake and to the west, high on a sloping pasture of Apple Mountain, Casper Antonin's quarter horses were grazing quietly. Farther to the south lay Lovers' Leap, two high peaks joined by a shaky, swaying bridge, where a pair of Winnebago lovers, denied the right to marry because they were of the same clan, had given the place its name by leaping hand in hand to their deaths on the ragged rocks below. She hadn't been on hand to witness the effects of this horrendous disaster, but Gunter had shown her the before-and-after photos of the tormented young couple; and the grief she'd felt could not have been more intense if she'd known them personally.

Often, since that fateful day, while perched on this same rounded rock by Wild Swans Lake, she'd felt their presences and heard their voices in the wind, voices that sometimes moaned grievously because of the pain they'd caused their loved ones and sometimes laughed joyfully because of their own happiness. She'd visited their graves up near Lovers' Leap more than once, but her acrophobia had kept her from crossing the dangerous bridge. She'd had no desire to be stabbed by the sharp, jutting rocks directly below.

"Mom used to call me her blonde Indian," she mused as she strained to hear the voices; but the breezes, though pleasant, were not strong enough to sustain the communication. So mentally placing gently pink wild roses on the graves, she opened the files of notes that Jorge had handed her and, returning abruptly to reality, reviewed the evidence on the famous theft.

Gunter must have had the files for a while, for he'd annotated some of the notes with his hieroglyphics; and as she tried to decipher them, she wondered why Brenda White would have jeopardized her career, and the careers of some of her colleagues, by engaging in flagrant misconduct. She could sympathize with Gunter's reluctance to help solve Lead Mine's crimes as well as those of Berger County, a large sheep-raising county which had been settled by the French and had been named for the shepherds, shepherdesses, and swains who had early cared for the sheep. Although the county was, in the main, peaceful, it provided shelter and anonymity for certain city criminals, some of whom found the Red-Eyed Bat, a disreputable night club a mile or so southwest of Lead Mines, a suitable hangout.

Lead Mines, too obviously named for the major industry of the region in the nineteenth century, was a charming town whose fine red-brick mansions had been left intact when railroad lines had replaced the old steamships and river barges that had plied the Lead Mine River, a tributary of the Mississippi, from the early eighteen hundreds until the Civil War. At that time the Mississippi had been closed to traffic, and lead mining had declined, causing the town's industry to die a wrenching death. It is perhaps a commonplace that good sometimes comes from depressing circumstances; there hadn't been enough money to tear down these choice old buildings, most of which were now listed on the National Register of Historic Places.

Lead Mines was decidedly an unusual town. Its main street was tiered like an oblong wedding cake, with the finest homes located on the two top tiers and the commercial buildings that catered mainly to tourists—antique and gift shops, art stores, eateries, bakeries, and other small businesses—on the wide lower tier that formed the main street, from which a steep wooden stairway rose to the top layer somewhat like the steps of a Mayan pyramid.

Because the town had no industry other than local commerce, it had no industrial sprawl and now survived primarily on its summer tourist trade. Among the neighboring hills, which rose in rolling but less rigid layers than the town itself, were a few small farms that provided fresh produce and kept the residents supplied with milk, eggs, and meat; these hills were also famous for their numerous hiking trails and their fantastic ski slopes. Lakes glistened like pools of aqua tourmalines in the dips and valleys, and it was to the one that bordered the Tillotson land that Pia Jo went in search of the solitude she needed to examine the files on the famous emerald theft. Odd that she hadn't even told Reo about the unsolved Roshnikov case. She would have, of course, if he'd shown a dab of interest; his thoughts had been, as usual, on his work alone.

Opening one of the files, she discovered that the Roshnikovs had supplied colored photos of the famous necklace and, in an interview with Brenda White, had described it as a chain of priceless matched emeralds in a setting of diamonds and other precious gems. Vladimer

Roshnikov's great grandfather had worked in an emerald mine in the Urals some time after the precious stones had been found imbedded in a bank of the Tokoveya River in 1830, and had not only left a fortune to Vladimer's grandfather, an only child, but had also left him the priceless emeralds, which had eventually come down to Vladimer in the shape of an undistinguished necklace.

More creative than his antecedents, Vladimer had himself designed the fabulous necklace of matched translucent emeralds interspersed with rare diamonds, and had had his design executed by a famous Russian jeweler as a wedding gift for Maxima. Valued at $100,000, the circlet was heavily insured; even so, Maxima had been devastated by its disappearance, for it was to her a symbol of her husband's devotion; and she'd confided to Brenda that its loss suggested the loss of his love. Moreover, the insurance company was so eager to have the collar back that it had sent a brash, young investigator named Tony Garnet, who was so hot after the $10,000 reward that he'd questioned all the Roshnikov guests and servants as well as most of the residents of Lead Mines and had pestered Brenda for details until they were ready to charge him with harassment.

"What I couldn't do with a bonus like that!" Pia Jo exclaimed jubilantly as she considered the attractive sum. "I could fund Reo's wild dream to go to Paris and see *fauve* art for himself. Or I could buy Soren's share of Mom's house."

-3-

As Pia Jo sat musing over the possibility of winning the generous reward, she suddenly recalled a bit of wisdom that Emeline had imparted before she'd enrolled at the University. "Don't do something merely for its end result, Pia Jo," her mother had said. "That's a sure way to enhance your chances of failing. Try to overcome each obstacle as it presents itself. It's better to learn from your mistakes than to rush ahead with overblown and unjustified confidence."

"In other words, I shouldn't go to college just for a diploma. I should make sure my diploma reflects my good work," she had paraphrased.

"That's a capsulized version of what I said," Emeline had agreed with a smile. "I guess I'm too wordy."

Pia Jo could apply this wisdom to her investigation, but how could she apply it to her personal life? Her goal was a close, understanding love relationship; would it help her achieve that goal if she told Reo about the money, or should she keep silent until she had it in her hand? Best not to say a word—after all, the Roshnikovs hadn't yet hired her to investigate the theft, and she'd probably need a contract before Reo'd believe her. Postponing a decision, she concentrated on Brenda's notes and Gunter's annotations.

The emeralds had disappeared on the evening the Roshnikovs had celebrated their twenty-fifth wedding anniversary and had invited their friends, most of whom lived in the red brick mansions on High Hill and Court Street in Lead Mines. Maxima had sung some of her operatic numbers, but they'd also hired a local orchestra as well as a pianist and soloist to perform the oldies they liked best, songs popular long before their marriage in 1970; but the party had not been catered; their servants had prepared the food. The guest list, written in a graceful hand, held the names of a dozen couples that had been invited to the fancy bash.

"Too many suspects!" Pia Jo groaned as she scanned the lengthy list. "Did Brenda get so tired of interviewing people that she chucked it in favor of group sex and marijuana?" But then she noticed the small asterisks beside some of the names and read the explanation at the foot of the page: only the couples whose names were starred were suspects—the others had left the party before the necklace was stolen. Brenda had questioned the Roshnikovs and the servants at length, but she hadn't interviewed the guests. In a side note, she admitted that she'd received her information from the Roshnikovs. Obviously, her heart wasn't in the investigation, for her jottings were fragmented and brief, and she hadn't prepared a cohesive report. One note said, "Necklace vanished from victim's neck—theft may not have been noticed right off." Thinking of Moll Flanders' nimble fingers, Pia Jo began to read the names of the five starred couples who were the prime suspects:

1) Ebony and Laurel Oleander: young Afro-Americans, sudden wealth, enough to buy a BMW and expensive furniture for mansion on High Street.

2) Elizabeth and George Wylie: middle-aged siblings, inherited mansion from parents but not much money. Turned mansion into home for retarded children, operate it on what? [A note in Gunter's handwriting said, "Close friends of Sven and Thelma—interview them].

3) Stan and Sandie Anderson: auto mechanic and wife who doesn't work. He was there as a soloist. She didn't enjoy party. Ill child, called sitter—her mother—2 or 3 times. Home on High Street not fashionable. Needs repairs. [Gunter's note: They dance with the Scandinavian Folk Dancers and Stan is virtually unknown as a soloist—why was he asked to entertain?].

4) Stefan and Sofia Constanta: elderly couple who live in Roshnikov's renovated Carriage House. Gypsy dancers—were entertainers in Rumania, then a Commie country. The Rs helped them escape.

[Gunter's note: Elderly gypsies dance? Would they steal from R's? Are gypsies honest?].

5) Reolo and Sidonie Alligretti: semi-retired Italian opera star and his stylish and wealthy French wife, who drips with jewels. Evanston couple, frequent guests at Cloud House. [Gunter: Could they be pretending they're rich?].

[Another note by Gunter: Why didn't B.W. consider couples one at a time? Why assume they worked together?].

Thinking that Gunter wrote the English language better than he talked it, Pia Jo went on to the single entry below the others:

6) Dag Amundson: piano player at the party, played while Stan Anderson sang. [Gunter evidently knew Amundson well for he'd added a lengthy comment: Also plays at the Red-Eyed Bat—hangout for bad guys and gals. Farms Asgard, has a fairly good financial reputation. Exercise nut and folk dancer. Seems well off but has been divorced a couple of times. Is generous—gives his sister Goldie and her kid a home].

Because they were so unusual, Pia Jo found the Constantas the most interesting people on the list, with the Oleanders second. "Why would the wealthy Roshnikovs invite poor gypsies to their anniversary party?" Pia Jo mused. "What do I know about gypsies anyway? The stereotype is that most of them are poor; that they wander from place to place; that they steal food if they're hungry; that they raise and sell horses; that they love loud colors, hoop earrings, and fringed scarves; that some of the women tell fortunes. But is the stereotype true?"

The Oleanders might have felt they were entitled to the emerald and diamond necklace as restitution to blacks by whites for former injuries. On the other hand, they were outstanding and successful—why should they harbor vengeful thoughts? The three other couples seemed even less likely suspects. Surely the Wylies, who had compassion for the retarded, wouldn't steal to meet their operating expenses—but their being friends of Uncle Sven and Aunt Thelma didn't make them innocent. What of the Andersons—were they embarrassed by their shabby home, which was evidently set in the splendor of the finer homes on High Street like a robin in the midst of peacocks? Or did their child need medical attention they couldn't afford? And the Alligrettis—why had Brenda even listed them as suspects? Was their wealthy display of jewels merely a sham? How could she know unless she investigated their finances? But she'd have to drive to Evanston to do that. And what if Brenda had questioned the servants extensively? They weren't likely to testify against themselves. She found Brenda's notes on them, annotated by Blue, in another file folder.

1 and 2) Dove and Ox-Eye Raintree: Winnebagos—cook and butler. Dove is from Black River Falls. Attended a school for chefs. [Blue had added: Well-trained but beneath Ox-Eye. A real thistle. Ox-Eye and I grew up in the Settlement; we attend Powwows together. He's 100% reliable]."

3 and 4) Chindee and Chearee Dgong: Cambodian houseboys, look alikes. They don't talk—seem mindless. Interview netted me nothing.

5) Horst Brenner: German immigrant, part-time chauffeur for Roshnikovs, rest of time works for Dag Amundson. [Note by Blue: Rumor has it that he fathered Goldie's two-year-old boy, Kaito].

Since he a was a Winnebago, Blue would naturally defend the Raintrees, especially Ox-Eye, Pia Jo reflected after reading the notes; she'd pay no attention to his biases, nor would she trust Brenda's perception where the Dgong houseboys were concerned. She could be prejudiced or in culture shock where foreigners were concerned.

"Insurance company bulldog watching all big fences," Blue had noted in a margin. "As of May 15th, no luck."

Watching the wild whistling swans that were skimming the water with such obvious pleasure, Pia Jo tried to come up with a plan but could only decide on her next step: to visit the Russians and see how they'd feel about her taking over the investigation as a private eye. What was the point of her pondering the case if they didn't agree to her investigating it? Oh, sure, she could continue the investigation as Gunter's detective, but then she'd be paid too little to satisfy Reo.

The evening meal brought mixed reactions from Reo; on the one hand, he praised the healthy chef's salad and crusty bread she served on earthenware in the homey kitchen; on the other, he disliked her tepid appreciation of his mod-art Paradise.

"It's a *pleasant* prospect," he mimicked sulkily. "What kind of praise is that? What you're really saying is that you hate it!"

"Of course I don't hate it! The positioning and shapes of the animals are fantastic. This is your best work yet."

"But you don't like the colors? You Scandinavians are all alike—cold-blooded and pale."

Tired of his insults, she was forced to defend herself. "Carl Larsson, the Swedish painter, loved color. It's true, he sometimes got carried away, but more often he used it realistically. I'm a Nature lover, Reo—you know that. I was born in these wilds, as you call them, and I love this area just as it is. I've been down by the lake admiring the wild swans—they're white, but they're still spectacular. Would they be more outstanding if they were red?" She'd rarely crossed him so openly, but he'd pushed her too far; she had the right to her own tastes, and she suddenly felt the need to defend them.

"There are black swans," he flared, stirring his herb tea so emphatically that it splashed over onto the tweed placemat. "But I'd paint mine gold—what could be more outstanding than that? If you prefer graphic art, get out your camera and take some pictures. Why paint what you can photograph?"

"Photographs are technically produced," she reposted defensively. "Paintings are the products of individual talent—Picasso's doves are terrific, but they aren't exactly like doves. And since the environment is such a pressing issue now, Nature paintings are coming into their own. Nature lovers—."

He got up and threw his napkin on the table disdainfully. "Nature lovers be damned! I'm sick of this prissy country life—I only consented to come because I thought I needed some privacy." Suddenly calming down, he took another tack. "Let's go back to our apartment tomorrow, Peejay. I feel more comfortable there—in fact, I miss the gang's kibitzing, and you'll never get over your grief out here. My paintings look best on city walls—and don't forget that you promised Luisa she could do your portrait this summer."

He had a point, of course; in fact, he had several good points: they did get along better on his turf than on hers; and perhaps she did think of her mother too much out here where her presence lingered like a sad benediction. Indeed, she had promised Luisa she'd sit for her—why not go back to the city with Reo first thing in the morning—it might save their relationship.

But what about the Roshnikov case?

She took a deep breath and plunged. "The police asked Gunter for some help in solving the theft of the Roshnikov emeralds, so Gunter suggested that I try. I more or less said I would."

If Thelma and Sven had been listening at Scandia, they might have heard his chortle. "You? If the police couldn't solve it, what makes you think you can? You've were only certified late last August, and you've been teaching Theatre ever since." But a new possibility sobered him. "What handsome sum is your hayseed brother prepared to pay for the safe return of the emerald necklace? If he'll shell out $500, you might consider it."

She didn't defend her brother; she was tired of making peace between them. "I wouldn't be working for him—I'd be working as a private eye for the Roshnikovs. They're offering a reward for the recovery of the emeralds."

"How much?" he asked skeptically.

"Ten thousand dollars."

"Ten thou—!" His mouth fell open. "My God, Peejay, of course you must try! This is the chance we've been waiting for—we need that money for our Paris trip. Look, why don't I go back to the apartment and get ready for the exhibit while you stay here and investigate?"

"What about my portrait?"

"Luisa can come up here and paint you. She'll love it—she makes me sick with her constant nagging about animal rights and the cruelty of zoos. And you can be sure she won't give you green teeth and blue hair."

Reo was at his best for the rest of the evening. While she did the dishes and he packed, he kept up a running conversation about the museums they'd see in Paris, the people they'd meet, the painting he'd do, the plays they'd attend. Ten thousand dollars! Fantastic! He'd known all along that he'd soon get the break he deserved.

"But I haven't recovered the emerald necklace yet," she cautioned. "The trail is ice cold—what if I never do?"

Of course he wouldn't listen. She'd helped Gunter solve a number of cases in the summers she'd spent at Innisfree, hadn't she? She should be overjoyed that she'd been handed such a simple assignment! Opportunity was knocking, and all she had to do was fling wide the door and welcome it with open arms.

"I'll be ready to exhibit by the end of June," he assured her with renewed confidence, "and I'll sock what I take in away for our return. I expect we'll be gone a couple of months, and we'll have to pay rent on our apartment while we're away."

She was surprised by his enthusiastic vote of confidence but not by his enhanced tenderness in bed.

- 4 -

Reo had no trouble getting up at dawn. As she helped him load his paintings and artist's paraphernalia into their tiny vehicle and watched him disappear down the long approach to the highway, Pia Jo had mixed feelings about the car. Since no train line ran from Chicago to Lead Mines, he needed it for his return trip, of course, but here there was no such thing as public transportation.

Later, when she walked up the hill to tell Uncle Sven about Reo's departure, to apprise him of her lack of transportation, and to ask him if he thought the Roshnikov case would be simple, he expressed an opposing view. Seated behind his large Scandinavian-design desk, the sun glinting on his silver-gold hair, he looked like her concept of Balder, the beloved Viking god. Her mother's younger brother, he was in his mid-fifties and seemed only to improve with age.

"Simple? Reo's idea, I suppose. After six months, how can it be simple to find a necklace that could have been redesigned by now? Besides, the trail will be cold as Stockholm in winter. But the Roshnikovs will help you. We know them slightly—in fact, Thelma and I saw her in a couple of operas in Chicago, and he's been very successful as her manager. What the heck? Why not go for the gold! I'll be rooting for you all the way." But when his thoughts returned to Reo, he was less reassuring. "So he took the car, which is at least half yours, and left you here to earn the prize all by yourself, did he?" His cultured voice held the disapproval he'd never before voiced. "And he expects you to spend it on him?"

"Artists need patrons—you know that, Uncle Sven. Thelma was once your patron, wasn't she?"

He nodded, coloring a bit, then rose to his own defense. "You're right, Thelma's inheritance bought both her and me our successes. But it was an investment, Pia Jo. I've repaid her ten times over."

"I know you have—and Reo will, too. You wait and see."

He nodded, unconvinced. "I won't hold my breath. In the meantime, how'd you like to drive my '57 Chevy Corvette?"

She stared at him, stunned. His three old cars were his pride and joy, and he rarely lent them out. She must be living in a dream state—first she'd been given the chance to earn $10,000, and now she was being offered the little runabout she'd always loved best. Perhaps *Dias* and/or *Dios*, did exist after all! Then she plummeted back to earth. "But that's not in working condition, is it?"

"I had the engine rebuilt after you left last summer, and it's in the pink. It's a little flamboyant for a detective maybe, but you can rent a more sober vehicle if you don't want to be recognized."

She roamed his office like an inquiring chipmunk, straightening out books that leaned and paintings that dipped. Brought up by a globe that was about half the size of Nero Wolfe's, she twirled it while she thought about his offer. Turning to study his face, she said earnestly, "I appreciate your offer, Uncle Sven, and I'll love driving the Corvette this summer; but I'm hoping I can soon afford a modest little vehicle of my own this fall. What I need now is information. What can you tell me about the theft of the emeralds?"

Leaning back in his handsome chair, he considered the matter thoughtfully while he tapped his desk with a fine monogrammed pen; then he straightened up, put the pen down, and began to search a side drawer in his desk. Drawing forth a paper, he held it out to her encouragingly. "Here's an article I cut from the *Courier's Interaction Magazine* after Gladstone's investigator—was his name Tony Garner?—failed to solve the case. I thought you might like to try for the reward once your mind had settled a bit. In fact, I suggested it to Gunter."

"I think his name was Garnet," she said as she began to scan the article, which was more than helpful since it not only gave the name, address, and phone number of the president of the Gladstone Insurance Agency, insurer of fine gems, but it also featured a photo of Maxima

Roshnikov, dressed to the nines and proudly wearing the stolen necklace. Pia Jo read the caption aloud. "Famous diva Maxima Roshnikov loses irreplaceable emerald and diamond necklace." She scrutinized the picture, which was in vivid color, then turned to the article and read aloud, "'A singer and actress of no small talent, Madame Roshnikov is shown here as Violetta in Verdi's *La Traviata*. Reolo Alligretti appeared as Alfredo.' I wish they'd included his picture—he's on Brenda White's list of suspects." She folded the article, put it in a pocket of her jeans, then added, "Gunter thinks role playing will help me dig out information I won't get as an investigator; but I'll have to decide what role to play when I call on each suspect, and that'll be a challenge."

"There you are then. By the way, Rex is coming up from Milwaukee on his vacation, and he'll probably want to discuss your plays with you. I wish you'd present one of them at the Lodge while he's here—I want him to see how talented you are."

She sighed in exasperation. As a matchmaker, Uncle Sven put Jane Austin's Emma to shame. "Uncle Sven, it takes players and money to present a play—and a lot of time. Can't I meet your publisher at a later date? I've got a case to solve."

"You'll have the case solved well before he comes!" He got up and took a set of keys from a wooden key holder on one wall. "This one's for the Corvette, and this one's for the garage. You can keep the Vette down by your cabin, but don't leave the keys in it. The thief who stole the emeralds just might have an eye on my three old beauties! Now go tell Thelma I said you could take it."

As she took the keys, she resorted to sarcasm. "Of course I'll leave the keys in the ignition. I want someone to steal it." As she went along the corridor that led past the many additions that Sven had, in the fashion of Solsidan, built onto Scandia, to Thelma's designing room, Pia Jo wondered what Rex Tremaine was like and what he thought about the plays she'd sent him for consideration. Sven hadn't failed to tell her about his publisher—how handsome, suave, and sophisticated he was and how high his literary expectations were. No doubt her offerings wouldn't get past his reader. One of these days she'd get a stereotypical little note that said, "Unfortunately your plays do not fit in with our publishing plans at this time. But don't be discouraged. Another publisher may think differently." And why should she be discouraged?

Hadn't she submitted the plays because Uncle Sven had been so deter-mined that she should? She was too realistic to think they'd capture the interest of a well-known publisher even though he was her uncle's friend.

She'd called Thelma earlier, and when she reached the designing room, which was filled with over-sized books, prints of famous art, and decorative objects that she loved to linger over, she found a note on the big bulletin board. "Pia Jo, Britt's gone to Lead Mines, and I'm work-ing in Cabin 3. Join me!"

Obeying her aunt-in-law's enthusiastic dictum, Pia Jo followed the path back down to the Colony and found her way to Cabin 3. Poking her head in the door, she breathed, "You're a genius, Aunt T. This cabin really does look like a Japanese Tea House, the *wabi* kind."

"*Wabi?*" Thelma asked as she finished putting a simple but elegant flower arrangement in an alcove. "Is that a Japanese word?"

"Mmm! When I did a paper on the *No* theatre at the University, I learned that the Japanese have two kinds of beauty—*wabi* and *yugen*. *Wabi* is the simple beauty of wild flowers or of a fisherman's shack, or possibly of our wild whistling swans—it's unpretentious and appro-priate for cabins like these. *Yugen* is the beauty preferred by the *No* theatre, the beauty of elegance, of silk kimonos and tame swans on a tranquil river."

"The rustic versus the elegant. Which type do you prefer?" The flowers placed attractively, Thelma lead the way to the kitchen and poured two glasses of lemonade from a carafe she'd brought with her from Scandia. As she accepted one of the glasses, Pia Jo's face grew sad. "I like both, but *yugen* has more sadness in it—it seems to say that anything that is sublimely beautiful will die. Mom had a beauti-ful soul, and she died. I can't deal with *yugen* right now." She sipped the lemonade as she explained that Uncle Sven was lending her his collector's Corvette. "Reo left this morning—he's going to finish his paintings in our apartment, and he's sending Luisa up to stay with me and paint my portrait."

"That's great! We love having Luisa around. We'll ask her to paint our portraits, too." Thelma's voice registered the pleasure she felt.

Mindful that she hadn't said they'd miss Reo, Pia Jo looked doleful. "Mind if I ask you a personal question?"

"No, I don't mind. Here, try one of these—maybe it'll cheer you up. Britt made them yesterday." When Pia Jo had helped herself to a big, date-filled cookie, Thelma further encouraged her to unburden herself. "So tell me what's bothering you."

"How did you and Sven get along when you'd been married three years? Was he tired of you?"

Thelma's gray-brown eyes held a serious twinkle as she tried to answer her inquisitor's wistful question. "We've had a few problems—in fact, quite a few. But I don't think Sven's ever been tired of me—I know I could never get tired of him. Are you saying that you think Reo's tired of you?"

"He's either irritable and insulting or he's cuddly and horny. There never seems to be anything else."

"Sven gets irritable when things go wrong, but he never insults me. I wouldn't stand for it. Have you told him you don't appreciate his insults?"

"Not in so many words. Right now he's happy because I'm going to try to win the reward for investigating the Roshnikov case—he wants me to spend the money on a trip to Paris. But what will happen if I don't win it? Cases are seldom solved when they're close to six months old."

Thelma considered the question as she munched on a cookie. "I guess you'll have to wait and see. Do you think perhaps you're growing apart? When you first met him, you were probably excited by his openly passionate, Italian nature. Maybe you want something else now—a deeper love that shows itself in its consideration, not in its demonstration."

"Then you agree with Sven that Reo's love is shallow and self-serving?"

"Not entirely. Sven thinks he knows people, and he's convinced that you and Rex Tremaine were made for each other. We can't measure Reo's love for you—we can only try to understand why he's so self-involved right now. Couldn't it be because he feels that you are achieving goals faster than he is?"

"But what goals am I achieving? I have a couple of part-time jobs, neither of which pays beans. How can he possibly be jealous of my non-achievement? He seems to want me to succeed in this investigation very much."

"Yes, but that will benefit both of you. But don't take my word for it—ask Luisa. She knows him a lot better than I do."

Pia Jo shook her head gloomily. "Luisa's a great friend, but she's no help where her brother is concerned. Sometimes she doesn't seem to like him at all."

"Just as you don't really like your brother Soren?"

"Touché! But I have much more reason to dislike Soren than she has to dislike Reo."

"How do you know? But let's talk about the Roshnikov case. Did you know that Sven and I saw Maxima perform the title role in *Tosca*—and that *we* were invited to their anniversary party last December?" Thelma's description of Madame Roshnikov's performance as a tempestuous diva who fell in love with a fiery rebel was so informative and absorbing that Pia Jo was able to tune out her anxieties and griefs and to concentrate on the possibility of a stimulating investigation.

- 5 -

The home of the Roshnikovs, *Oblachnyi Dom* (Cloud House), was the finest red brick mansion on High Street. Like the other mansions, its windows were of leaded crystal, and fine panes etched with classic designs bordered each gently arched entranceway. Unlike the other mansions, the leaded crystal had been imported from Russia, along with the doors, which had brass hinges and knockers that gleamed like jewels in the morning sun. By Pia Jo's standards, the grounds were not large; the farm she'd grown up on was immense by comparison, and her mother's gardens at Rendezvous of the Four Winds were easily as large as the Roshnikov lawn. But its landscaping was spectacular; several types of full-foliaged maples dotted the lawn, spirea bushes trailed their pristine blooms, and huge irises and lilies in new and breathtaking hues bowed regally from their sculptured beds. Beds of peonies and hydrangeas would soon be blooming, and the grass itself was as well groomed as an aristocrat's blue-ribbon Pekinese.

She had called ahead to ask for an appointment; even so, she was startled by Ox-Eye's abrupt appearance. The Winnebagan must have been able to see through the door with those large, near-black eyes, which now had a hostile expression in their smoky depths. She had learned long ago not to stereotype Native Americans; and it did not surprise her to find him far less voluble than Windy, far less trusting than the Whitewaters, and far more intimidating than Blue Feather.

For this initial interview, Pia Jo realized that she not only had to be herself but that she also must present herself in the best light possible. Since she knew that the Roshnikovs were outraged at the Police Department for their failure to retrieve the valuable necklace, and since she couldn't investigate under the aegis of the sheriff's department, she'd decided to state the reason for her visit as briefly as possible, then wait to select an approach that would enlist their interest and inspire their confidence. Therefore all she said was "I'm Pia Jo Borg—I phoned the Roshnikovs earlier. I'm here about the emeralds."

His response was clipped. "The Roshnikovs will see you."

Thankful that the necklace was an open sesame to the mansion's owners, she followed him through a long hall lined with gilded sconces backed by flying Cupids, gilded mirrors with frames wrought with tiny flowers, and huge paintings of the stars of great operas dressed in grand costumes, into a drawing room where two cunningly-rendered white marble Cupids adorned the sides of the immense marble fireplace and three others posed daringly on the tops of marble columns of varying heights, their eyes bandaged, their bows and arrows ready. From the deep-rose velvet drapes to the thick, deep-rose carpet, the room carried out its classically romantic theme.

The man who stepped forward with an extended hand was himself a mid-sized Cupid with a rounded belly, a pink-cheeked face, and Wedgwood blue eyes. All he lacked was a blindfold, a diaper, a bow and arrow, and a quiver. By way of contrast, the woman who stood to one side was tall, imposing, and stylish; her proud bearing suggested that she knew exactly how to command an impressive audience. As soon as Vladimer had shaken Pia Jo's hand and had offered her a plump, old rose chair, the diva stepped forth as if making a grand entrance and said resonantly, "I'm Maxima Roshnikov. I take it that you are related to Sheriff Borg."

Feeling like a bootblack in the presence of an empress, Pia Jo fidgeted on the sculptured upholstery and delivered her own carefully rehearsed speech. "Yes, Madame Roshnikov, he's my brother. But I'm not here on his orders—I'm here because I'd very much like to investigate the theft of your emeralds on my own, and I need your cooperation."

"You mean as a private eye? But you do have investigative skills, do you not?"

"Yes, I spent twelve weeks in Springfield, and I was State Certified in criminal investigation late last August. I prepared a resume in case you'd like to know more about me." She took some papers from the Winnebago tote bag she was carrying, handed them to the diva, and waited for her response.

When Maxima had scanned the resume, she handed it to Vladimer, her expression less grim. "I see you have a Master's degree in the Fine Arts and quite a bit of experience in Theatre. That could be helpful." She paused to express her deep displeasure at the lack of progress in the case. "Vladimer and I are hugely disappointed in the detective Chief Gramm sent to investigate the theft of the emerald necklace, a woman named Brenda White. She seemed highly qualified at first; but as time went by, she not only lost interest in the case, but she was also relieved of her duties because of misconduct. Chief Gramm informed me that he'd had eight officers, including Ms. White, but that he had to let her and two others go after a disgraceful party in her apartment; so he now has only five to cover all the shifts. And the insurance investigator didn't prove efficient, either." She looked at Pia Jo sternly. "I hope you won't disappoint us as they did."

Pia Jo smiled her most winning smile as she gestured toward her resume. "You'll note that I included four character references, none of whom are blood relatives. You might ask Sheriff Borg to tell you about some of the cases I helped him solve before I was State Certified. Since I plan only to work part time, he's starting me out as a detective; but I can advance to chief investigator if I decide to work full time."

Vladimer had been reading the resume carefully, and now he inserted a few comments of his own. "In a nutshell, you got your degrees several years ago and have been teaching part time during the fall and spring semesters. But since your income from part-time teaching was inadequate, you worked for the sheriff summers and also took courses in criminal investigation. You completed your course work late last summer and were State Certified. So why can't you investigate this case for the sheriff? Since Chief Gramm is now shorthanded and has asked for his help, the jurisdictional question seems resolved."

Because Vladimer was obviously the shrewder of the two Roshnikovs, Pia Jo addressed him directly and bluntly. "To be honest, I'm here to try for the reward, and I can't do so as a Sheriff's detective. The going rate for officers is less than $10 an hour."

"Good Heavens! Is that all officers make?" he expostulated. "That's a damn shame!" His mind made up, he turned to his wife with an amiable but decisive smile. "Ms. Borg is a trained investigator, Max. She could be the answer we've been looking for. What do you say we hire her and pay her the $10,000 if she retrieves the necklace and it's still in good shape?"

It was obvious that Maxima relied heavily on her husband's managerial skills, but she seemed to need social as well as proficiency assurance. "Aren't you also related to the Tillotsons?"

The mention of her uncle and aunt gave Pia Jo the extra confidence she needed. "Yes, Sven's my uncle. They're letting me use Cabin 6 at Innisfree as a base for my investigation." Since Uncle Sven had encouraged her and had lent her one of his treasured vehicles, she assured herself that her statement wasn't exaggerated.

Maxima was clearly impressed. "Ah, yes, a charming couple, so knowledgeable and socially acceptable," she said in a rich contralto as she glissaded around the room the better to view the slender, fair, and surprisingly-qualified girl who was partially occupying the huge, old rose chair. "Vladimer, do give her a contract and an expense account—I wish very much to wear my emerald and diamond necklace when I appear at La Scala in July."

Vladimer, it seemed, had unexpected facets to his personality, for he suddenly switched from the sublime to the ridiculous. "You can wear peacock feathers to Italy, m'dear—you'd look stunning in peacock feathers," he observed dryly. "We'll have 'em dyed red—."

"Peacock feathers? Steal a peacock's beautiful tail? You know how I feel about—." She stopped in mid-sentence and emitted a sound that was a cross between a groan and a chuckle. "There he goes again with his outlandish suggestions. I must warn you, Pia Jo, that Vladimer is a practical joker. He likes nothing better than to present a totally ridiculous idea in a serious way." She turned back to her husband and showed her annoyance. "Behave yourself, Vlad. Stop wasting our investigator's time."

Vladimer promptly became serious. Clearing his throat importantly, he said in a businesslike tone, "I trust you've been giving the theft some thought. We will, of course, expect frequent reports; and if you have a plan, we'd like to hear it."

Thanking the insomnia she'd suffered the evening before for giving her a plan of sorts, Pia Jo said briskly, "I've already gone over Brenda's list of major suspects and your impressions of them; but since I need to form my own opinions, I hope to interview them, and others, myself. The biggest obstacle is that I can't examine the crime scene or evaluate the suspects against the background of the party—it would be a great help if I could observe them as they interact on a gala occasion."

She paused to breathe and to consider the Roshnikovs' reactions to her ideas. Seeing that they were both listening closely, she hurried on. "If you want to help, you might stage another party and invite all the suspects as well as some other couples who aren't implicated, for example, the Tillotsons, who couldn't attend the first party because of my mother's death. Since the sheriff is my mentor, I'd like him and his chief deputy to attend as guests; but they should have dates so the other guests won't feel they're being observed. The sheriff can bring my friend Luisa. And of course, Chief Gramm and his wife should also be invited."

"And you?" Maxima asked.

"My fiancé's in Chicago, but I'll find someone to escort me—maybe Blue."

"The Winnebago deputy? You'd come with *him*?" The diva sounded a trifle disdainful.

"Why not? He's very attractive and my good friend. The important thing is to convince everyone that the party is bonafide and not a reenactment of the first party, so you'll have to make some changes—perhaps hire different entertainers and plan new events. But if the entertainers are also suspects, they should be rehired. Could you possibly create a special occasion by honoring someone who deserves to be honored?"

For a long moment, the expressive brown eyes consulted the glittering blue ones, and Pia Jo thought she heard Cupid's wings flutter. Obviously Vladimer's love of the ridiculous had not diminished Maxima's love for him. Now she nodded in his direction.

"Vladimer gave me the necklace—he must decide on a guest to honor."

Her husband's choice was prompt. "Maxima's niece, Yentl Androvi, is coming to live with us next week. She'll be teaching music at the Community College in Prairie du Loup, and she'll also have a studio here. We raised her as our own child, and we want her to become reacquainted with our neighbors and friends so she won't feel lonely while we're in Italy."

"Was she present at the first party?"

"Yes, she came with her fiancé, Nikita Morotski, but she wasn't the guest of honor."

After they'd discussed the suspects and set the date of the second party for the evening of June 3rd, Pia Jo drove back to Cabin 6 euphorically, a signed contract and an advance of $500 in her pocket. "Money really makes wheels roll," she said with the overconfidence of untested training. "Since they eliminated all the competitors except the insurance investigator—what's his name, Tony Garnet?—this case is going to be like playing with tinker toys."

Because Gunter, too, had demanded frequent reports, Pia Jo invited him to dine on vegetarian pizza from a local pizzeria that evening. "You eat way too much meat," she informed him tartly. "If you die early, Buster Bigelow will rear your son." Since his wife, Helen, had left him for the wheeler-dealer Bigelow, it was a potent argument; he griped but accepted, and over their pizza, she recounted the details of her visit to *Oblachnyj Dom*, described Vladimer's penchant to make jokes over serious subjects, and presented her plan.

"I'd no idea you'd grab the rat by the tail so fast," he said inelegantly. "It might work—but I see some flaws."

"What flaws?" she demanded testily while her indeterminate eyes, which could be blue, gray, green, or a combination of all three, searched his deeply-tanned face as she bit down hard on a wedge of thin-crusted spinach and mushroom pizza.

"How're you gonna observe all the guests at once? You got eyes in the back of your head?"

"That's where you and Blue come in—and maybe Chief Gramm. You're going to observe some of them—unofficially, of course, and surreptitiously."

"Takin' us for granted, ain't you? An' what about Dag Amundson? Did you make sure he'd be there?"

"The man who played the piano at the Roshnikov party? I asked

Maxima to make the second party different in some respects so that the guests won't suspect that it's staged, but I'm sure she'll ask Amundson to play."

"An' he'll accept because they don't squeeze every penny before they shell it out, an' because he loves the oldies they'll ask him to play. He's gifted as hell but can't make it with the girls."

"Why's that?" she asked as she reached for the notebook and pen that she'd popped into her Winnebago tote bag along with Brenda's notes on the case.

He helped himself to another piece of pizza, took a huge bite, and chewed part of it meditatively before he responded. "Prob'ly because his skin an' hair lack pigmentation an' his eyes are sort of pink. He wears blue contacts, an' on special occasions he uses make-up, but he's more 'r less accepted his looks."

"I've never liked my looks!" Pia Jo said as she scribbled rapidly. "He couldn't have snatched the necklace while he was at the piano; but he could have had an accomplice. I understand that Maxima missed her necklace right after she'd sung a song. What was the other soloist doing then?"

"Anderson? I suppose he was dancin' with his wife. I don't know, and Brenda's notes were like stick men," Gunter grunted as he got up to refill their cups with the strong brew she always made when she knew he was coming. "I wonder who certified her as an investigator."

She moved the dishes out of the way, drew the files from her tote bag, and scanned them cursorily. "But he's probably paying alimony to a couple of wives—or don't men pay alimony these days?"

"Maybe not alimony—but they would have had a share in Asgard, an' he would've had to pay 'em off to keep it. When Helen and I were members of the Folk Dancers, Dag used to talk about his two wives. He's desperate for a woman—maybe he figured he could buy one with th' necklace." He gulped his coffee, burned his tongue, and muttered, "Hot damn!" When the pain wore off, he added, "Can't see why women don't stay with him—lots of Scandinavians have white hair an' skin. They may look a lil anemic, but so what? Besides, at forty he's got the body of a young athlete. By the way, he thinks you're a real looker."

"Me?" She tried in vain to remember when she'd seen the man Gunter had described. "Have I met him then?"

"No, but he saw th' pictures of you an' Mom on my bookcase, an' he asked if you were available. I said I wisht you were—an' I do. Not that I'd want you to give him a tumble; but he wouldn't expect you t' shack up with him, like your present jerkimo."

"Shack up! Jerkimo! You'd better lay off Reo—or I won't let Luisa go with you to the party."

Gunter came to instant attention. "Luisa's comin'? When?"

"She should be here tomorrow night." She was in danger of catching on fire from the rage in her eyes. "By the way, how would you avoid having Reo for a brother-in-law if you married Luisa?"

"Who's talkin' marriage, lil sis? The word frightens me to death."

"Oh, I get it—it's all right for you to 'shack up' with a girl, but I'm too young! Well, hear this, big bro—no flighty jerk is going to hurt my friend Luisa. She's the marrying kind." Having delivered this ultimatum, she returned to the earlier thread of their conversation, and a cunning look came into her eyes. "Yentl Androvi's to be the guest of honor, but the party isn't until June 3rd, so I've still got plenty of time to charm the handsome albino. Can he generally be found at the Red-Eyed Bat?"

"Yeah, he plays there on weekends." He rose to go, then did a quick turn-around. "Now hold on! No sister of mine is goin' to a place like that, no way. I promised Mom I'd look after you, an' that's what I'm goin' to do!"

Pia Jo regarded him sweetly. "You seem to have forgotten that I've been on my own in the big city since I was eighteen. Oh, don't glare! I'll interview him at Asgard."

"On what grounds?"

"He was a material witness."

"Okay, but remember you ain't actin' in an official capacity, so don't demand that he see you. An' since he ain't a prime suspect, mind your tone. Don't interrogate—just interview." After he'd delivered a few more unnecessary admonitions, Gunter hurried off, his mind filled with Luisa; and Pia Jo pondered the questions she'd ask Dag Amundson two days hence—the following day was out of the question since Luisa was coming by bus and she had to meet her in Richton. By the time she'd changed the bedding and put soiled clothing in a hamper for Rilka Beerbahm, Innisfree's laundress, to pick up in the morning, she'd devised a plan.

The next morning, after Rilka had picked up the soiled clothing, Pia Jo swept, dusted, picked a bouquet of fresh lilacs from a bush behind Cabin 6, showered, and changed clothing; then she drove the twenty-five miles to Richton to meet Luisa. When they'd shared a big hug, Pia Jo explained why she was driving Uncle Sven's 1957 Corvette, after which she issued a quick invitation. "Come on! I'm treating you to lunch at Mandy's—they have a great salad bar."

"Good! Then you can tell me about this case you're going to investigate. I can see why Reo was willing to leave you at Innisfree all by yourself—he loves money!"

"Don't we all? Just don't start on Reo, and I won't start on Soren!" Pia Jo bargained. When they'd filled their plates and seated themselves by a window, she took out Brenda White's notes on the case and, over their salads, she described her private eye role in some detail. On the way back to Innisfree, she concentrated on a description of the suspects; and back in Cabin 6, while Luisa unpacked her luggage, she laid out her plan for the evening.

Luisa's response was vehemently negative. "You're not serious!" she reposted passionately. "There's been a murder at that place—a double murder if I remember right. It's not safe for a woman to go there alone!" Some girlish escapades had quelled her Latin blood; curiously, it was Pia Jo, the cold-blooded Swede, who was the more adventurous of the two.

Pia Jo's theatre make-up case lay open on the dressing table, and she was applying make-up with a heavy hand. Looking at herself from side to side speculatively, she finally nodded, reached for a red wig with long, flowing curls, and began to settle it over her own short, fair hair.

"I don't believe this!" Luisa stormed while her dark eyes snapped. "Wait'll Reo hears that you went to the Red-Eyed Bat looking like a fancy whore!"

Swiveling around, Pia Jo did her best to pacify her cautious friend. "Reo knows I'm on a case, Lu. He's expecting me to win the $10,000 prize—he'll understand if I take unusual measures."

"Unusual measures? Lunatic chances, you mean. I'm calling Gunter!"

"No, wait, Lu, please. Why don't you come, too? There's safety in numbers, and I won't wear the dinky skirt if you'll come with me. It's no good interviewing Dag Amundson as myself at Asgard—I need to catch him off guard, and I don't want him to recognize me if I interview him at Asgard later. By the way, Gunter's to be your escort to the Roshnikov party."

Luisa's eyes clouded over. "I don't know, Peejay—he's just been divorced and he's hurting. I don't want to catch him on the rebound."

"You hate his bad grammar, you mean. He can speak good English if he wants to—his letters are close to flawless. He's just become accustomed to identifying with the locals," Pia Jo retorted as she combed wildly through the contents of a large cedar chest, tossing disguises hither and yon in her eagerness to find the right disguise. "Here they are—the outfits we wore hiking in the hills when you vacationed here last summer! I'll remove this make-up—most of it—and wear this totally blah outfit if you'll go with me. I'll even wear the black wig—you can wear the red one." Tossing the red curls to her friend, she clapped on a demurely bobbed ebony wig. "We'll both flirt with him and be as coy as teenagers."

After considerably more coaxing, the cautious Luisa agreed to wear the old trousers and shirt, and in the interests of seduction, the curly red wig. "We can't take the Vette—he might see us in it later," Pia Jo decided as they helped one another with their disguises. "I'll ask Blue to give us a ride in his pickup truck. He can be trusted not to tell Gunter."

- 6 -

The Red-Eyed Bat Night Club was well outside Lead Mine's limits and was therefore under Gunter's jurisdiction; he and his officers had raided it more than once.   Recalling former clashes of a formidable nature, Blue wasn't as easily persuaded to cooperate as Pia Jo had predicted.   On the contrary, he swore he'd tell Gunter if she and Luisa went to the notorious hotspot unprotected.

"Who knows what crime figure'll be lurking about? And I guess you know that the bat's blinking red eye is a secret signal announcing that naughties are available. If Gunter found out I let you girls go there, he'd have me up for insubordination and you for conduct unbecoming an officer."

"What's happened to you, Blue?" Pia Jo scoffed. "You used to be a good guy. Anyway, I'm not one of your officers yet—I'm a private eye; and if Holmes can wear disguises, so can we."

"I *am* a good guy, and you're living in never-never land!" Blue snapped, but his indecisiveness suggested that he, too, had a favor to ask. "I'd go with you myself, but I've got a date with Clover—that is, if Maize will let her go with me. What's that woman got against me, Pia Jo? I could understand her animosity if I were a member of the Bear clan, but she knows that we Thunderbirds are an 'above the earth' clan. Hey, she likes you—why don't you put in a good word for me?"

Pia Jo saw an opening and darted through. "I will—if you'll give us a ride to the Bat tonight and don't tell Gunter."

Blue continued to protest vigorously. "You know very well he finds out everything." But eventually he did a complete turnabout. "Oh, all right, go if you must! You can probably trust Dag—he's been good to his young sister. If you have any trouble, latch onto him and he might protect you."

"If you say one word to Gunter, Blue, I'll warn both Maize and Clover that you can't be trusted with women."

Forgetting for a moment that he was a Winnebago, Blue resorted to profanity. "She-devil!" he groaned. "You know damn well I'm a one-woman man." Nonetheless, he agreed to give them a lift.

Night had drawn its shades and the sky was dominated by ominous black clouds when Blue, dressed in a tee shirt bearing the words "Life's too short not to be a Winnebago" and a pair of faded jeans, picked up the two sleuths in his ancient pickup, "The Wild Duck," and drove them to a little-used side-road that was overgrown with weeds and newly-sprouted trees. Pointing them to a faded Indian trail that would take them to the road across from the Red-Eyed Bat, he praised them for wearing backpacks to give credence to their concocted identities, warned them against the red-eyed bats that were said to live in and around an old shack in this particular woods, then got back into his truck and left them to the mercy of nocturnal beasts. When from its dark interior came the deep, penetrating howl of some animal, perhaps a coyote or a wolf, Pia Jo got out her torch and surveyed the area in its vague, dying light.

"I thought private eyes were supposed to have powerful torches and lots of extra batteries," Luisa whispered hoarsely. "A mole couldn't find its way by the light of that bitty, old thing!" Shivering, she added, "This isn't a good plan! I saw a special on vampire bats once—they kill livestock by sucking their blood. Let's go back before they suck our blood!"

"And you're supposed to be an animal rights activist! You're the one who told me all about bats, how they eat up to six hundred mosquitoes an hour and control night pests; but when you even hear about one, you turn and run. And didn't you say that vampire bats are native to Mexico and South America, not to Illinois?" Pia Jo scoffed. Then she abruptly shifted gears. "We can't use a bright light when we're trying not to be seen! What if someone catches us trespassing?"

But Luisa was having second thoughts about the value of bats. "I didn't say I knew anything about red-eyed bats," she confessed with a shudder, "What if they have rabies or—or get in our hair?"

"Then we'll buy new wigs. You're worse than the cowardly lion, Lu—bats don't get in your hair, and those around here don't have red eyes. Blue just said that to frighten us off. Look! Over there—move off the path a bit and you'll see a light."

"I'm going back." Louisa had stopped in her tracks and was looking at Pia Jo resentfully. "I don't like it when people call me a coward."

"I'm sorry, Lu! I'm worse than the cowardly lion—I just pretend I'm brave. If I thought there were coyotes or wolves in this woods, I'd run like hell. Please don't go back."

Somewhat mollified, Luisa caught up with her friend. Groping their way slowly through the uncharted area by the dim light, they tripped over rocks, hit their shins against fallen logs, felt the smart of unseen vines slap them across their faces, and paused now and then to listen to the sounds of unidentified animals scurrying from their path. Once in range of the yard lights, Pia Jo switched off the torch, jammed it into her backpack, hoisted the pack to her shoulders, and beckoned Luisa to accompany her.

The black bat swinging on the sign by the entrance of the disreputable night club reminded Pia Jo of a creature from a Stephen King story; its flashing red eyes were purgatorial, as was the club's dim interior, lit only by red lights that cast fiery shadows on the faces of the occupants. Approaching the somewhat more brightly lit bar, Pia Jo addressed the suave, silky bartender in a sultry Southern voice. "Whe' ah we anyway? We've been hikin' in the hills, an' we got lost. How fah ah we from Joseph's Lodge? We-all ah stayin' the yuh."

The men in the bar picked up their ears, while the fingers of the man at the piano lagged. Two floozies in a booth giggled shrilly while their half-drunk conquests guffawed.

"Joseph's Lodge? That's a good five miles to the south, young ladies. Don't you have a compass along?"

"A compass!" squealed the redhead. "We fuhgot a compass, Bella. Reckon us city gals don' know much about hikin' in th' hills."

"Where you from anyway?" a half-shikkered client asked, his eyes lighting up like brushfires, his voice hoping they were far from home.

"Verginyuh!" supplied the sultry voice of the brunette. "If we could jes' use yoah phone—."

"Sorry—it's out of order," the suave bartender, a double for Poe's Prince Prospero, said too quickly for truth.

"Then could we hyuh someone to take us home?" simpered the redhead.

"I got a better idee," said a barfly, leering hungrily. "You two kin come spend the night with me."

"Can it, Jute!" the bartender warned, evidently recalling a previous occasion. "You heard what the sheriff said last time he was here—if he hears of any hanky-panky in my place, he'll close me down. Why don't you buy the ladies a drink or two?"

Several voices were contending for the honor when the white-haired man at the piano thumped the keys loudly. When the place quieted down, he said in a soft, musical voice, "I'll be glad to give the ladies a ride to Joseph's Lodge on my way back to Asgard." Ignoring Jute's loud taunt that Joseph's Lodge wasn't anywhere near Asgard, he rose, bowed gallantly to the lost females, and introduced himself. "I'm Dag Amundson, and I'd be proud to play your requests free of charge."

The two girls were all interested relief. "Really?" trilled the red-head. "What a nice man you ah! Isn't he a nice man, Flo?"

The brunette twittered and agreed. "Now an' then a gal does run into a very nice man. Can you play 'Come Tiptoe through the Tulips with Me'?" It was the silliest song Pia Jo could think of at the time. Why would a romantically inclined person want to tiptoe through the tulips? Why not go the long way around?

However, Dag found nothing silly about her request. He at once swung into "Come Tiptoe," and even sang the words, fully aware of his talented fingers and his musical voice. "And if I kiss you in the garden / In the moonlight, / Will you pardon me? / Come tiptoe through the tulips with me." As he sang, his eyes caressed their faces one at a time as if he were trying to decide which one he preferred; and although they deplored his eagerness, they could not but admire his gifts. It seemed that in denying him hair color, Nature had compensated by making him a fine figure of a man and by pouring music into his soul. And his contact lenses had transformed his eyes to a vivid blue.

After performing "Carry Me Back to Ole Virginie" eloquently for the redhead, he turned and called, "Burl, take over here, will you? I want to buy these young ladies a drink." At his request, a striking black man with a baby face moved to the piano and began to play and sing Nat King Cole's "Mona Lisa." When the two Southern belles had heard a few bars of the song, they regarded Burl curiously and respectfully, then hurried to join the waiting Dag. A younger bartender, a silky replica of the older one, immediately followed them up the crimson steps and stoically took Dag's order of a bottle of red wine, and since he was sure they were starving, huge bowls of popcorn. As they listened to Burl's mellow voice singing perceptively, "Do you smile to tempt a lover, Mona Lisa, / Or do you only wish to play a fetching part?" the girls looked at each other quizzically, then relaxed and lost their fear.

When they'd exchanged chitchat about Lead Mines, Burl, Nat King and Natalie Cole, and Sheriff Borg, who was, according to Dag, "a nice enough fellow but a snoopy, unbending sheriff," the brunette said, "A farmuh in the hills told us an amazin' story about the theft of a valuable emrald braclet in Lead Mines a while back. He said the insurance company's offerin' a big rewahd."

"Fancy that!" chimed the redhead, like a grandmother clock. Then she tossed her long curls coquettishly and added, "I'd shoah like to put that rewahd in my hope chest."

The words "hope chest" drew Dag's blue contacts to her face magnetically. "Hope chest? You planning to get married? Where's your engagement ring?"

"Oh, noah," squealed the redhead, "I haven't met the right man yet. Now don' get me wrong—I've met a lot o' willin' men, but they ah all so poor."

"Now isn't that the truth!" chirped the brunette. "A gal's got to think o' her future, you know. I'd shoah look twice at the man who won that prize, wouldn't youah, Flo?"

"Would I!" The redhead's eyes took on a dreamy, speculative look. "I do believe I'd look twice at the man who was clevah enough to steal the braclet! Th' ownahs must of collected th' insurance by now. The farmuh said they ah very wealthy, and they want the braclet back fo' selfish reasons."

The eager pianist had been listening to this exchange intently. "It wasn't a bracelet," he finally amended. "It was a necklace made of emeralds and diamonds surrounded by little pearls. I played for that party—I saw it on the lady's neck."

Upon hearing his proud claim, the girls plied him with questions; and soon he was telling them about the lush beauty of the emerald necklace, which, he averred, was almost as appealing as a fetching woman. Under the influence of a second bottle of wine, he said grandly that emeralds were merely green fire, while a beautiful, seductive woman is red fire. Then he looked directly at the redhead and asked boldly, "Would you even marry me?"

Flo's eyes flew to his face. "Even marry yo', sugah?" she asked in shocked tones. "Why, you'd be the first ah'd marry. You ah a han'some man. We could have a sweet honeymoon on th' money the emralds brought in, couldn't we, honey lamb?"

The brunette took instant offense. "Hey, Flo, give a gal a chance, would you? Ah'd marry him, too, an' ah've saved $5,000. We could take the necklace out uh the country an' get rid o' it on my savin's— that is, if you-all have it, kitten."

At that point, the two girls looked as if they were about to throw wine in one another's faces, and perhaps they would have if Dag hadn't silenced them with a hoarse question. "You two mean it? No kidding? You'd both marry me if I had some money of my own?"

"Not both of us—that 'ud be bigmy—but you sure could have yoah choice." The girls now nodded at each other agreeably, their faces reflecting their mindlessness.

"Would it have to be marriage?"

"Weelll, nauw—ah'd have to think about that," the redhead said slowly.

"Me, too," echoed the brunette. "You have any idea who stole th' emralds so we could steal 'em away from him?"

"Oa her?" added the redhead eagerly.

"Do I? My head's full of ideas!"

"Who do you suspect?" in unison.

"The butler, that's who. The one they call Ox-Eye. They can't be trusted—those Indians from the Settlement. They hold grudges. If he or Dove took it, they'd think it was their due. After all, the Natives were treated like dirt."

"But could he work fast enough? The thief must of been awful quick with his—oa her—hands," mused the brunette.

"He's a juggler, that one is. I've seen him juggle at the Winnebago Powwows. The man's fingers are faster'n lightning."

When they both looked at his hands, he sensed their unspoken question and put them in his pockets. "Sure, I have fast fingers— what piano player doesn't?" Suddenly he began to cry. "But I'm a tin man." The wine, which he'd almost chugged, had loosened his tongue. "There it was right before my eyes—a $100,000 emerald necklace all studded with diamonds and pearls!" he moaned. "If I'd reached out when I walked past her, I could've had it in a flash. But I didn't have the nerve. The thief must have had both nerve and fast fingers."

"You girls, Joseph's outside waiting for you," a harsh voice informed them before they could speak again. "A farmer in the hills called him and said he saw you wandering along a path headed in this direction."

The girls stared at Blue, who was accompanied by his favorite female, Clover Whitewater. "What ah you doing here, deputy?" Pia Jo demanded, almost forgetting her phony accent. "I tol' Maize that you two were playing cahds with Flo and me at the Lodge." She was enjoying her role, but when Blue tipped his head toward the stairs threateningly, both she and Lu got up, thanked Dag sweetly in their phoniest accents, said they'd call him first thing in the mahning, and hurried down the steps.

As they passed the Afro at the piano, Pia Jo whispered in her own voice, "How did you know we were acting, Mr. Burl?"

"Just call me Burl. I'm from Virginia—nobody talks like that there," he whispered back. "I reckoned you were undercover for the sheriff."

"Go see Sven Tillotson," Pia Jo urged. "Wild Swans Lodge needs a pianist."

Burl's chuckle seemed to come from his toes. "What'll I play on? Last time I was there he'd gotten rid of that tinny old piano."

"Don't worry—I'll use my chawm!" she said with a wink and hurried after Luisa. Blue's angry voice followed them as they departed: "I heard what you said to those two dingheads, Dag. What do you mean, the Indians at the Settlement can't be trusted? You know damn well they've lived in peace with the whites. They bought the Settlement with money they earned themselves, and white settlers backed them when they refused to go to the reservation." He took a notebook from his pocket, urged Clover to sit down, seated himself beside her, and barked an order. "Tell me what you know about the theft of the emerald necklace, Dag!"

When he and Clover joined the dingheads in his pickup later, he explained, "When I told Clover what you were planning to do, she said we'd better follow you or I'd be on probation for a year."

"Did Dag tell you anything?" Now caught up in the adventure, Luisa asked eagerly.

Blue shrugged. "He's drunk—he doesn't know a thing. I left him sobbing because he hadn't stolen the necklace when he'd had a chance to do so. He said he could have made it with one of you if he'd stolen it."

Pia Jo looked at him sadly. "He's an alcoholic, isn't he? That's the real reason the girls don't give him a tumble."

Blue nodded. "It's *a* reason! Dag's his own worst enemy." He looked at his watch and groaned. "I've got to get Clover home—you girls'll have to ride in back. Don't complain—no one forced you to come here tonight."

Later, when they'd doffed their disguises, creamed off their make-up, and were sipping tea in the kitchen, Pia Jo looked at her friend questioningly. "Shall we have a go at the servants tomorrow?"

"You can!" Luisa said firmly, reverting to her cautious self. "I came here to paint your portrait, remember? When you're gone, I'll do a sketch of Boffo. Where is she anyway?"

"Thelma's keeping her inside until Gunter finds the dog or wolf that killed Martin Diver's sheep. Martin's on a vendetta of some sort— he's already shot two of his neighbor's dogs even though there was no evidence that they were near his sheep. Batty old menace—he'll probably shoot his neighbors next."

"Surely he wouldn't come to Innisfree and shoot a pedigreed Sheltie from the Shetlands?"

"Who knows what a madman will do? He might think Boffo's a pit bull in disguise. Sure you won't come tomorrow? You were smooth tonight."

"I'm sure—I'll just keep your home fires burning. And don't be gone all day—I want to get started on your portrait."

After saying, "Goodnight, Luisa—I've got to be up with the dick-cissels to write a report on tonight's adventure," Pia Jo went to her room and set her alarm. After donning a nightshirt, she jotted down some questions to ask Gunter in the morning, "What's Ox-Eye really like? Why on earth does Burl play in a scruffy place like that? Was Amundson really drunk or merely putting on an act?"

- 7 -

The song of the dickcissels—"dick cissel, dick cissel"—awakened Pia Jo; slipping from the sheets, she rushed to the window to see if she could catch a glimpse of the unusual yellow-breasted sparrows with their black bibs. Emeline, who'd thought they resembled meadowlarks, had pointed them out to her the previous summer and had suggested that they buy binoculars and go bird-watching; and when she'd been too busy to comply, her mother had bought an inexpensive pair of binoculars and had gone with friends. She had the binoculars now; knowing that she could use them in her sleuthing, Gunter, who was temporarily living at Rendezvous, had confiscated them before Lena, Soren, or one of their numerous children could sneak them out behind his back.

"Yes, there they are!" she breathed triumphantly. "I wish Luisa and I could take time off from our work to go bird-watching. I'll ask her." But when she peered into Luisa's bedroom, she found it unoccupied. "Am eating breakfast at the Lodge," a note on the counter informed her. "We're out of groceries."

Provisions were indeed scarce, but Pia Jo found oatmeal and some dry dark bread that was adequate for toast. As she prepared the oatmeal and toasted the bread, she considered a course of action based on the notes written in Brenda's ornamental calligraphy somewhat augmented by Blue's no-nonsense scrawls regarding the servants at *Oblachnyj Dom*. She had no intention of ignoring Ox-Eye and Dove as suspects even though Blue had defended them loyally; but this was Winnebago country, and she could learn more about them easily enough.

The Cambodian twins were a different story; Brenda had learned only that they were identical and that they painted tiny nature scenes—flowers, birds, butterflies, bees, fish, and the like—on eggshells and peddled them in the village on their bicycles when their services weren't needed at *Oblochnyj Dom*. Dgong eggs, they called them, mimicking the famous Fabergé. She'd added that they seemed to have most afternoons off.

"I'll interview the Raintrees first," she decided as she added brown sugar, cinnamon, and a bit of skimmed milk (the last in the container) to her oatmeal. "But if Dove is as hard to approach as Ox-Eye, what role shall I play?" The only fact she'd gleaned from Blue's notes was that Dove served as treasurer for a group called "Friends of the Winnebagos"; anyone who gave a $20 donation could become a "Friend" and would receive a pin with a thunderbird design to signify membership. Although Sven generally frowned on soliciting, he knew that the Friends had helped many needy Indians in the Settlement and on the Reservation; he'd therefore allowed members of the group to call at Scandia and at the cabins and ask for donations during the previous week. When they hadn't found Pia Jo or Reo at home, they'd left a request on the door, along with Dove's address. Instead of sending her donation in the mail, she could bring it to Dove in person.

Having settled on an approach to the Raintrees, she turned her thoughts to the Cambodian twins. With a generous expense account, she could afford to buy some decorated eggs, but thoughts of Reo discouraged the idea. Delicate little Oriental designs were not his idea of Art. When she'd commented on the tasteful use of color in a print by a female Japanese artist, he'd shrugged dismissively and had contradicted the recent study that said women were genetically more perceptive, color-wise, than men. Time, he'd insisted, had proven the artistic superiority of males. But she had no time to think of Reo's ego now—she had to decide on an investigative plan, and even though she wasn't on the case in an official capacity, she knew that Gunter expected copies of her reports; besides, she loved to write, and they might be required if the Roshnikov case were to come to court. After scribbling a response on Luisa's note, she hurried out to the mini Corvette and drove to his office at a speed that would have set a state cop's teeth on edge.

Gunter, who'd been called to Martin Diver's farm in the middle of the night because a German shepherd had killed two of Martin's valuable merino sheep, wasn't in a cheerful mood. When Pia Jo learned of the attack, she asked, "Why didn't you send one of your officers?"

The question did nothing to improve Gunter's glum spirits. "Because Martin was sure the dog was Casper's Rasputin, an' he was threatenin' to shoot both Casper an' th' dog, that's why! Martin's a time bomb ready to go off, an' you have to handle that kind with kid gloves." Gunter was close to being a time bomb himself. "Must you look so cheerful this early in th' mornin'?"

Pleased that he was reading Emeline's gift of a thick book on criminal psychology, she pacified him as best she could. "I'm upset myself, but I'm practicing what you preach—that I should wear my best face when I interview suspects."

"An' what're you upset about?"

"I'm upset because Brenda was totally uninformed about the Cambodians—I don't have enough background material to decide on a role to play when I interview them."

He was definitely not pacified. "How'm I sposed to know anything about Cambodians? That's what the Roshnikovs are payin' you for, ain't it?" he demanded irascibly. "To find out things about people?"

"Yes, and that's what I'm trying to do, Rhubarb. You've told me yourself that I should know something about suspects before I interview them. I also need to know how Dove will react to my playing the role of a Friend of the Winnebagos."

Blue was busy at a fax machine, but now he turned and offered his insight. "Dove's taken courses in Domestic Arts and is willing to cook for whites if she makes enough money; but she claims she was raped by a wealthy white man once, and she hates all whites because of it. She's probably accept your donation, but she won't be grateful."

"At least she's devoted to her own people. What can you tell me about Ox-Eye? When I met him, he was chillier than a cold water fish."

"I'd reserve judgment if I were you—he doesn't always put his best face forward. He's a juggler for one thing; I've seen him juggle dainty glass cups and not break a single one. He gets teased because he drives a 1987 *Comanche* Jeep, and he's closer to his dog than he is to people. It's a valuable dog, and he trained it himself; in fact, it's so obedient and well-behaved that the Roshnikovs let him keep it in his quarters at Cloud House."

"What kind of a dog is it?"

"A Siberian Husky, a male. He named him Chukchi after the Chukchi people of Northern Siberia. He's a sled dog, and he was on a winning team in an Iditarod race."

"So Ox-Eye likes strong, rugged things and may seem cold but is capable of affection. You might teach my dear brother to be a bit more polite." To forestall another explosion, she handed her report to Gunter. "Here are my notes on our vamp act last night. It was highly successful. Did Blue tell you?"

It was Blue's turn to erupt, although less vociferously than the sheriff had. "If I remember right, you swore me to secrecy," he growled, looking warily at his boss over the rim of his coffee cup.

Gunter glanced at the report but reacted without reading it. "No, Blue didn't tell me! I won't have you corruptin' my deputy, Peejay, an' you can't ask him to help you win that reward!" But curiosity got the better of him. "What vamp act?"

"Seducing Dag Amundson at the Red-Eyed Bat, what else? It's all here in my report. I need to make a copy for the Roshnikovs, but I'd like you to comment on it first."

Gunter's protest filled the office. "I warned you not to go to th' Red-Eyed Bat! Blue, what the hell do you know about her shenanigans?"

"He came as our bodyguard," Pia Jo said innocently. "We were perfectly safe. You know I wouldn't do anything to worry you, Gunter."

"Like hell you wouldn't." He skim-read the report and tossed it aside. "This is storybook stuff—a lot of damn foolishness. You'd better have 'em give you a signed contract—they might fire you after a few more acts like this one."

She grinned mischievously as she retrieved the report and photocopied it on a small office machine. "I have a signed contract and an expense check for $500!"

"Well, then, whadda you need us for? Get outta here or I'll arrest you for impedin' us in th' performance of our duties."

As she left the sheriff's office with a copy of her report, a walkie-talkie, a notebook and pens, and a small tape recorder in her tote bag, she decided not to share any more information with Gunter until she was well into the investigation—he was too busy with his own cases. Gearing down to take the steep ascent to High Street, she felt a tiny sting of remorse over bothering him; after all, he'd probably spent a sleepless night worrying about Martin Diver's frightening temper. She would have felt a great deal better if she'd heard him and Blue cracking up over her unorthodox methods when she was safely out the door.

It was ten-thirty when she reached *Oblachnyj Dom;* and when, donation in hand, she asked Ox-Eye if he and Dove could spare a few minutes to answer a few questions about the theft of the emerald necklace, his response was as wooden as an orange crate.

"I'm helping Dove prepare lunch," he protested. "The Roshnikovs expect it to be punctual. Can't you come some other time?"

How long does it take a professional cook to make lunch for two people, she wondered, but she answered diplomatically. "Since the Roshnikovs have hired me to find the emerald necklace, I'm sure they won't be angry if lunch is a little late today." As she spoke, a tall, thin, brown-skinned woman wearing white trousers and a white jacket joined Ox-Eye. While her uniform was like that of any trained chef, her thick black braid, which was very long and hung down her back, was Native American.

"You must be Dove!" Pia Jo said with a warm smile, extending the donation check. "Reo and I weren't home when your members called last week, so I thought I'd bring you our donation in person. May I come in for a few minutes?"

Dove did not return her smile, and her response was as rude as Blue had said it would be. "I'll just take the donation," she said crisply, reaching out for it, "and you can be on your way."

Her smile subsiding, Pia Jo withdrew the check. "I'm here to interview you about the theft of the emerald necklace," she said in a tone that meant business. "I shall have to discuss your lack of cooperation with the Roshnikovs if you refuse to comply."

Dove's attitude did not improve, but she did stand aside. "If you must bother us, come into the kitchen. We have to keep on with our work."

The kitchen was large, conveniently stocked, and cheerful. Handing the donation to Ox-Eye, who accepted it without comment and passed it on to Dove, Pia Jo seated herself at the end of a table filled with enticing food. "You're welcome," she almost said when Dove put the donation in a basket on a shelf without thanking her or giving her the usual lagniappe for a donation, a thunderbird pin. "What do you think we can tell you?" Dove asked as she picked up a knife and went back to slicing plump, white mushrooms.

"Let me summarize what I already know about you—you can correct me and add to it. You are Ox-Eye and Dove Raintree, the cook and butler at Oblachnyj Dom—."

"Brenda White already interviewed us," Ox-Eye pointed out as he popped a pan of Cornish hens into the oven and turned the dial to the required heat. "We can't add anything to what we told her."

"Since she's been discredited as a police officer, I can't depend 100% on her report," she explained, clearing a place for her tape recorder, turning it on, and recording her name, the names of the interviewees, and the date. "You're from the Settlement near Innisfree, aren't you, Ox-Eye? And Dove, I think Blue said you're from Black River Falls."

"He said right." Dove's laconic response was delivered in a "this is too much" tone of voice. "In case you don't know, that's in Wisconsin," she added sarcastically.

Pia Jo ignored this assault on her intelligence. "Have you worked here long?"

"Five years."

"Do you like working here?"

"It's a job," Dove said without bothering to disguise her reservations. "They pay well enough."

I'll bet they do. "What do you remember about the anniversary party that was held here last December?"

"It was like any other party. Madame gave us a menu. We bought the food and prepared it." Dove's short, choppy sentences held less emotion and less information than a Dick and Jane response.

Ox-Eye, who was now stirring what appeared to be a batch of gingerbread, added a morsel of information. "Because the crowd was so large, we served it buffet style in the dining room adjoining the drawing room. The houseboys went around with trays of drinks."

"Did you hear the commotion when Maxima discovered that her necklace was gone?"

"How could we?" Dove demanded, her malice undisguised. "We weren't allowed to mingle with the guests."

"Where were you?"

Ox-Eye took over the duty of responding. "We were here in the kitchen. The houseboys removed the empty bowls, brought full ones in, and supplied clean dishes, and we all cleaned up the mess after the guests left."

"And you couldn't hear the commotion from out here?"

"We heard her scream that her jewels were gone, but what could we do about it? We aren't law officers."

"I see. Did you notice anything unusual that night? Were the Roshnikovs sober?"

"We don't gossip about our employers," Dove snapped scornfully; but when Pia Jo explained that pertinent information isn't considered gossip, Ox-Eye nodded briefly and said, "They drank more than usual, but they hold their liquor well."

Pia Jo turned off the recorder, thanked them, and scrawled her address and phone number on a piece of paper. "If you think of anything else that might be helpful, please call me," she urged as she handed Ox-Eye the paper. She'd noted that he was more cooperative than Dove, though in a stand-offish way. "Would it be possible for me to interview the houseboys before I leave?"

"They have the afternoon off," he offered in a deadpan voice. "I heard them talking in their own language, but I think they were discussing their bikes. They may have gone for a bike ride."

As Pia Jo thanked them and left the kitchen, she felt the keen blade of disappointment. Obviously they didn't consider her a friend of the Winnebagos; in fact, they seemed prejudiced against her whereas she wasn't the least bit prejudiced against them.

Fearing that she'd missed the houseboys, she was about to get into the Vette and leave; but when she glanced about, she saw them, mounted on ten-speed bikes, preparing to descend the hill. Thankful that she could interview them before lunch, she hurriedly got out of the car and approached them deceptively. Since she knew nothing about them, she'd decided to size them up in a leisurely fashion before she questioned them about the Roshnikov party. "Are you the artists who paint eggs?" she asked in a friendly fashion.

They were in no hurry to answer her—in fact, they stared so intently at the white Corvette, its red interior, and the red blaze on its doors that she soon realized that the car interested them more than she did. The realization gave her an opening. "You like it? It belongs to my uncle, and it's a 1957 Corvette, a collector's car. He's a very nice uncle—he's letting me use it until I can afford to get a car of my own."

When they still didn't answer, doubts began to crawl about in her brain like centipedes. What if they hated cars? Or red? Or Americans? Or blondes? "One of these days I'm going to buy a book on the reactions of foreigners," she told herself firmly before she tried again. "Would you like to ride in it?"

This suggestion worked like a charm. When they both said "Yes" at the same time, she urged them to leave their bikes where they were and climb in beside her; since they were small, there was room in the two-door vehicle for both of them. In a few moments they were descending to the highway, and she was heading for an old-fashioned ice cream shop on the other side of Lead Mines. The car had a top, but Uncle Sven had left it off for the summer, so the wind was in their hair and the sun was warm on their necks.

It was as good a time as any to emphasize another interest that they had in common—artistic endeavor. "I'm Pia Jo Borg. My Aunt Thelma collects decorated eggs, and only yesterday she remarked that she'd heard you do beautiful work. I'd like to buy a couple for her birthday next week." Had Thelma heard this remarkable statement, she would have been amazed. She was a September child who collected antique plates.

When they still said nothing, her perambulatory doubts took on speed. What if they'd been to Scandia peddling their eggs and had been turned down? But then she remembered that the Colony was a good five miles from the town. It was doubtful that they'd go that far on their bikes to sell eggs. Or was it?

She pulled in at the ice cream parlor and asked, "Do you like ice cream?"

"Yes!" they chorused. Accompanying them inside, she suggested that they order whatever flavor they preferred and ordered a maple nut cone for herself. When they had silently and leisurely finished the last bite, she popped her own last bite into her mouth and said, "Okay, back to Cloud House. I want you to show me your eggs."

As the ice cream had disappeared, so had some of their reserve. "Okay!" they said as one. Back at the Roshnikov residence, one of them said, "Come with us, please," then added politely, "I'm Chindee, and this is my brother Chearee." Getting out of the car, they led her through a side door into the servant's quarters.

Their room was large, cozy, and neat. It had twin beds; twin dressers; a wooden cart holding baskets of decorated eggs all exquisitely Oriental in design and color; a work table filled with paints, brushes, and works in progress; and a small entertainment center. Compared to Cambodia's rude dwellings, this room must seem like the Eastern Heaven to them.

Her pleasure was so obvious and her admiration so genuine that she trumped her own ace. One by one, they showed her the fragile objects, each as impressive in its own way as the others. Since they looked expensive, she asked fearfully, "How much are they? I hope I can afford a couple."

"We ask $20 each," Chearee said silkily, "but you a nice lady—we sell you two for $20—if Chindee say okay." As she looked from one to the other, Pia Jo could not tell them apart; they were facsimiles of one another in appearance and dress, echoes in voice. Then she noticed that Chindee had a small black dot, a birthmark, beneath his left eye.

"How easily they could impersonate one another," she marveled silently. "Chearee could use a marker to draw a little black dot under his eye. Could they have somehow been involved in the theft of the emerald and diamond necklace?"

When Chindee had graciously agreed to the price, Pia Jo selected two eggs, one decorated with golden butterflies, the other with cherry blossoms, for Thelma's imaginary birthday. When, using extreme care, they'd each wrapped one of them and placed them side by side in a small box, she paid them and started for the door. "But you haven't interviewed them yet," she paused to remind herself. "Think, Pia Jo, think!!" And then an idea came like rain to parched earth. "Do you like picnics?" she asked eagerly. "My friend has just come from the city, and we're having a picnic to welcome her this afternoon. Would five miles be too far for you to come on your bikes?"

For a long moment, they consulted one another with their eyes; then they shook their black heads in unison. "Five miles not too far," Chindee said politely; and Chearee concurred elegantly, "We not been so far, but we try."

"Great! Can you be there by one? I'll give you directions." Taking a pad from her purse, she quickly drew them a map, then said, "See you at one," and hurried out the front door. She had a picnic to plan and guests to invite, and both tasks must be done in record time.

-8-

Swinging the Corvette around, Pia Jo sped to Herman's Food Mart on the edge of Lead Mines and promptly bought hard rolls, lean ham, low-fat cheese, pickles, and a bag of varied fruit for her impromptu picnic, then added large cartons of vegetarian baked beans and cole-slaw, ruefully paying for them with some of her retaining fee, which she dearly wanted to save for the Paris trip. Plastic plates that could be washed and napkins took another chunk, but she consoled herself with the thought that her expenditures were investments that just might net herself the cheering sum of 9,500 additional smackeroos!

"Okay, so they're gorgeous eggs!" Luisa conceded none too graciously, "but a spur-of-the-moment picnic just when I want to begin your portrait? I just wish your moments would take off their spurs!"

As she spread her purchases out on the kitchen table in Cabin 6, Pia Jo resorted to praise and bribery to gain her friend's cooperation. "But you work so fast, Lu—you finished Boffo and this fantastic pencil sketch of a blue-footed booby in two days! You've wanted to paint a booby from the snapshots your parents sent you from the Galapagos; and now you can, blue feet and all. Don't be mad, Lu—if I win the reward, I'll bring you a fantastic souvenir from Paris. We have to eat sometime—besides, I'm inviting Gunter and Blue."

"Good grief!" Luisa protested with a groan. "Why didn't you say so?" Promptly forgetting the unusual and humorous bird she'd been working on, she charged into her bedroom to look over her wardrobe, leaving Pia Jo free to telephone her invitations, which met with surprisingly positive responses. Since Luisa was to be present, even Gunter approved of her plan. Thelma, always helpful in an emergency, sent Britt over to lend an efficient hand; and when she arrived, she was loaded down with pound cake, strawberries, and whipped cream for a strawberry shortcake. This was not the first time that Britt Larson, Thelma's distant cousin who had come from Sweden to work for her and Sven, had saved the day.

"I hope you won't mind if we bring some guests," Thelma said when Pia Jo telephoned Scandia to extend the invitation. "We'd already asked the Wylies to lunch with us. George is working on an article on Lady Gregory, and he wants Sven to critique it."

Pia Jo's permission reverberated enthusiastically along the line. "By all means bring them along. They're on Gunter's list of suspects—did you know that?"

Thelma's response was drenched with disapproval. "When you meet them, you'll realize how ridiculous that is. They spent their personal inheritance on a home for retarded children—I'd just as soon suspect Gunter or Blue. Or even you!"

Leaving Luisa to doll up for Gunter, Pia Jo and Britt swung into action, moving two picnic tables together to form one long one, covering them with a white tablecloth (which Thelma insisted on furnishing for the comfort of her stylish guests), and loading them with enough food for a small smorgasbord. Sven too came bearing gifts—a basket containing two bottles of fine, chilled wine, cloth napkins, and sparkling wine glasses; and the tray of *hors d'oeuvres* that Britt had prepared for the lunch with the Wylies. This being a picnic, the good-humored, rawboned woman fully intended to enjoy her own labors, something she would not have done had the Tillotsons entertained their guests formally at Scandia. But what evolved was not a simple picnic—it was a sparkling feast.

The guests arrived promptly at one, Chindee and Chearee on their ten-speeds; the Wylies in a sleek station-wagon that matched their tall, slender elegance; Gunter and his chief deputy in an official white and plum "Sheriff of Berger County" vehicle. Pia Jo smiled surreptitiously when she saw their crisp navy uniforms mingling with the Wylies' classy clothes, the sports outfits Sven and Thelma favored, the Cambodians' immaculate white garb, Luisa's pale green shirt and darker green

Capris, and her own scuffed blue jeans. "If we only had masks," she mused, "this would be a costume party." The soft-pink country roses Elizabeth brought provided the proper ambiance; and the decorated eggs, festively wrapped, gave Pia Jo an opportunity to wish Thelma a happy birthday and to welcome Luisa to Innisfree.

Thelma, who'd been apprised of the birthday deception, said truthfully, "I couldn't have gotten a lovelier birthday gift, Sweet Pea. Bess, you really should buy some of these eggs."

"Oh, but I have—six of them." Turning to Pia Jo, Bess teased inelegantly, "Your name is 'Peuh Jo'? Does anyone ever call you 'Pee' or' Pee-Pee?"

"A few kids in my elementary school tried that! They made up a song called 'Pee-Pee's in the Parlor Peeing Purple' and tormented me with it for days. Finally I got mad and locked them in the woodshed while I ate the goodies their mothers had packed in their lunches. When they didn't return to class after recess, one of the other kids told on me, and I had to go and let them out."

She laughed as she recounted the incident, and her audience laughed with her. "Were you punished?" George wanted to know.

"Emeline's response was unusual. She thought they'd demeaned me when they called me 'Pee-Pee,' and she wanted them to feel what it's like to be demeaned. So she helped me make up a poem with a nasty stanza devoted to each of them. One stanza was about Harold, who never washed his hair. He didn't, either—his scalp smelled rancid. Then there was Nancy, whose nose ran into her food—I'd refused to eat *her* goodies." Pia Jo paused and was thoughtful as she recalled the event in more detail. Then she added with a chuckle, "Mom did make me bake a cake and bring it to school to replace the goodies I'd eaten, but that wasn't punishment—it was sweet revenge. I made my favorite kind—chocolate—and ate the biggest piece myself." Having confessed to a misspent youth, she called enthusiastically, "Dig in, everyone! This is a feaste, so don't count calories."

"I ought to tell you some of the tricks Emmy and I pulled when we were youngsters together," Sven chuckled as he and Thelma joined the Wylies and picked up plastic plates. "She liked to write—I wonder if she recorded any of them."

While the guests "dug in," Pia Jo appraised them all covertly. How could the Wylies, whose presences were so courtly, possibly be thieves? And if they were thieves, how could they be so at ease in the company of the law officers? Seldom had she seen two more striking people; both had light brown hair worn mid-length; both had large, strong teeth; both were highly educated; and both had the polished manners of diplomats. Clearly, too, Thelma and Sven idolized them.

"I've been away so long that I've lost touch with Thelma and Sven," she mused as she noted the camaraderie of the four older picnickers. "They've been so decent to me—how can I suspect their close friends?"

Realizing that feelings don't solve crimes, she temporarily shelved her mental inquisition of the Wylies, whose surname did little to quell her fears, and focused on the others. Gunter was seated next to Luisa and was mimicking and miming Martin Diver for her entertainment; Britt was eating near the Dgong twins and was listening while they talked with Blue about their life in Cambodia. Moving closer, Pia Jo joined their conversation.

"How do you like living in Lead Mines?" she asked, striving for the right combination of interest and objectivity.

"We miss our family, but we make more money here," Chindee said in his careful Cambodian English.

"We like money very much," Chearee chimed in.

"Well!" Pia Jo expostulated inwardly. "So your focus is on money rather than on America's other advantages! Does that mean you'd steal to get more?" But her tone was carefully noncommittal when she asked, "Are your parents very poor?"

"They are velly, velly poor," they said, echoing each other.

Their response brought Ching, an Oriental student at the University, to Pia Jo's mind. "I once knew a young man from Taiwan who sent his parents money on a regu—."

In their eagerness to reply, they didn't wait for her to finish. "Oh, we do that!" Chindee blurted. "Every month," added his echo.

Sensing the importance of her inquiry, Blue joined in the questioning.

"You send them quite a bit, do you?"

Startled by his uniform and official tone, their eyes met and telegraphed caution; for a long moment, it seemed as though they were going to take refuge in silence. Then Chindee said defensively, "We get free room and board, so we send half our wages."

"That seems like a good arrangement," Pia Jo hastened to assure them. "I'm sure you can live well on the rest." Pacified, they fell to eating, and the conversation turned to Cambodian food; but when they'd finished eating, they mounted their bikes and left before Pia Jo could question them further. Turning to Blue, who was washing down a huge helping of strawberry shortcake with wine, she warned him off. "I'd gained their trust—and then you frightened them with your uniform and official voice. Now they'll never tell me anything."

"I was just trying to help," Blue returned defensively.

"If you want to help, check their spending habits—find out what those bicycles cost, or have Windy do it if you're too busy. And Blue, how would the emerald thief go about selling such an expensive necklace? Would any of our suspects know anything about disposing of stolen goods?"

"Maybe the Wylies—or the Oleanders. They've been around the most. The diamonds and emeralds would have to be separated and reset in other ways. The necklace couldn't be sold as it is, and since no reports have come in on similar gems, Garnet thinks it's been stashed somewhere."

"Are you saying he's still on the case?"

"You bet he is, at least covertly. He's watching the known fences."

Although Pia Jo knew nothing about fencing stolen goods, she could empathize with the Cambodian twins, for she did know what it was like to be poor. Emeline had had to struggle hard to keep her four children together and to prevent creditors from foreclosing on the farm. Pia Jo had wanted to get a job after high school and become self-sufficient, but her mother had urged her to take courses, work part time, and save for her education. And although more than one well-off man had proposed marriage, Emeline had refused to marry for security. Instead, she'd continued to be resourceful. Skillfully, she'd turned her talent for gardening and her love for the environment into a steady, if small, source of income.

Her thoughts returning to the present, Pia Jo could see a strong similarity between herself and the Cambodian twins. "No matter what their ethnic background might be," she mused, "people are much alike.

Obviously the twins feel as strongly about their parents as I feel about my mother. If they stole the jewels, it would be a Robin Hood sort of theft. The same is true of the Wylies—if they stole the necklace to help provide a home for unwanted retarded children, would it be right for me to expose them? Which is more important, the luxuries of the rich or the necessities of the poor?"

- 9 -

Because Gunter and Blue had duties to perform, the picnic ended rather abruptly; Sven and George soon said "Goodbye," "Thanks so much," "Compliments to the Chef," and "We enjoyed the break from duty," and hurried off to Sven's study to discuss George's paper on Lady Gregory. However, Bess lingered, and guiltlessly, since several devoted and trained volunteers were available to take over when she and George needed a change of pace from their charges.

"I didn't help prepare the food, so I'll clean up," Luisa said firmly. "Britt will help me, won't you, Britt? You three sit there and visit for a while."

Obedient to her command, Pia Jo, Thelma, and Bess sat for another hour, sipping blush wine and talking about Pia Jo's work in the theatre and her part-time fall and winter job at Halcyon College in Chicago. Although it seemed a great opportunity to interview Bess about the emerald necklace, Pia Jo was loath to do so for fear she might offend Thelma. But Bess was so interested in Pia Jo's teaching and its rewards that it was some time before Pia Jo was able to focus on the investigation. When Bess asked, "But can you make enough money teaching part-time to support yourself?" Pia Jo found herself explaining her precarious financial situation at some length.

"Far from it," she answered somewhat heatedly. "You're looking at one of the most-exploited people in the United States. I have a Master's degree and have done some post-graduate work, but I'm allowed to teach only two courses a semester, and I get paid $1,500 a course.

Since summer courses go to full-time teachers or part-timers with se-
niority, I make the huge sum of $6,000 a year teaching. I take pride
in my work, but I get no fringe benefits, no privileges, and minimal
respect from the Administration and the full-time teachers. As one of
the Adjunct Faculty, I rate with Hindu Untouchables in the College
Caste System."

Bess looked at her in astonishment. "But Thelma tells me that you
were a first-rate student and are a dedicated teacher."

It was difficult for Pia Jo to remain dispassionate. "My employers
don't consider brains or merit reasons for higher wages," she said with
a sigh.

"But teachers can't live on $6,000 a year!"

"Right—they can't. So some of them teach several courses at wide-
spread colleges and become burnouts."

"And there's no chance for advancement?"

"Very little. Hiring committees rarely hire new teachers from the
ranks of the Adjunct Faculty—they say they want fresh blood in the
department. And full-time teachers with tenure are fixtures for life—
not even presidents or prime ministers have it so good."

"It's the same at the University where Sven teaches part time,"
Thelma added. "He and I have met several tenured teachers, and it
isn't clear to us why they're such a privileged class. We're lucky to have
private funds."

"And you? Do you also have private funds?" Bess asked Pia Jo with
what seemed like an insatiable thirst for information.

"Gad, no, I'm a pauper! I stay in Cabin 6 now and then because
Sven and Thelma don't charge me rent."

"And you didn't inherit anything when your mother died?"

"Not yet. We know that we'll each get an equal share—Elise, Soren, Gunter, and I—after her debts are paid. But because Emeline was
an environmentalist and was very concerned about what would happen to Rendezvous after she died, she left a two-part will; the first part
stipulated that we will all inherit but that Rendezvous can't be sold for
six months because she wants us to consider its destiny carefully; and
it also specified that Gunter could live there rent-free during that six
months to help him recover from the expense of his divorce. Emeline's
attorney, Mr. Blanding, is meeting with us sometime this month, and

he's going to read us the second part and let us vote on what to do. Unless we all agree to sell the place to a wealthy developer, which I will never do, our individual shares won't be all that much."

Bess looked at her thoughtfully. "Yes, I know Josh Blanding—he's fair but a bit on the rigid side. You'll have a little money, and you'll have your job with Gunter, so why teach when you're so poorly paid?"

"Good question!" Pia Jo admitted ruefully. "I guess it's because I love to teach and I love my students. But I hate being jobless, as I am at present. It makes me feel restless and insecure."

"But she's not quite jobless," Thelma corrected and thus deftly brought the conversation around to the desired subject. "She's investigating the theft of the emerald necklace for the Roshnikovs. They're going to pay her the $10,000 reward money if she solves the case."

Her friend's response was immediate and seemed sincere. "That's wonderful—I hope you find the thief. George and I have often wondered if anyone would try to retrieve the jewels—in fact, we discussed doing a bit of investigating ourselves. I would like to take the children on an educational trip, but funds won't permit."

"You too, Brutus?" blinked across the screen of Pia Jo's mind. The need for extra money seemed to be universal.

"Why didn't you—try for the reward, that is?" Thelma asked Bess. "Your overhead at the home must be very high."

Bess nodded. "It's high, but we're fortunate to have a few wealthy donors. We felt that it would take a trained investigator to recover the necklace, and we were busy with our own pursuits. George isn't paid much for critiquing famous Irish writers, but he has a contract; and we both work very hard at the Home. Have you made any progress, Pia Jo?"

"A little. It would help if I could get an objective picture of the anniversary party you all attended last December and some input on the suspects." Taking her notes and tape recorder from her tote bag, she added, "I'd like to consider this an interview and tape it if you don't mind."

When Bess assured her that she sometimes contributed articles on the Home to the society pages of the *Courier* and that descriptions of gala occasions were right up her alley," Pia Jo pressed a button and then asked with a roguish grin, "What can you tell me about the Oleanders, the Andersons, the Constantas, the Alligrettis, and the Roshnikovs?"

Bess's large teeth flashed in a delighted smile. "That's a tall order, but I'll try to set the scene. It was late evening, but the moon and stars were shining on the snow, so it was surprisingly light out. It was the holiday season, and a huge evergreen tree decorated with clear lights and blue stars in a variety of sizes and colors dominated a corner of the great hall; but Maxima is a Russian Jew and Vladimer is extremely unorthodox, so they used a mix of themes. The Classical columns that held the Cupids were twined with garlands of fresh evergreen boughs; some windows held menorahs filled with white candles while others held fat bayberry and pink potpourri candles encircled with boughs. The Cupids on the mantel were crowned with wreaths; tall vases held both flowers and Stars of David on stems; and flying cherubs swung from the chandeliers. The Roshnikovs probably got a wicked delight out of shocking the more conventional guests by combining themes so extravagantly."

Pia Jo and Thelma were smiling over the images Bess had conjured up from her memory. "It's an eclectic world," Thelma said thoughtfully. "I'm sure most of us pick and choose what we prefer to believe."

"With so many priceless paintings and objets d'art to steal, it's a wonder the thieves took only the emerald necklace," Pia Jo mused, her thoughts on the case.

"That was a puzzler for a lot of people," Bess agreed, "but they probably thought that a necklace would be easier to conceal. The Roshnikovs obviously learned that crooks don't just live in big cities. They had a heavy wrought-iron fence with pointed peaks and a burglar alarm system installed after the theft."

Pia Jo nodded. "I noticed their precautions when I interviewed them."

Once again summoning the ghost of Christmas past, Bess resumed her narration. "Fires were blazing in all three of the big fireplaces in the drawing room—I recall remarking how the flames were reflected in the huge mirrors and thinking how dramatic the setting was. In the dining area, a long table was gaily decorated and filled with exotic food—chiefly Russian, and Jewish. A huge bouquet of pink and white poinsettias [she pronounced 'poinsettias' correctly] occupied the center of the table, and this was flanked by matching candles of various sizes; on either end there were epergnes filled with out-of-season iced grapes, berries, and nuts. A man with white hair was seated at the grand piano softly playing oldies but goodies, chiefly of a romantic nature, all very danceable tunes."

"That was Dag Amundson. Didn't he play any rock 'n' roll for the young adults?" As Pia Jo asked the question, she thought of her own earlier penchant, and Reo's continuing fondness, for loud music, an addiction that had cost her the higher decibels of her hearing and would perhaps affect Reo even more drastically.

Bess knitted her brows as she tried to recall the evening's music. "Yes, there were some Elvis tunes—'Love Me Tender' for one—but apart from Maxima's niece Yentl and her fiancé, the only young adults there were the Oleanders, a striking black couple who were celebrating his promotion at some bank; and the Andersons, who weren't all that young. He sang a few numbers, and she kept calling the sitter to see how their sick child was. I recall Ebony's remarking that his promotion would help them buy furniture—they'd recently bought one of the mansions on high hill; and Stan Anderson said that he and his wife had only one child, and she was frail."

Pia Jo had been inwardly sketching the scene while she listened to Bess's recital, but now she paused to ask, "Did all the guests dance?"

"The Oleanders did—all evening—except when they were eating or drinking wine or drinks made with vodka. They seemed to love to dance and were exceptionally good at it. The Andersons danced once or twice, but mostly he sang or brought drinks to the man at the piano—Dag Amundson? George danced with Sandie once, and I think Dag danced with her, too, when Yentl's fiancé was at the piano. Sandie seemed less anxious when she was with Amundson—they appeared to be talking earnestly."

Pia Jo nodded. "They are all members of the Scandinavian Folk Dancers. Gunter and Helen were members, too, but he dropped out when they separated and so did Helen—she runs with a different crowd now. My brother Soren and his wife, Lena, also belong."

"And you?"

"I belonged years ago." She didn't add that she'd left the group to avoid Soren and Lena, who were avid folk dancers. She'd been furious when they helped themselves to some of Emeline's belongings before her express wishes could be known, and she'd feared that she's say too much if she encountered them at close range. No doubt they would have taken everything of value if Mr. Blanding hadn't suggested that Emeline freeze her estate for a six-month period of reflection.

Shutting out the disconcerting memories, Pia Jo asked, "When exactly was the emerald necklace missed? The police detective's notes state that some of the guests had gone home before it was stolen—that's why I'm concentrating on those who stayed longer. What happened after they left?"

"Yes, some early birds went home. The rest of us gathered in the drawing room to hear Maxima sing Russian love songs and to snack on the remains of the feast. Maxima was standing by the tallest wreathed column, the one that holds the largest Cupid, waiting for the albino to finish playing the introduction to her song. Suddenly she gasped and turned as white as the Cupid behind her. 'My emeralds!' she said in a strangled sort of way. Then she screamed, 'Vladimer, my emeralds are gone!'"

"Could she have been acting? She's been an opera star, you know, and sometimes people steal their own jewels—or have them stolen—to collect the insurance."

But Bess doubted the possibility. "She seemed genuinely shocked, and so did Vladimer. She's a star, but he's not an entertainer. He's her manager." Bess further testified that the guests were entirely congenial and that none of them seemed the thieving sort; but knowing that a house with an innocent façade may harbor a cunning criminal, Pia Jo wasn't convinced. "Could the clasp have broken?" she wondered.

"The police were called, and Chief Gramm considered that possibility, but he had the house searched from attic to basement, and the searchers came up with nothing."

"Who did the searching?"

"Two of the police officers—I don't know their names. Vladimer insisted on searching with them—he was afraid they wouldn't be thorough."

"How did you react to the Rumanians? Brenda's notes said they were comics of some sort."

"The Constantas?" Bess asked with a look of amusement. "They were both comical and serious. At the party they let everyone else dance each number sedately and romantically; then they appeared in their outlandish costumes and hammed it up until we were all in stitches."

"Can you describe the costumes?"

"Sofia was wearing a long black skirt, a gold top, and a red chiffon scarf with gold fringes. She used the scarf to cover part of her face coquettishly at certain times during their act. She had numerous gold bracelets on her arms—she said she was wearing one for each year they've been married. Their dark skin and big hoop earrings reminded me that they're gypsies—and the way he made objects in the room disappear and appear. He was just as versatile with his black coat as she was with her skirt."

"When were they serious?"

"When he did sleight of hand tricks. But during their ballet dance, just when we were admiring their incredible poise, he dropped her with a thud. When she berated him in a language I couldn't understand— I suppose it was Romany—he became as crestfallen as a bird with a broken wing."

"But aren't they elderly?"

"In their eighties, I think. George thought she was wearing a thick corset of some kind and that she'd hidden the necklace in it. He wondered why Chief Gramm hadn't made her and Stefan strip."

Good point, Pia Jo thought. The Constantas, with their sleight of hand talents, their loose clothing, and their gypsy background, were indeed likely suspects. But she merely said, "A suspect can't be arrested without probable cause—suspicions aren't enough. And since the Fourth Amendment gives people the right to privacy, Chief Gramm would have needed a special search warrant to force them to undress. Did the Roshnikovs seem to patronize the Constantas?"

"Not at all! Maybe that was because persecuted groups stick together."

"What motive could the Constantas have had for stealing the necklace?"

Bess looked skeptical; it was clear that she did not doubt the Rumanian gypsies. "When people are in their eighties, what need have they for expensive jewels?"

Pia Jo conceded the point but asked seriously, "If you were to finger one of the guests as the thief, which one would it be?"

Bess didn't reply until she'd reviewed the evidence of her own senses and arrived at a fair judgment. Her answer, when it came, was a total surprise.

"I'd finger the Cambodian twins. At first I didn't know there were two of them, and I almost flipped when I saw one of them standing across the room and the other one passing a tray nearby. They were serving the guests, and every few minutes they'd stop and stare at the jewels and then look at one another in a sort of telepathic way—George remarked on it, too. They're small and move so silently that they startled me more than once by their interchangeable identities. Their white coats were roomy enough to conceal the necklace, and besides, they were the most deprived of all the guests."

Wondering is she shouldn't also interview George, Pia Jo said, "I'll keep that in mind. By the way, when did the Russians move here?"

"It must have been in 1969. He bought the place the year before they were married, which he said was in 1970. He mentioned it in the little anniversary speech he gave. His grandparents had hated Communism and had managed to smuggle their antiques and jewels to Finland long before the take-over. A man from Finland owned their house on High Street before they bought it—it had come down to him from his grandfather, an official in the lead mines when they were still being worked."

"And they stay at Cloud House all the time?"

"No, she still accepts some roles, and they have to travel so she can appear in them. They have other houses, but they both insist that Oblachnyj Dom is their favorite." Spying her brother, Bess rose to leave. "Here's George come for me. I loved your picnic, and I hope you'll visit us some day. George and I occupy the third floor of the Home—Thelma, you and Sven must bring Pia Jo next time you visit us. And Luisa, too!"

- 10 -

The last of the guests had departed, the lawn had been restored to
its former state, and Pia Jo was seated by the kitchen table of Cabin 6
listening to the tape of the word picture Bess Wylie had so generously
painted of the Roshnikov party. "How did you and Gunter make out?"
she asked Luisa absently as she turned off the tape recorder and filled in
her rude sketch of the Roshnikov drawing room with Maxima singing
in front of the wreathed column that held its largest Cupid.

"*Make out?* Really, Pia Jo, you ought to reread the Alice stories—
your use of language is far from precise," Luisa responded crossly; but realizing that her comment was too glum, she amended it hastily. "Sorry!
I'm just discouraged because he's so afraid of love. I haven't been hurt
by it as he has—my love affairs have never reached the marital stage,
while Helen does everything she can to hurt him. She's justifying her
decision to keep Ulf away from him—claims he's a bad influence because he swears so much and was untrue to her with a Winnebago girl.
She's right—he does swear too much, and he uses atrocious language;
but was he untrue to her, Peejay?" Luisa had met Gunter two years
previously, when she'd visited Pia Jo and Reo in Cabin 6; but he'd been
married to Helen then, and in spite of their unacknowledged attraction
to one another, she knew little about him.

"She wants to think so!" Pia Jo's voice reflected her genuine indignation. "Clover drops in at the office now and then, especially when
Maize isn't home; but it's to see Blue, not Gunter. One night when Blue
wasn't there, Gunter gave her a ride home, and she forgot her sweater

in his official car. It had a Winnebago bear design, so of course Helen guessed whose it was. He swore there was nothing between them, and Clover did, too; but Helen refused to believe them—she'd never gotten over an attorney named Buster Bigelow from Prairie de Loup, and she jumped at the excuse for a divorce. She and Buster are already married, and Buster has started proceedings to adopt Ulf. Since Gunter dearly loves his son, he's having a rough time of it. Helen left him just before Mom died, and even though Mom had always been good to her, she wouldn't attend the funeral or let Ulf attend."

"No wonder he's bitter. Doesn't he have any legal rights?"

"Yes, he does have visiting rights. But they're trying to teach Ulf to regard Buster as his dad, and Ulf is so confused that Gunter doesn't visit him often. Please be patient with him, Lu—he thinks you're extra special, but he's had a rum deal. Excuse me—I have to call him about some new info I have on the theft. We'll have leftovers for dinner, won't we?"

"Right—we won't have to cook. I'll set the table while you make your call."

Gunter's response was harried. "Bring your notes and the tape to my office after supper—I'll be back by then. The beast that killed Martin Diver's sheep—it's killed some of Jake Bosun's, too. Jake described it as a big German shepherd with a nasty temperament an' a taste for blood."

Since Gunter had been forced to sell the house he'd had built for his family and divvy up the profits with Helen, he'd accepted Emeline's offer to live at Rendezvous for six months; and although Soren and Lena had been generous to themselves with Emeline's furnishings, they'd left the ones they hated most. Gunter often stayed at his office after hours to avoid the memories they evoked.

"I'll be there at seven then," Pia Jo assured him and hung up.

Gunter had a tale of his own to tell when she joined him in his cluttered office later. When he and Officer Bert LaFarge viewed the carnage at Jake Bosun's farm, Jake's wife told them that both Jake and Martin Diver were convinced that Rasputin had killed their sheep; so they'd taken their deer rifles and had gone to the Antonin ranch to shoot the dog. Mrs. Bosun was frightened—her husband had a bad temper and so did Martin Diver. Who knew what would happen next? She'd trembled violently when she answered their quick questions.

Gunter had pushed the gas pedal to the floor and had turned on his siren, and they'd reached the Antonin ranch just in time to prevent a murder. Rasputin already lay dead in the yard, killed by two shots, one from each irate farmer's rifle. Antonin, a huge man with a bushy red beard, was furiously accusing them of killing an expensive watchdog without conclusive evidence. The two farmers had their rifles trained on him and only put them down when Gunter threatened to arrest them for "assault with intent to kill."

"I ain't the only man hereabouts who owns a German shepherd," Antonin had yowled. "A dog's innocent till he's proved guilty, ain't he? You bet I'm pressin' charges, Borg! Now get them sons o' bitches off my land so I kin bury my dead." After Bert had taken pictures, secured the crime scene, and called a vet, they'd left the rancher mourning by the dead dog.

"How can they be sure Rasputin killed the sheep?" Pia Jo asked before she began discussing her own investigating. The rancher's son Alexei had been her closest chum when they'd attended high school in Prairie du Loup, and he'd viewed his father in a highly favorable light.

"No doubt about it—when Jake caught the German shepherd killin' his sheep, he didn't have his rifle along; so he wounded the dog's eye with a sharp stone. Since the dead dog's eye was swollen shut, we got our proof. Besides, both farmers identified Rasputin by the wavy streak on his face. Now what's goin' on with you?"

When she'd gone over the notes she'd taken after interviewing the Raintrees and the Cambodians and had played him the tape of Bess's lively testimony, he said, "She'd make a good witness, that one. Good work so far, peanut. Whadda you want me to do?"

Pia Jo's temper flashed like a neon light. "You can answer some questions, popcorn. Where can I find out if the Wylie Home for Exceptional Children really does have some wealthy sponsors? Oh, I know—Sven and Thelma swear by the Wylies, and they seem close to perfect to me, too; but I can't rule them out."

"Go ask George for a list of their sponsors. If he refuses to give you one, he'll become a suspect."

Pia Jo shook her head at her own incompetence. "I thought of interviewing him, but I didn't want to offend Sven and Thelma." She wrote "Interview George!" on a new piece of notepaper, then asked, "How can I find out where Ebony and Laurel Oleander work and whether their present earnings justify their buying a houseful of expensive furniture and a new car after purchasing a mansion on High Street?"

"That's easy enough—I bank at Prairie du Loup Savin's an' Loan, an' Ebony's waited on me more'n once. Laurel used to work at Country Furniture in de Loup—mebbe she still works there or they can tell you where she works. Why don't you check 'em out?" Gunter's question was ample notice that he needed to concentrate on his own cases; but to make his message stronger, he also riffled impatiently through some papers on his desk.

"Can't. I called their home, and someone named Fiona said that Laurel's father had a stroke and they'd flown to New Jersey to be with him and her mother. Will their employers give me some information?"

"Fiona's probly their cook or housekeeper. I dunno about their employers. Investigatin' ain't easy, Peejay. You can't pick answers off a vine like ripe grapes. Any other questions? If not, I got work to do."

"Just one. Do you have any idea when the Scandinavian Folk Dancers are performing next?"

"Yeah, Soren was in last week an' asked to put a poster up. I said 'No' an' meant it—I don't allow advertisin' in here unless it's about criminals." He drew a brightly-colored poster featuring Scandinavian folk dancers from under his desk calendar and handed it to Pia Jo. "It'll be in three weeks—on _Midsommer's Dag_, June 24th— an' you may be sure he an' Lena'll be there." He didn't try to disguise his hostility. "He told me to vote for sellin' Mom's house to the highest bidder when we meet with Blandin'—he an' Lena are chompin' to get their share. I said I had a mind o' my own. Why'd you ask about him—he ain't your favorite relative."

"I wondered if he'd give me some background on Stan Anderson. Their names were both on a list of dancers Sven gave me, so they must know each other. I haven't checked Anderson out yet—I don't know where he works."

Gunter emitted a cynical sound, a cross between a grunt and a sigh.

"Yeah, Soren an' Stan might be in it together—you know how materialistic Lena is. I know where Stan works—don't forget I used to dance with that bunch o' yokels."

"Well? Where does Stan work?"

"You ever tried lookin' people up in a phone book? He works at the Eberle Brothers Gas Station—he repairs cars an' trucks."

Pia Jo folded the poster, put it in her tote bag, and turned to go; but thoughts of their other sibling drew her up short. "Have you talked to Elise lately? I called her to see if she'd go to Mom's grave with me, but she was too busy. She and Arturo did send an elegant white rosebush."

"I know—they sent it to Rendezvous, an' I brought it to the cemetery." Pushing his papers and his chair back, he got up and stared out a window as though it had a magic pane that would explain his older sister's behavior. "It ain't healthy the way she caters to that loser—she just shuts her eyes to his shenanigans an' shuns us like the Amish when we try to talk about them. He ain't even tryin' to make her happy!"

Pia Jo sighed. Elise's familial attentions had dwindled to drips since her marriage to the Bolivian, Arturo Vargas. As a girl, she'd been somewhat reserved, but her marriage had made her downright introverted. How could she adore a man who was openly untrue to her? But Elise would brook no interference—she blamed herself because she couldn't get pregnant and Arturo was desperate to prove his virility. He'd proved it all right—he had three children by a more fertile woman.

"Why don't you divorce him so he can marry her? Don't you think the children need a father?" Pia Jo had asked indignantly, her thoughts on her own fatherless childhood. "Anyway, why do you want to share a husband?"

Behind the chilly reserve, Elise was strangely passionate. "He's legally *my* husband and *he loves me*! Besides, my need for him is greater than theirs. Do I tell you how to run your life? Please, Pia Jo, try to respect my privacy."

Pia Jo had obeyed, of course, but her heart had ached for her unhappy sister. Drawing courage from Gunter's pensive stance by the window, she paused by the door to ask, "You still interested in Luisa? She said you're mourning the loss of your wife and son."

"I'm interested as hell, but I'm scared to death that history'll repeat itself. I rush to see her, an' when I see her, I talk about th' last thing I should talk about—my ex-wife's disloyalty. Seems like I should be more cool than that."

She wanted to comfort him but didn't quite know how. "Luisa isn't Helen, Gunter," she finally said. "She's got staying power—look at how long she's been my friend! But you're right to get over Helen before you get serious about Luisa. If Reo and I ever break up, I'll probably have to spend five years getting over him. And don't worry about Ulf. He's confused but he still loves you. That shyster Buster Bigelow isn't worth one of your toenails!"

He grinned at her, a lop-sided grin. "Thanks, lil sis—I needed that. Good luck on th' case!" Catching a glimpse of Sven's collector Corvette, he added, "I ain't so sure it's a good idea for you to drive that car—it's too noticeable an' it'll be cold as holy hell in winter. You'd better buy your own car when you collect that cash."

Musing with a grin that Gunter had his own vision of hell, she hurried out to the objectionable vehicle, got in, and glanced at her watch. Since it was only eight p.m., she sat for a while reviewing her progress and reflecting on how few people she knew in Lead Mines or its surrounds. She'd grown up on a farm some ten miles north of Prairie du Loup and had attended high school there by bus. Her mother hadn't sold the farm and moved to Rendezvous of the Four Winds until she was seventeen and about to graduate from high school.

"Damn!" she muttered as the hand of her mind moved ahead a space, "I forgot to ask Gunter if he knows anything about the Alligrettis. He probably doesn't—they don't even live around here. Best to get their Evanston address from the Roshnikovs—after all, they're close friends. But what now?"

Should she call on George Wylie? Not tonight—she didn't want to bother Sven's friend and literary associate when he was off duty. Ebony's banker? Laurel's employer? A glance at her watch told her that the bank and the furniture store would be closed—it was nearly eight p.m. The Andersons? Yes, the Andersons—they'd most likely be home in the evening.

- 11 -

As the little Corvette steamed up the incline that led to High Street, Pia Jo gave some thought to the role she'd play and decided on that of a person getting reacquainted with the Scandinavian Folk Dancers in the hope that she could perform with them on *Midsomer's Dag*. When the time came actually to perform, she'd find an excuse not to; dancing with Soren, Lena, and Dag held no charms—she no longer fit in with their crowd.

"Mark Twain would be proud of me for refining what he called the fine art of lying," she chuckled as she slowed down to enter the approach to Number 17. "I'm becoming as devious as a double agent." As that thought slipped away, another nibbled at her consciousness. "Must be good drainage up here. Good thing the land slants enough not to trigger my acrophobia."

The Anderson house was not a brick house, and it wasn't as large or impressive as the mansions it neighbored; moreover, it badly needed some repairs and a coat of paint. A black and brown Ford van of indeterminate age and nondescript appearance was parked in its driveway. If the Andersons had stolen the valuable necklace, they hadn't as yet reaped the financial benefits that its sale would have brought.

A pretty blonde woman of perhaps thirty-five whose mouth drooped at the corners answered her ring and waited politely while she introduced herself and showed her the poster advertising the Scandinavian Dancers. "Soren Borg is my brother—I've come because I danced with this group when I was in high school, and I'd love to dance with them again." She crossed her fingers in a pocket of her jeans as she told this barefaced lie.

"You're the sheriff's sister then," Sandra Anderson observed, her gray eyes becoming friendly. "Come in! Stan, the sheriff's sister is here asking about the folk dancing."

Stan Anderson, as fair as his wife, entered the room, and Pia Jo noted the curly blond mustache that adorned his upper lip and the long, curly sideburns that gave him a slightly rakish look. He was definitely the Errol Flynn type. A little blonde girl of perhaps ten came skipping in at his side. Although fine-boned and delicate, she looked as healthy as a newly-ripe peach. As Pia Jo repeated her desire to dance with the colorful group, her mind flung its contents about like a mixer of Lotto numbers: this child is well; Bess Wylie said she was sick, but that was six months ago—children recover quickly. He looks like a roue, but looks can be deceiving. Yes, she has a pinched look, but maybe that's because she's tired of being poor. Her clothes are faded—they must need money. If he's a close friend of the lusting Dag, can he be trusted? Hold on—that's the fallacy of guilt by association. His wages must be pretty low—he had a strong motive for stealing the emeralds.

"You want to join our group? Hey, Dag'll be bowled over when I tell him. We practice every Saturday and Sunday afternoon in one of his meadows. So you're Soren's sister—funny he didn't say nothing about your wanting to join. He's a funny man—always has a joke to play on someone. And Lena—she likes to cook and brings us all the food we can hold. Gunter should come even if Helen divorced him; she does all her dancing at the Country Club now. Julie, come here and meet Pia Jo Borg—she's auntie to all those little Borgs you play with when their mama and papa dance."

"Their mama is so fat she looks like a buffalo when she dances," the little girl said innocently and was instantly shushed by her father. "Hush now, girl—Lena's a right good dancer, and it's not nice to call people fat. Have a chair, Pia Jo." He indicated a ragged, green armchair that had seen years of hard service and had also been used as a cat post. "I don't expect you have a costume, do you? If not, you better get your order in right now. Goldie Amundson makes 'em—she's Dag's sister and the best dancer in the group. You just give her a pattern and some cloth, and she'll do the rest. Expect your costume'll be like Soren's and Gunter's——."

She interrupted this gush of information firmly. "Thank you, but I was a member in high school, and I kept my costume." As Stan seated himself on a worn sofa that matched the worn chair and Sandie brought in a tray of cookies and pale nectar, she wrestled with the problem of how to get the conversation around to the theft of the emerald, but without success, for Stan was overflowing with a description of the fun they had after their practices—how they go to Dag's farmhouse and sing gospel and patriotic songs and roundelays and heaven only knows what else while Dag plays the organ and his sister Goldie serves them ice cream and goodies of all kinds. "You'll have to meet Dag—I heard him asking Soren about you."

"Really? It's too bad I already have a fiancé." Seeing a tiny opening, she dived for it. "These cookies are super, Mrs. Anderson—homemade, aren't they? Dag? Is his last name Amundson? Where've I heard that name before? Oh, I remember—Gunter mentioned that he'd played the piano at the Roshnikov anniversary party—I read about it in the *Courier* when I was here for my mother's funeral last December. That paper was so full of articles on the theft that there was little room for her obituary."

Stan was looking at her with deepening interest. "Why, yes, he did play at that party, and I sang a few songs. At first I wasn't asked to sing—the Roshnikov woman is an opera singer, and she was going to do all the singing; but Dag's playing is the best in the County, and he said he wouldn't play unless I sang and Sandie was invited, so they had to give in." He paused to reflect but didn't let the reins of the conversation go. "Mrs. Roshnikov has a niece who's a pro at the piano, and the niece's boyfriend's a composer; but they wanted to dance at the party."

Daringly, she played out her line. "I envy you! I'd love to attend a party like that! You must have been in seventh heaven, dancing around and around that lovely, decorated ballroom, you in a glittering gown, Mrs. Ander——."

"We only danced a couple of times," Sandie interposed impassively, "and my dress was a yellow lawn I've had for ten years. Stan repairs cars—we don't have money for glittering gowns. Julie was very ill then—I spent the evening worrying about her and calling my mother, who was sitting for us. Julie, why don't you pick up your paper dolls?"

"She looks well now," Pia Jo observed, smiling at the pretty child whose blonde ponytail bounced as she ran around the room picking up paper dolls from hither and yon and stuffing them into a box that was already overflowing with paper dolls.

"She's fine now, but at that time she had a bronchial infection that was threatening to go to her lungs. Since she's our only child and we can't have another, we were probably overly concerned."

Wondering why she and Elise didn't try the *in vitro* method or whether it cost too much or hadn't worked for them, and feeling she'd learned all she could through playing this particular role, Pia Jo rose, thanked them kindly for their hospitality, and shook hands with Stan. "I'll see you at practice next Saturday, then!" she promised, trying to disengage her hand. "It's going to be a busy June—I'm going to the Winnebago Powwow at the Settlement with Clover Whitewater on the 24th—."

Stan finally dropped her hand and found his voice. "You can't go to the Powwow," he insisted. "That's the day of our dance."

Pia Jo's eyes grew big and round as she asked, "How could I have forgotten? Oh, dear, that means I'll have to forego the Folk Dancing this year. I'm helping the Winnebago children present a play on that day." The lie came easily to her lips and she felt only a small ripple of guilt; after all, she'd promised Clover she'd direct a play at the Settlement *some day*—why couldn't it be on the 24th? "I'm so sorry I bothered you—and so glad Julie is well." This much at least was sincere. "Goodnight!"

Although she left quickly, she still overheard Stan's disgruntled question, "What real Scandinavian would prefer an Indian Powwow to folk dancing with her own people? Soren told me she's a fancy pants troublemaker who'll most likely block the sale of his mother's house out of pure meanness. He sure knew what he was talking about."

-12-

As she stood under the shower prior to going to bed, Pia Jo reflected on her visit to the Anderson house. "I trust her, but I don't trust him—he's a ladies' man for sure. She looked embarrassed when he said Dag had had to wrangle a singing spot for him and an invitation for her. Why weren't they among the guests to leave early when their child was so ill? And, since Sandie's mother could no doubt have been trusted to call them or a doctor if Julie had gotten worse, why had she called home so often?"

When she described the evening and put the questions to Luisa the next morning, her friend said, "You aren't a parent—you have no idea how anxious parents can become, especially over an only child. He may be a lady's man who ogles a shapely visitor, but that doesn't make him a thief. From what you've told me, I can see a weak marriage, but I can't see a solution to the crime."

Pia Jo's sigh nearly lifted a nearby curtain. "You're right—I can't assume that he finagled a solo spot just so he could steal the necklace. From what he said about the fun they have at the Amundson farm, he probably loves to sing." Feeling strongly that she'd done Stan Anderson an injustice, she changed the subject. "Do you have any idea how I could find out who the Wylies' wealthy donors are? Gunter thinks I should ask George for a list; but if I do, Thelma and Sven might think I don't trust them to choose trustworthy friends."

Luisa took time to consider the question before answering. Then she said, "You can't be that sensitive. Why not ask Thelma or Sven what to do? That will at least show them that you're not eager to question their friends."

"Good idea! I'll give Sven a call." But when Luisa reminded her that they were invited to Scandia for a Belgian waffle brunch at ten, she decided she had time to go to Prairie du Loup Savings and Loan to see what she could learn about Ebony during his absence. Luck was with her, for when she arrived at the bank, she was referred to Morgana Willoughby, who'd been Emeline's trusted loan counselor.

"Pia Jo! How are you, dear?" Morgana greeted her. "I was so sorry to hear about your mother's death—the place always came alive when she walked in. What can I do for you today?"

Seating herself before Morgana's desk, Pia Jo didn't hedge. "Frankly, I'm looking for information. I'm working on the Roshnikov jewel case, and I wondered if you could tell me if—."

It was definitely to Pia Jo's advantage that the Roshnikovs had a large account there. "Maxima told me recently that the case had been shelved—I'm sure she's elated that it's been reopened," Morgana said, leaning forward and adding in an undertone, "Confidentially, she had the emerald necklace in a safety deposit box here prior to the party. When she and Vladimer came in after its disappearance, they were very upset."

Pia Jo's thoughts mounted a carousel at this bit of information. Could she read something into the fact that the lovely and valuable gems had been accessible to Ebony while they were in storage? But they weren't stolen from the bank, so what did that matter? Even so, he could have loosened the clasp so they would be easy to steal. Here was information that must be weighed carefully, but she'd better weigh it at her leisure and not jump to a hasty conclusion.

"I'm trying to establish the motives of the suspects," she began, but Morgan intercepted her. "Wouldn't the motive be a need for money in every case?"

"Generally it would be, but a love for fine jewels could be a motive, or a need to hurt someone—in this case, either Maxima or Vladimer. I've been trying to reach Ebony Oleander—I understand he works here."

It didn't take Morgana long to get her drift. "Ebony's an honest, trusted employee—he'd never steal anything," she said a bit heatedly.

"But he and his wife are living on High Street and have just bought new furniture and a new car. Aren't those expenditures a bit beyond his income?"

Morgana was quick to offer a viable explanation, and in so doing, gave Pia Jo the information she needed. "Yes, they do seem high, but he and Laurel just took out a loan for $50,000; and don't forget that she works, too. Besides, his salary will be much higher as Vice President, a position he's expected to get shortly." Morgana had no sooner made this statement than she reproved herself guiltily, "That's confidential information. We observe the Right to Privacy here." But in self-defense she soon added, "I expect the Law has a right to know."

"But I'm not the Law on this case," Pia Jo thought a little guiltily, then bit her tongue down hard on the information. Smiling gratefully, she thanked Morgana for her cooperation and returned to her car. There she paused to consider the Oleanders in the light of the testimony she'd just heard, but she couldn't come to a sensible conclusion. How far would $50,000 go towards the purchase of a mansion on High Street, a new BMW, and membership in the Country Club? It would depend largely on their parents and on Laurel's contributions.

Her next stop was at The Country Furniture Store, which featured a wide range of furniture, from Pioneer to Country and Western. Moving about from exquisite to merely ordinary pieces, she almost forgot her errand; but when a well-dressed male asked her if she were interested in something special, she shook her head and stated her business. "I'm Pia Jo Borg, and I'm investigating the theft of the Roshnikov jewels. I have a question about Laurel Oleander's income."

"Borg? Borg? Are you related to the sheriff?"

"I'm his sister and one of his investigators, but I'm working on the Roshnikov case as a private eye." She showed him the I.D. that Gunter had presented her to use as his investigator.

Taking the I.D., he scrutinized it carefully; then said with a pronounced sniff, "This doesn't identify you as a private eye."

"You're right, it doesn't, but you may call the Roshnikovs if you doubt my right to gather information regarding the case." When his reluctance seemed to be wavering, she pressed her advantage. "But I'll be brief. Laurel Oleander was at the party when the emerald necklace was stolen, so I have to consider her a suspect. She and her husband recently purchased a home on High Street, and they also bought expensive furniture and a new BMW. I'm wondering whether she got a rake-down on the furniture and whether her salary, when added to his, would be sufficient to cover these expenditures."

"You're begging the question," he snapped sarcastically. "How can I answer that when I don't know what his salary is?" Then he added, "Her husband is—."

She nodded in quick perception. "Yes, he's about to be promoted. However, his salary alone doesn't warrant that kind of expenditure. She must have to make a substantial contribution."

She finally perceived the truth. He wasn't the owner, he was merely a salesperson; and, judging from his hostility, Laurel more than likely earned more than he did. He pointed out that Laurel had a right to privacy but added, "She works on commission and her income varies. I would imagine that she and her husband are deeply in debt." The idea must have delighted him, for he smiled when he said it.

"And the rake-down on the furniture?" she reminded him.

"They didn't buy their furniture here—she said our furniture wasn't appropriate for an antebellum Civil War home," he sneered. "She was looking for Victorian, but can you imagine—she planned to add an Afro twist. Have you ever heard of anything so ridiculous?"

"She sounds like an original thinker," she said politely but firmly, then thanked him and left; but once outside she said, "Creep!" loudly enough for a woman on the street to look at her doubtfully. In the car, she did some rapid figuring in her head and concluded that even with their combined income, the Oleanders were stretching their budget beyond the breaking point. "Maybe they're heavily in debt," she mused, "or maybe they have generous parents." Jotting down her findings briefly, she labeled and dated them. While backing out of her parking spot, she glimpsed the offensive salesperson eyeing the 1957 Corvette suspiciously.

"Appearances are deceiving," she admitted. "Someone who didn't know the circumstances might conclude that I stole the emerald necklace to buy this collector's car." As she headed back to Lead Mines, she applied that bit of reasoning to the suspects she'd interviewed. None of them *appeared* courageous enough to be a jewel thief on a big scale. Petit larceny perhaps, but grand larceny? No!

"The comic Constantas are next. If they're just an innocent old couple, I may as well kiss that $10,000 goodbye!" But when her stomach groaned loudly, she suddenly remembered the brunch at Scandia and her plan to ask Sven about the Wylie donors. She'd have to drive back to Innisfree before going to Lead Mines to interview the Constantas, but she didn't mind—Britt's cooking was worth the extra miles.

Luisa had preceded her, and Britt was already serving her and the Tillotsons when Pia Jo arrived; but they welcomed her heartily anyway. While they sat around the big, square kitchen table drinking coffee and eating the waffles with fresh fruit, they discussed the case, and Thelma asked, "Who's your prime suspect?"

"I've interviewed Dag Amundson, the Andersons, and Bess Wylie, and I've asked around about the Oleanders, but so far no one stands out as a prime suspect. They all seem to need money; and since they were all at the party, they all had opportunity and no alibi." She described the events of the morning, then continued. "I'm going to interview the Constantas next if I can think up a convincing role." She changed the subject abruptly. "How's George's article on Lady Gregory coming, Uncle Sven? She's a favorite of mine—I would love to read it."

"It's being published in a scholarly journal soon—I'll get you a copy. George is a careful researcher—he spent two months in Ireland visiting Cooles and learning all he could about Lady Gregory for himself and Yeats for me. I haven't been to Ireland for a while, and new things keep turning up."

"Did he bring you any valuable information?"

"Oh, yes, enough to fill out my own work. Why do you ask?" Sven was looking at her appraisingly.

"Because I can't figure out where he got the money to stay in Ireland for two months when Literary Criticism pays so little. I know you and Thelma aren't going to like it, but I must get a list of the Wylies' wealthy donors, and I don't know how to go about it."

Sven looked at Thelma quizzically, and when she nodded slightly, he said, "George is coming around in an hour or so—I'll sound him out." He finished his waffle, then asked, "Sure you won't direct a play for Rex Tremaine at the Lodge this summer, Pia Jo?"

"I wish I could—it would be a challenge. But Reo's expecting me to return to Chicago when this crime is solved."

"Do I have to leave when you do?" Luisa demanded. "The cabin's ideal for painting, and I want to do a dozen landscapes."

"You can work on my portrait while Thelma's decorating Rex's suite and Peejay's hot on the trail of the thief," Sven offered magnanimously. "I'll be free when George leaves."

"I'm sorry, but I have to finish my blue-footed booby, and Pia Jo wants me to do her portrait next—it's to be a birthday gift for Reo. But I'll do you and Thelma together after that."

After they'd discussed blue-footed boobies to their satisfaction, Pia Jo took a last luscious bite of her waffle and strawberries and then affirmed, "This breakfast was fit for the Valkyries, Britt. May I use the encyclopedia on your computer, Uncle Sven? I need to glean a few facts about Rumania."

- 13 -

A few facts gleaned on Sven's computer, Pia Jo borrowed his camera with its infrared attachment to supplement her Polaroid in case she needed to take night pictures, noted that he had plenty of high speed film in its case, took leave of the brunchers, and drove into Lead Mines, where she went directly to the Constantas' small house on High Street. The building, set far back from the street, no longer resembled the Carriage House for the Roshnikov mansion. As she entered its driveway, she was struck by the unusual deep-purple roof which slanted over white boards that were almost smothered in purple lilacs, their heavenly clusters angelically perfuming the small front lawn. Drawing the Polaroid from its case, she followed a winding sidewalk around to the front entrance, mentally rehearsing for her new role as she did so.

As she was about to climb the steps, a short, elderly woman dressed like an immense bee in a bright yellow and black wind suit, emerged from the lilacs with a large, stunning bouquet in her arms. "Dearie, you scare me!" she exclaimed, stumbling backward when she saw Pia Jo standing on the walk near the door. "Is something you want?" she asked in a mixed English and Balkan accent.

"Your lilacs are gorgeous! I'm Pia Jo Borg—my mother has had a stunning flower garden on her place near Prairie du Loup every year for the past ten years. She always wanted to plant lilacs near her garden studio, but she died before she could realize her dream. I'm hoping to buy my brothers and sister out, and if I can, I'm going to plant lilacs in her memory; but I haven't the faintest idea what kinds to plant. May

I take some pictures of yours, and will you tell me where I can buy the best root stock?" Pia Jo finished the long speech breathlessly and managed to seem eager for a reply. Since Emeline had long ago planted a variety of ethereal lilacs by her garden studio, her speech was sheer prevarication; but what the heck—all's fair in loving and sleuthing.

Her eyes fixed on the camera, the elderly woman smiled eagerly. "Oh, yes, please, missy—you take pictures of lilacs and me, then you come inside and we talk. I go in now and put these in water."

"What a way to get some free pictures taken!" Pia Jo mused as she complied with the unusual request. The pictures taken and developed, she tapped on the door and was instantly admitted. It was one of those occasions wherein friendly ghosts take over and direct the course of events. Having plunked the stems of the lilacs into a pail of cold water in the sink, Sofia Constanta accepted her share of the outdoor snapshots gratefully, looked at them avidly, then ignoring her caller's first name, she called loudly, "Stefan, come here and meet Jo Borg."

The elderly couple were oddly alike, both of them short, grayhaired, pleasant-faced, color-conscious, and profoundly interested in life. Stefan was as impressed by the Polaroid shots as Sofia was. He was even dressed like her in a yellow and black jogging suit; and they were both hospitable in the extreme, which surprised Pia Jo, who had always considered gypsies suspicious people. Soon she found herself seated in a well-worn but comfortable chair, remarking on their colorful artwork, which strongly reminded her of Reo's, and taping the interview while they eagerly answered her questions. They seemed unusually hungry for company.

Yes, they'd come from Rumania—from Botosani on Russia's eastern border. They'd been entertaining in Odessa on the Black Sea when the Roshnikovs docked there on their way to visit Kiev ten years ago. They were gypsies, yes; some 600 years ago (who knows exactly when?) their ancestors had lived in northern India, until a terrible war with Moslems had ruined the land and forced them to leave. But they weren't nomads—they'd wanted to leave Rumania because the Commies had expected them to renounce their gypsy customs. They'd gone to Odessa hoping to find a way to escape, and yes, they loved all kinds of dancing but especially folk dancing.

"I understand you met the Roshnikovs at a folk dance in Odessa?"

Pia Jo asked skeptically. "Do wealthy divas like Maxima go to folk dances?"

"No, no, that they did not do," Sophia hastily denied. "Five years ago she come to Odessa to sing in opera, and we go there because Stefan's great niece Olga had small part in it. Olga read in paper Roshnikovs were from America, so we follow them to place they eat, and we ask if they help us escape to America and help find us work."

Stefan took over the recital. "When they ask what we can do, we say, 'Dance!' 'No, no,' they say—dancers do not make the money. But when they ask if we are from north where kelims are made, we say 'Yah, we make and sell the kelims.'"

"Kelims? What are they?" Pia Jo asked, glancing about eagerly to see if she could spot one.

They pointed proudly to the boldly colored carpet under their feet, a woolen rug hand-woven with old world flowers and birds.

"So you made enough kelims to pay for your escape? Did the Roshnikovs help you?"

The words tumbled out of them almost too rapidly. Yes, the Roshnikovs had helped them enter Bulgaria and cross Greece dressed as folk dancers and had also made the Carriage House available to them; and they had earned a good living by making kelims and selling them to shopkeepers in Lead Mines.

"And when we can, we dance! We are in eighties, but we dance!" Stefan concluded proudly.

The opening Pia Jo had been waiting for had arrived. "I suppose the Roshnikovs ask you to dance at their parties. Did you dance at their anniversary party last December, by any chance?"

Oh, yes, they dance at anniversary party—they play violins, and they dance to song piano man with white hair play, and they request "Blue Danube" because Danube flows through Rumania to Black Sea. When they had talked at some length about the Blue Danube, leaving out the articles that should have preceded their nouns and adding some that shouldn't, Pia Jo steered them deftly back to the party. "I heard that some of Maxima's lovely and expensive jewels were stolen that night. Did you know that a reward is being offered for their return?"

Yes, they knew about theft of green fire. What shame they didn't see thief! They owe Roshnikovs everything—they wish they could have prevent such great loss!!

"I'd love to buy a kelim for the apartment I share with my fiancé," Pia Jo remarked, falsely enthusiastic. "He'd love them—they're so colorful."

Sophia, whose eye was on the main chance, suddenly had an idea that pleased her very much. "You shoot pictures of kelims and show to boyfriend, Jo Borg," she urged excitedly. "Stefan, come here and be with me in picture." As Pia Jo smiled and posed them prettily, she reminded herself that she was a sleuth, not a photographer; so while she waited for the print to develop, she looked around and evaluated their belongings as best she could with an untrained eye. Excepting a few heirlooms in a glass-encased curio cabinet, nothing looked particularly expensive other than the kelims; and these had cost them only their labor and the money they'd spent on the wool. Wouldn't it be far-fetched to suspect this bubbling couple of stealing the Roshnikov emeralds?

Before she left, she snapped a final picture of the couple standing under the heady lilacs by the door, developed the print for them, accepted their invitation to come for lunch someday, and said goodbye. As she drove away, she almost crossed the Constantas off her mental list of suspects. They seemed as harmless as babes in the woods and as constant as their name. But a small sliver of doubt remained—they had not, after all, shown her their bedroom—perhaps the emerald necklace was hidden there.

When she backed out of the Constanta's driveway and drove past the Oleanders' fine home, Pia Jo quickly filed the visit with the Rumanians away in one of her mental cubbyholes. When she'd borrowed Uncle Sven's camera, she'd had a vague idea that she should check out the Oleander possessions in their absence, and what better time to do so than at night when her breaking and entering wouldn't be so obvious? "I'm lucky—he wouldn't lend his expensive equipment to just anyone." Drawing to the curb, she took her phone from her tote bag and made three calls, one to Maxima, one to Gunter, and a final one to Scandia.

"Yes," Maxima assured her. "Yentl is here and is excited and pleased about the party. Vlad and I sent the invitations yesterday."

"It's still set for June 3rd?"

"Yes, Saturday night, and it's to be formal! How are you coming with the investigation?"

Needing to impress the Roshnikovs, Pia Jo gave her a brief overview of what she'd accomplished. "I've interviewed Dag Amundson, the Andersons, and the Constantas, and I've gathered some info on the Oleanders—they're next on my list. But I've got *nada* on the Alligrettis. Zilch. I'll have to go to Evanston to interview them. I'll need their address and phone number."

But Maxima disliked this idea intensely. "The Alligrettis are our close friends—we can't understand why Brenda White included them as suspects when Sidonie has more valuable jewels than she'll ever be able to wear!" she said indignantly. "They weren't pleased to be questioned last December, and I don't want you to offend them by barging into their home and grilling them like common criminals."

"But they're material witnesses, Madame Roshnikov. They may have seen something they don't know they saw."

"Oh, for Heaven sake, call us by our first names. Look, why don't I ask them to come a day early? You can interview them here if you're careful not to let on that the party's being staged."

Pia Jo was disappointed. She loved Evanston's University, which she would have attended if finances had permitted; she loved its gracious old homes and its lakeshore; and she enjoyed eating at a vegetarian restaurant there—it was one she and Luisa had visited often and looked forward to visiting again. But the return of the necklace was all that mattered to Maxima, so she responded matter-of-factly. "I need to assess their wealth by getting a look at their home."

"I've been there often—I can tell you what their home is like. In fact, it's regularly included in tours of gracious homes," Maxima insisted impatiently. "And that dimwit Garnet told me that Gladstone's have insured Sidonie's jewels for millions. Why can't you concentrate on the suspects who need money?"

In the light of all the concentrating she'd already done, it was an unreasonable question; but Pia Jo couldn't afford to take offense. "The Oleanders are next on my list," she said appeasingly, "but they're out of town and won't be back for a couple of days. I'll give you a report on my progress when I have more time. What I'm most concerned about now is detecting undercurrents, and I can't do that until I see the suspects together. Do you have another necklace you value highly and a paste copy of it?"

"Indeed I do—among other pieces, I have an antique necklace with a large pendant of pink diamonds and pink pearls in my safety deposit box."

"Pink diamonds?" Pia Jo was astonished. "I thought all diamonds were colorless."

"My dear," Maxima said importantly, her impatience gone, "you need to brush up on your gemstones. Diamonds come in many colors—the Conde Diamond weighs fifty carats, is shaped like a pear, and is a lovely rose-pink. It was awarded to Louis de Bourbon, the Prince of Conde, in 1647 for his services to France in the Thirty Year War. My pink diamond necklace was made in England in 1870 and is valued at $180,000. Vladimer gave it to me, along with a matching ring, when we'd been married ten years.

"The set must be worth a mint!" Pia Jo surmised, scarcely able to imagine a necklace that was worth considerably more than the Roshnikov emeralds. In fact, she hadn't been able to visualize the emeralds adequately.

"The set is worth $250,000! We keep both pieces in a safety deposit box, or in our safe if I plan to wear them. Vlad won't let me wear the originals unless I have a bodyguard. What's your plan?"

Pia Jo thought briefly of Ebony's probable access to the safety deposit box in the Loup's Savings and Loan before she responded to Maxima's question. "I plan to bait a thief. We must circulate the rumor that you aren't daunted by the theft of the emerald necklace because it was fully insured, and that you'll be wearing the pink diamonds. But you'll really be wearing the copy. I hope it looks real. It does? Great! Here's what I want you to do."

- 1 4 -

The word "formal" had alarmed Pia Jo—her one formal dress was in Chicago and was too inelegant to wear to a party at the Roshnikov's mansion, and she couldn't afford a new one. The situation called for a conference with Luisa, but it would have to wait until she'd made her other calls. Her call to Gunter elicited the information that Blue had gratuitously contacted a Winnebagan friend in Black River Falls and had learned that Dove had been doing good deeds at the Wisconsin reservation she came from. She wasn't much liked up there—she'd acquired her skills at a Milwaukee school for chefs and had snubbed her old associates because of her certification and her job with the Roshnikovs. But she seemed to want to get back in their good graces; and since she made good wages, Blue didn't think her good deeds were out of line.

"What kind of good deeds?"

"Lunches at restaurants, movies, trips to Ho Chunk."

"Gambling can get significantly out of line, dear bro. Reo and I went to Ho Chunk once, and we lost our grocery money. Uncle Sven told us to go hungry, but Thelma let us run up a tab on her at the Lodge. How does Blue know how much she makes?"

"Ox-Eye told him. They're close friends. Admit it, trinket—she does check out."

She thanked him for the information, but when she'd disconnected, she railed, "Is that what he calls checking out? Somebody's got to be guilty, and I'm going to find out who it is!" When she dialed Scandia, Sven answered and said he'd kept his promise to "sound George out" about the donors to the school for exceptional children. "It was easy—I merely asked him, academically, if he thought it would be wise to reveal the identities of his wealthy donors when he writes the retrospective of the Home he's contemplating; and he said it definitely would—the Roshnikovs, Portnows, and Barnabies love receiving credit for their good deeds. His retrospective will feature a full account of the Home and the donors' involvement with it. They stage a huge picnic for the kids in some big park every Fourth of July, and they'll love the recognition they'll receive. By the way, the Home also has a long list of less-wealthy owners. George gave me far more information than you'll need—it was as easy as slipping on ice."

Since Sven's tone mildly suggested that she could easily have interviewed George herself, she became defensive. "He's a literary critic—how was I to know he'd consider writing a retrospective of the Home? So the Roshnikovs are wealthy donors? Hoo-ha! That lets the Wylies out—they'd never chance stealing from a wealthy patron. Thanks, Uncle Sven. I know you're busy, but please take time to record what you learned for me and date it. And please put Thelma on."

After asking her when he'd become her assistant private eye, he complied with her second request. "Thelma, dear," she said sweetly, "I need a little favor. I have to do some investigating tonight, and I don't want Gunter or Luisa to know what I'm doing. When I call you and ask if we can borrow formals for the Roshnikov dance on Saturday night, please invite me over to look at your old ones. I'll think of a reason to come without Luisa."

"No way! My old formals would never suit either of you. Besides, you're doing something illegal and dangerous—I can tell!"

"Please trust me, Thel! I swear I won't be in any danger—be a dear and play along. And promise you won't tell my tart uncle. He's getting more like a Granny Smith apple every day."

"But dear, you aren't trustworthy when you're investigating. Oh, all right—give me a call and I'll invite you over." Having won Thelma's reluctant cooperation, she dialed Gunter a second time. "I forgot to tell you that the party at Cloud House is on Saturday night, bro dear—and it's formal! Your invitation is in the mail."

"Formal?" Gunter's groan made her phone quiver. "That means I got to rent a tux!"

"Exactly! And Blue, too."

"Not me! I ain't goin'."

"Yes, you are, Gunter, or I'll have to find another date for Luisa. Now here's the drum—." But she kept back a few drumbeats for her own purposes.

At Cabin 6, she found Luisa preparing a light late lunch. "I thought you might get back in time to eat with me. The Tillotsons asked me to stay for lunch, but I had a yen for your unreliable company. What's new?"

Over broccoli and cheese soup and English muffins, Pia Jo brought her friend up to date.

"A necklace worth $180,000! I'm glad we're invited—it's time we began moving in the right circles."

"You're to go with Gunter. I left him grunting violently because the party's formal."

"Formal? Oh, no, whatever shall we wear?"

"I've thought of that—why don't you work on my portrait this afternoon, and after dinner I'll call Thelma and ask her if we can borrow a couple of her formals? They won't be suitable as they are, but Britt's a wizard with the needle. And Lu, dear, while I'm at Thelma's, please call Gunter and talk him into renting a tuxedo. If he and Blue go in their uniforms, the thief will think they're hired guards."

When Luisa had hesitantly agreed to this request, she began a portrait of Pia Jo; and as she worked, the two discussed the case. "Was Dag Amundson really drunk the night we went to the Red-Eyed Bat, or was he acting?" Luisa wanted to know. "Burl Stoker saw right through us—for all we know, Dag might have, too."

"I've wondered about that, and I've decided to interview him again tomorrow morning—at Asgard—that's what he calls his farm. He named it after the Viking home of the gods." Not being a person who likes to sit still for any length of time, Pia Jo fidgeted a lot and had to take several breaks; even so, the afternoon passed pleasantly enough. While Luisa tried to give her nose some verisimilitude, her squirming friend silently made plans for her evening's foray into the unknown.

When they'd consumed their soup and English muffins, eaten

rice pudding, and done the dishes, Pia Jo called Thelma, mentioned the formal problem, and accepted her invitation to look over her old gowns. Then she reminded Luisa to call Gunter, explained that she was in a hurry and would take the car, and drove up to Scandia the long way around.

"Why'd you drive?" Thelma asked when she let her in. "I thought you liked exercise."

"I do, but I need the car for an errand I have to do tonight, and Luisa would have heard me if I went back for it. I just wish people wouldn't be so nosy where I'm concerned. A private eye should be a *private* eye."

At Scandia, to pass the time until darkness fell, Thelma roped her into persuading Sven to go shopping with her in Madison the following day. "You girls are welcome to my old gowns—but only if Sven will help me pick out a couple of new ones. Since you're so deviously persuasive, you'll have to persuade him! He has exquisite taste."

Pia Jo's devious powers of persuasion came into full play during the next half hour. When Sven protested that he couldn't afford new clothes, she called him a skinflint and demanded to see his old tux. "Just as I thought," she said when she'd examined it closely. "Look at this shiny rear end! You can't attend a glamorous party in that old rag!"

"*That old rag* cost me a small fortune. If we hadn't both been skin-flints, how would you have gotten your Master's degree?"

"Oh, I agree—it's an admirable trait! How about if I pay for your new tuxedo with some of my $10,000 reward?"

"Oh, for Heaven's sake, Sweet Peuh—I'm not that hard up! All right, you win. Tomorrow Thelma and I will go to Madison."

Much to Pia Jo's satisfaction, Thelma's wardrobe provided instant gratification—a calf-length, night-blue sheath for Luisa and a silver mesh for herself—and though Britt didn't much approve of *décolletage*, she pleasantly agreed to remove the sleeves, lower the necklines, and slit Luisa's dress up the side and Pia Jo's up the back.

"I vill bring the formals to your cabin in the morning," she offered. "Dare I vill fit dem on you and make da renovations. But I vill sew dem at Scandia—vare no vun vill breat down my neck."

When darkness finally fell, Pia Jo returned to the Corvette, her inquiry kit stashed in her tote bag. Fully aware that Gunter would frown severely on her *modus operandi*, she drove to Lead Mines in a roundabout way so as not to raise her uncle's suspicions. She knew what it was like to have them both come down on her at once—it was sheer hell! After driving up to High Street and parking to the rear of the Oleander mansion, she removed a case of lock picks and her flashlight from her bag, attached the light to the camera, and slung the camera over a shoulder; then scaling a high brick wall, she approached the house under the cover of the bushes, nervously aware that a vicious dog might attack her at any moment. No dog appeared, but she tripped over a soft creature that snarled in displeasure. When she realized that the snarl was not that of a trained pit bull but of an offended feline, she let out a jagged sigh of relief. Clouds obscured the moon, but the light from the widely-spaced street lamps soon revealed a cat that was blacker than the night itself, with starlight reflected in its spotted yellow eyes.

"Go away, Cat!" she ordered in a loud whisper. "This is not your night to howl." Approaching a side door, she verified what she had earlier surmised, that it had a lock not readily accessible to the manipulations of burglars—she had to try various lock picks until she found one that worked. The door slid open, but its thick chain stubbornly refused her entrance. Feeling glum, she went around to the back door and tried again but with no more success—the door was obviously heavily bolted or barred on the inside. There was no help for it—she'd have to try the front door, which was too vividly limned by the corner streetlight to disguise her movements. But as she advanced in its direction, the jet black cat streaked by her like a Norn and seemed to disappear through the basement wall. Looking more closely, Pia Jo almost broke into tears of joy—the Norn had vanished through a partially open basement window!

Stooping down to survey the opening, she discovered that with a little patient manipulation, she could open the transom-shaped window wide enough to slip through. Being especially careful of the expensive camera, she climbed through the aperture and swung herself to the basement floor.

The basement was tenebrous; no dim moon or sparkling stars penetrated its abysmal gloom. Chiding herself for not remembering to put new batteries into her old flashlight, she snapped it on and stealthily made her way up the stairway and into the kitchen through a door that had no doubt been left ajar for the treasured pet.

The house was immense; as she went from room to room on the lower floor and then climbed the stairs and went from room to room on the upper level, she snapped pictures of the expensive furniture and the rich draperies that adorned every room. Even the paintings looked original; but since she knew nothing about African artwork, she had no way to determine their worth. But without the artwork, they must have had to spend more than $25,000 on furnishings alone! However, none of the dressers, closets, or desk drawers held the emerald necklace, nor did the jewelry chest that stood on a chiffonier, a chest as tall as a midget and as filled with costume jewelry as a fancy boutique.

"I could really make a haul tonight if I were a thief," she mused. Descending to the lower floor, she suddenly drew back, for the front entrance light had gone on and a woman's voice was saying, "Nox hasn't been fed—we'll have to speak to Fiona," while Nox was meowing up a storm and a man's voice was soothing both the cat and the woman.

"Lady Fortune, be with me now!" Pia Jo breathed prayerfully as she crouched down behind a living room couch. "How'll I get past them and back down the basement stairs?" But there was an alternative— they'd left the door to the front entrance wide open; only a screen door barred her way to the freedom of the out-of-doors. Reaching over the back of the couch, she requisitioned a black plush throw and wrapped herself and the camera in it; then, grateful for the thick gray rug, she crept from behind the coral couch to the shelter of a graceful black goddess. Making sure that she hadn't been discovered, she crept to the shelter of a gleaming black god. Peering around the long, muscular legs of the black god, she saw that the Oleanders had fed Nox and played with her to their satisfaction and were about to return to the living area. There was no help for it—she had to make her move without delay. Dashing for the screen door, she dived through it, rolled down the front steps, and crashed on the sidewalk below.

"Did you see that, Eb? Something black just ran across the living room and out the door. Big and black! O my God! Maybe a wolf got in through that basement window! Are wolves black?"

Fearful for Sven's camera, Pia Jo didn't wait to hear the man's reply; instead she struggled painfully to her knees and crawled behind the BMW parked in the driveway. But she dared not linger in the protection of the luxury car. No doubt they'd call the police! Stifling her groans, she rolled into the shelter of a prickly hedge and lay there suffering from her numerous bruises until they gave up searching the grounds. Leaving the thick plush throw under the hedge and hoping against hope that it wouldn't retain her fingerprints, she hobbled to the Corvette, checked out the camera, expressed gratitude to Lady Fortune for preserving it intact, and returned to Cabin 6.

"Where have you been?" Luisa demanded when Pia Jo limped into the living area of Cabin 6. "When I called Sven an hour ago, he said you were on your way home. I was getting ready to call Gunter—you're hurt! What happened?"

When she heard what Pia Jo had been up to, Luisa examined her shoulder, pronounced it sprained but not broken, and excoriated her for her foolhardiness. "I wish they *had* called the police," she said sternly. "Chief Gramm wouldn't have been as easy on you as Gunter is." Then she relented. "No, I don't, but what good did it do to break in and take photos? Since they were obtained illegally, they can't be used as evidence; and if you show them to Gunter, he'll know what you did."

But Pia Jo didn't think the night's adventure was wasted. "The pictures strongly indicate 'probable cause,' and they could convince Gunter that a search warrant is necessary. The Oleanders must have invested a lot more than $50,000 in down-payments on their home, furniture, and car," she explained. After she'd swallowed pain pills and soaked in the tub, she felt a little better. Even so, her aching shoulder awakened her every time she rolled on it, and she spent an exceptionally uncomfortable night.

- 1 5 -

After awakening Luisa at dawn, Pia Jo thoughtfully donned a white knit shirt with a scalloped collar, knotted a subdued yellow scarf at her throat, pulled on pale yellow trousers and white sandals, and stepped back to study her appearance. She'd decided on the demure outfit so that Dag wouldn't recognize her as one of the Southern charmers he'd previously encountered at the Red-Eyed Bat. "It'll do," she finally decided as she dabbed a bit of AnaïsAnaïs on her wrists and throat. She seldom wore perfume, perhaps because it made her think of Lena, who saturated her clothes with various scents and often smelled unpleasantly stale. But the light perfume enhanced her feminine appeal.

At her friend's sleepy protest over being roused so early, she explained, "I thought you might want to come with me to Asgard—I'm planning to question the Amundsons this morning."

"Why so early? I'll bet his cows aren't even up." Luisa yawned as she turned her back and pulled the sheet over her face.

"It's planting time—Dag'll probably be in the fields by seven, right after he milks the cows. Well? Are you coming with me?"

Luisa tried reasoning her out of it. "You're going to be a mass of aches and pains today—can't you put it off until tomorrow?"

"No, I can't. Maxima wants me to get this show on the road, and I want to be able to tell Reo that I've made real progress when he calls."

"Well, then, you'd better go alone. If Dag sees two of us, he might remember us."

"You have a point," Pia Jo admitted. "Go back to sleep. I'll eat breakfast at The Swans Nest." Over her coffee, juice, and whole-wheat toast at the restaurant in Wild Swan Lodge, she secured directions to Asgard from Alvin Stein, the overweight young man who was highly gifted in the culinary arts, after which she hurried off to fulfill her responsibility. It was a beautiful, full-foliaged, end-of-May day with soft breezes blowing and crabapple trees blooming on either side of the highway that led to the farm; but while she admired the charms of the countryside, her thoughts were primarily on the approaching interview. Her biggest anxiety was that Dag would recognize her, but she quelled her doubts by assuring herself that today she did not in the least resemble the silly young woman who'd worn a black wig, heavy make-up, and a sturdy hiking outfit at their first meeting.

When she saw the name on the mailbox, she turned abruptly into the driveway, drove up to the house, and sat for a while surveying the buildings, which, though old, were fairly well cared for; and the lawn, which, though neat enough, lacked an artistic touch. Evidently the Amundsons had other things on their minds than the care of shrubs, flower gardens, and lawn ornaments. She was thinking so hard of Emeline's love for garden art and remembering that it was Memorial Day that she was startled when a voice with a German accent asked, "Do you vant someting, Miss?"

Aroused from her reverie, she turned her head in the direction of the voice and saw a large, ungainly man with fair hair and intensely blue eyes who surely could not be an Amundson.

"Yes, I do—I would like to talk to Dag Amundson." Getting out of the car, she offered him her hand. "You must be Horst Brenner. I'm Pia Jo Borg, and I'm investigating the theft of the Roshnikov emeralds. Is Mr. Amundson at home?"

"I'm right here," said another voice, and Dag, lured by the sound of a young female voice, sprang through the door like Heathcliff pursuing Kathy. "Hello! So you're Pia Jo! Come in! Come in! Horst, since you're not a suspect in the theft, you might as well start seeding the corn." She was amused to see that Dag almost seemed glad to be a suspect since it put him in close proximity to a young, unmarried woman.

But he was brushing his employee off too hurriedly to please Pia Jo.

Turning to Horst, she asked, "Aren't you the Roshnikov chauffeur? If so, don't go far. I want to ask you some questions."

"Wait out here," Dag ordered him. Then leading her to the front entrance and into a long narrow shed that had been built on to the main house, he held the door open and called, "Goldie, put another cup on the table—Miss Borg's here and would like some coffee."

Thinking suddenly of her Uncle Willum, who had called coffee "Swedish gasoline," she refused his offer as she followed him into the shed. "Thanks, but I've had breakfast." Pausing briefly in the shed, she was startled by the large number of Viking tools and weapons that were displayed on the walls. Since she had seen more than one Viking exhibition, she recognized them at once.

The kitchen was large but low ceilinged and had a round table in its center; the curtains and the tablecloth were of blue-and-white checked gingham, and a wide blue-and-white checked border adorned the walls just below the ceiling. The table was set with blue plates. Why not yellow, she wondered, remembering that Sweden's colors were yellow and blue. When they came to America, the Amundsons had obviously brought their natal country with them; for, like the shed, the kitchen held numerous reminders of Sweden.

Drawing out a chair for her, he poured what probably was coffee into a blue mug and called loudly, "Goldie, this stuff's been on the warmer for hours. We don't want to poison Ms. Borg." Seating himself near her, he began to ply her with unsought information. "I played the piano at the Roshnikov party. Everybody who is anybody in Lead Mines was there, and a few out-of-towners. If you like, I can give you a list of the guests." He appeared educated and certainly was courteous enough.

A chubby girl with a kewpie doll face and a long, corn-blonde pony tail tied at the nape of her neck with a hot-pink scarf sauntered into the kitchen, a little, white-haired boy trotting at her heels. Her expressionless face suggested an untutored mind. "I'll have to make new coffee, and I've got three costumes to sew," she said peevishly as she held up the bodice of a colorful peasant costume.

"Well, make it then," Dag grunted, but Pia Jo objected firmly. "Thank you, I'll drink this." She took a sip and instantly regretted her offer—sheep dip would have been preferable. "Are you Goldie?"

The girl looked at her oddly. "How'd you know?"

"Stan Anderson told me you live here with your brother and your little boy."

The girl observed her little boy proudly. "His name is Kaito and he's two. If you don't want new coffee, I'll get back to my sewing. I'm making costumes for the Scandinavian Dance. Goodbye. Come on, Kaito." She took the child's hand and led him out of the kitchen. Pia Jo followed her with her eyes. "'Kaito' is an unusual name. Was he named after his father?"

Dag's negation was vigorous. "No, but it could be German. She has a big imagination, and she still plays with dolls," he said, gesturing toward a long, scalloped shelf that held a variety of elves, trolls, and peasant dancers. "She's too young to be a mother."

"How old is she?"

"Seventeen. But she was only fourteen when she got pregnant. She dropped out of school, and when she refused to name the father, my parents kicked her out. That's why she's living with me."

"You were kind to give her a home. She seems genuinely fond of the child."

"Oh, she is, though he's more like a little brother than a son." But his sister was clearly not his immediate concern. "So you're Soren's sister! And Gunter's! That must be why you look so familiar."

Sensing that he was about to get personal, she changed the subject abruptly. "I was surprised to see Mr. Brenner here—I was planning to interview him at Cloud House."

"He only works there when they need him—he works for me during my busy seasons. Gunter said you have a fiancé, but you're not wearing a ring."

Feeling that the question was out of line, she decided she'd better let him know right off that she wasn't available. "My fiancé thinks rings are for weddings—he gave me this locket instead." She drew a silver locket studded with tiny pearls and chips of diamonds from under the yellow scarf and opened it to reveal small, oval pictures of herself and Reo. Ignoring his disconsolate expression, she began a discussion of the case. "When were you aware that the emerald necklace had been stolen?"

"When Madame Roshnikov screamed. I was finishing the introduction to her song, and I looked up at her to see if she was ready to sing. When she put her hand to her throat, I realized that she'd lost her necklace."

"You think she merely lost it—that it wasn't stolen?"

"Seems obvious to me. The clasp was probably weak and it slipped from her neck. Someone saw it happen and picked it up—isn't that as good an explanation as any?"

"Yes, but the person who picked it up didn't return it, which makes him or her a thief. What happened after she screamed?"

"Her husband tried to calm her, but she was hysterical. He sat down with her on a couch and told Ox-Eye to call the police. Ox-Eye said we were not to leave until Chief Gramm had talked to us. When he came, he had a female detective along—pretty woman, name of Brenda something or other. I heard she's no longer on the Force." He paused for an explanation but went on when she said nothing. "Ms. Roshnikov had given me a Russian songbook with English translations, and I stayed at the piano and played until they came. That Brenda woman asked some questions while another officer searched the premises for the necklace. It got pretty late and many of us had to get up early the next day, so she had us write our names, addresses, and phone numbers on a sheet of paper and then let us go." When Dag focused on the theft, he was quite articulate.

"Did you see anything unusual or suspicious before or after the theft?"

"No, but if anyone stole it, it must've been one of those Jews— Yentl and her boyfriend. She's a poor relative, and you can't trust a Jew with money."

Pia Jo's opinion of Dag fell markedly at this nasty, hateful remark. "Don't gentiles like money?" she asked, her voice edged with disgust. "I know I do." Then reminding herself not to lose her temper, she changed the subject. "I understand that Yentl and her fiancé are talented musicians and that the Roshnikovs are having a party in honor of Yentl on Saturday. Since she and Nikita will be there as guests, not performers, I expect you'll be asked to play. I suppose you will play even though Maxima is Jewish?"

"Oh, I'll play," he assured her doggedly. "They pay well."

She couldn't refrain from observing sarcastically, "So *you* like money, too?"

He looked at her skeptically. "You're not much like Soren, are you? Can I go now? I have work to do."

She thought, "And you aren't much like Raoul Wallenburg, are you?" Aloud she said, "Thank you, Mr. Amundson. If you think of anything else, please call me. I'm staying at Innisfree, and this is my number." She scribbled a number on a piece of notebook paper, said "I'll interview Horst outside," and preceded him out the door, leaving the bitter, rancid coffee to burn a hole in her cup.

Outside, he hurried off in the direction of the barn while she joined the big, blond German, who was sitting on a bench under a huge elm tree waiting for her to interview him. It wasn't much of an interview—he told her in broken English that it had snowed on the morning of the theft, and he'd blown out the driveway and the walks with the Roshnikovs' snowblower. They were expecting guests from Evanston, and they had him clean out an unused stall in their garage so they could park their car inside. They'd called the Salvation Army to come and remove the objects they'd been storing, and he'd helped load a couch and a chair on the Army's truck, after which Frau Alligretti had hired him to stay near her and guard her jewels during the party.

"And after the necklace disappeared?" she asked, her pen poised. She'd forgotten her tape recorder, so she was forced to take notes.

He'd gone with Frau Alligretti to Herr Roshnikov's office and stood guard while she checked the contents of the safe. She was glad she'd left her most valuable jewels in her safety deposit box at the bank. The next morning Frau Roshnikov sent Dove to his quarters with a tray of fancy leftovers. That's all he knew.

While she finished making entries in her own peculiar brand of shorthand, she wondered if Maxima had asked Horst his political views before hiring him. But he didn't seem at all like a skinhead. "So you only work here during farming weather? Does Dag treat you well?"

The big German shrugged elaborately, looked embarrassed, and finally admitted that he worked at Asgard to be close to Goldie. He wanted to make sure that Dag was good to her and the little boy. Yes, he loved her and wanted to marry her, but she was interested in a smooth-talking married man. Who? That he pretended he didn't know. When she let him go, he hurried in the direction of the barn, softly singing a Rhine River tune about a Lorelie.

The interviews over, Pia Jo sat in the Corvette and amended her skimpy notes. Her gut feeling was that the man Goldie wanted most was Stan Anderson, and she felt deeply sorry for both Horst and Sandie. No wonder Sandie looked so hopeless and devastated! However, the interviews had netted her little beyond the realization that here were three people whose thoughts were more on unrequited   love than on the theft of the Roshnikov jewels.

When she got back on the highway, she again remembered that it was Memorial Day and decided to bring her mother a bouquet of fresh flowers. Driving to Lead Mines, she parked in front of Flowers and Feathers, a floral establishment that featured both floral bouquets and exotic birds. What a good idea, she mused as she peered into a screened-in greenhouse where canaries, parakeets, hummingbirds, and even a few colorful parrots were having a field day amid the lushly blooming flowers. The place reminded her a little of the Milwaukee Domes, especially the one that features Midwest flowers and shrubs. She'd gone there with Sven and Thelma the previous summer, on a day when Sven had an appointment with his publisher. That was the day that Sven had first tried to interest her in Rex Tremaine. Over lunch he'd raved about Tremaine's charms and attributes so much that she'd almost wished she'd stayed home.

Since the symbolism of red roses had repulsed Emeline after Gustav Borg, whose passion had been short-lived, had deserted his family and had not been heard from again, Pia Jo selected a bouquet of white wood violets with lavender veins and had them tied with lavender and white ribbons, thinking as she did so that they deserved their reputation of having the scent of sanctity. When she'd paid for them, she brought them to the cemetery and exchanged them for the dead lilacs that were still on the grave. Stopping to read the cryptic message on the headstone, she asked, "Who put it there, Mom? Who loved you like that?"

It was a mystery that would have to wait its turn. And then an even bigger mystery nibbled at her consciousness. "Where are you now?" Remembering that Emeline, whose experiences had made her highly speculative about religion, had requested a non-sectarian funeral featuring universal poetry rather than sermons, Pia Jo resolved to read her manuscript on religion, which was still in a chest in her garden studio at Rendezvous of the Four Winds. But that resolve would also have to wait its turn—she had a case to solve now, and her relationship with Reo to salvage. Leaving a memory kiss on the violets, she returned to Cabin 6.

-16-

When Britt had renovated the two formals and had gone back to Scandia, Pia Jo held the silver mesh gown up to her body and lamented, "It's a shame I have no one to impress with this fabulous dress. You're lucky—you can enjoy the romance of the occasion with Gunter. I wish my sposo were here."

"You could call him and ask him to come—but then what would you do about Blue? Frankly, Peejay, Blue's got twice the character my dear brother has, and he's just as good-looking."

"Maybe so, but he's Clover's; besides, Reo's much more exciting."

"Have it your own way, but when Reo breaks your heart, don't blame me."

"What makes you think he will?"

"Because he's more child than adult, that's why. Did I ever tell you that our parents paid for that snazzy red Camarro he wrecked before you met him? And how did he repay their generosity? By ripping off some valuable paintings they'd bought in Italy!" Luisa said hotly.

"Sposo told me that the Camarro had a faulty steering wheel and that they didn't pay him for some paintings he did for them."

Luisa could not have looked more disgusted. "Oh, he's good! The body shop man said that the steering wheel got bent in the accident, and his paintings were supposed to be gifts. Anyway, they weren't worth one-tenth as much as the Italian paintings were."

"But he was young and irresponsible when he did those things. He's matured since then."

"Have you ever wrecked a car your parents bought you? Or helped yourself to anything they treasured?" Luisa demanded, her eyes sparkling with indignation.

"No, but girls grow up faster than boys. Besides, my dad skipped out and left my mom with all the debts—we had to drive junk cars and frame inexpensive prints ourselves."

"Don't you think they've given Reo a hundred chances to grow up?" Luisa demanded irately. "I wasn't going to tell you this, but just last month he called Dad and asked for a $10,000 loan to pay for a trip to Paris. He insisted that you and he need a vacation and the trip would be part of his education. Of course Dad turned him down."

Pia Jo took a minute to digest this bit of news. "No wonder he's so eager for me to solve the Roshnikov case," she finally mused. "It must be very important to his career to see Paris. Let's not fight, Lu. Go ahead and denounce Reo—I'll just have to keep your jibes in perspective."

Putting the investigation on hold until the Roshnikov party, Pia Jo spent the next two mornings speed-walking the trails in the hills behind Wild Swans Lake with Luisa and Alvin Stein, who had been sampling too much of his own and Britt's expert cooking and was eager to lose weight. Al, who made no romantic demands on either of them, was an ideal companion, full of camaraderie and wacky theories about the case. Afternoons, Pia Jo sat for her portrait, and evenings the two young women read drama and discussed Pia Jo's plays or speculated about Rex Tremaine, of whom they knew little. June 3rd was slow to arrive; however, the young investigator's desire to get on with the case was granted on the morning of the 2nd, when Vladimer phoned to announce that the Alligrettis had arrived and she was to interview them at 1:00 p.m.

"You didn't tell them I'm investigating the case, did you?" she demanded in a burst of anxiety. "If you did, I'll be interviewing two clams."

"Of course I didn't," Vladimer denied a bit resentfully. "Where's your confidence in me? I told them you were writing a play based on the case and needed every bit of drama you could wring from it. Being a highly dramatic person, Reolo suggested that you make it an opera—I had to tell him that I doubted you had any experience with librettos. But dress wildly when you come—they're never impressed with the ordinary."

This suggestion sent Pia Jo into a panic. "Wildly? What do you mean—wildly? Shall I wear a costume?"

Vladimer's laugh boomed over the telephone wire. "You needn't go that far. I suggest rainbow Capri pants of a silky material with uneven calf-length hems, a lavender blouse, and several strands of beads—if possible green, pink, and yellow."

Pia Jo shuddered. "I haven't anything that wild—unless I dress up in one of Reo's paintings, maybe his *Rainbow over Chicago's Famed Navy Pier* or his *Architecture from a Cruiser on the Chicago River.* We've had enough trouble getting formals ready in the time allowed. How can I ever get an outfit like that together?"

She heard what seemed to be a mild scuffle at the other end of the line; then Maxima's voice said sternly, "Give me that phone, Vlad. Stop teasing her. If you wore an outfit like that, Pia Jo, Sidonie wouldn't speak to you. If you have a sort of classy black outfit, that would be fine. Didn't I tell you that Vlad loves to mislead others so he can be amused?"

Berating herself inwardly for falling for Vladimer's practical joke, she answered with considerable relief, "I have a black and white silk pant suit that fits the description—Thelma and Sven gave it to me for my last birthday. Will that do?"

"That sounds suitable. And don't be put off by Sidonie's uppity attitude. She's lived in France, and she thinks Russians and Americans are low-class. After your interview, I want you to stay and give me a report on your progress."

"With them there?"

"No, no! They'll be preparing to meet friends at *Chez les Célèbres* in Prairie du Loup for dinner. Sidonie loves to show off her jewels. Be sure to be on time this afternoon—she's always late herself but has no patience with others who aren't prompt."

As she related the conversation to Luisa while pressing the black pantsuit with its black and white waistcoat, Pia Jo couldn't help think-ing that Sidonie Alligretti must be a thoroughly unpleasant person. It would be a challenge to get any useful information out of her. When she voiced her doubts, Luisa comforted, "Just sizing them up might be enough. If I were you, I'd let them do most of the talking."

Dressed in the stylish pantsuit, Pia Jo rang the Roshnikov doorbell promptly at 1:00 p.m. and followed the formal Ox-Eye into a private sitting room. After he announced her as Ms. Borg, Maxima introduced her to the Alligrettis as her young playwright friend. Feeling like an amateur, Pia Jo put Luisa's advice to good use. The Alligrettis were accustomed to being the center of attention, and she had only to say, "I'll appreciate your giving me your fresh ideas," and they were off on a race to see who could lend the highest drama to the theft of the emeralds; in fact, they seemed to want to star in her play themselves, the arrogant Sidonie no less than the aggressive Reolo; for while he was an opera star, she'd been on the stage and, according to Maxima's previous information, hadn't had a good role for quite some time.

The two were a study in contrasts; whereas she was pencil-slim, fragile, and lovely in a patrician way, he was built on a large, unwieldy scale, and though regal and impressive, wasn't exactly handsome. And while he emphasized his suggestions with mellifluous, tenor examples of arias he had sung, she emphasized hers with dramatic renditions. This was especially apparent when she suggested a soliloquy on the theft something on the order of Hamlet's "To be or not to be" oration and he immediately sang it with operatic impact. "To steal or not to steal—that is the question!" His soliloquy didn't ask whether it was nobler to steal or not to steal the emerald necklace; instead it concentrated on a wily thief who got away with it.

To avoid looking like a private investigator, Pia Jo had decided not to tape the interview but to take notes instead. So while she made use of her bewildering shorthand, Sidonie offered suggestions on how the female lead should be dressed in the play, what songs she should sing, and what other jewels she should wear. She didn't like Reolo's comment that the play should be entitled *Green Fire*—that title was way too common. It must be titled *Temptation*. This suggestion sent Reolo into an operatic reverie on the tempting power of green fire, which was the birthstone for May, and on the human desire to own such a valuable and seductive jewel. His knowledge of emeralds was fantastic; he said, for example, that the ancients believed they imparted to their wearer a supernatural ability to tell fortunes, and that they also quickened intelligence, enhanced eloquence, and increased honesty.

"I have an emerald stickpin and cuff links, and I do believe they enhance my operatic eloquence," he added with pompous pride. "I gave Sidonie a ring with an emerald stone to enhance her dramatic impact."

"The ancients also thought that emeralds had the power to distinguish true love from false—they were said to burst into flame when they were near poison," Sidonie added.

"Do you believe these claims?" Pia Jo asked while she wondered how they could remember them all. But she soon answered her own doubt—they were used to memorizing long speeches and songs.

Sidonie shrugged elaborately. "I have three strings of emeralds— they certainly suggest the fire of love."

"Or jealousy," Pia Jo countered, but only in her mind. She'd been led to believe that red was the color of passion.

When the hour was up and the Alligrettis had retired to their suite to dress for their dinner at *Chez les Célèbres*, Pia Jo looked at the Roshnikovs helplessly. "They certainly are interesting people, but what am I to make of all that information?" she demanded in confusion.

"They make a hobby of studying gems," Maxima assured her. "Ask them about sapphires some time, or pearls."

"What do you honestly conclude from your interview?" Vladimer prompted. "First impressions are often important."

Not knowing the Roshnikovs well, Pia Jo weighed her answer carefully and decided to be rigidly honest. "For all their wealth, I found them rather pathetic. They were eager to have *me* write a play that would be a vehicle for their special talents—they actually seemed to be auditioning for the parts. With talents and connections like theirs, why would they value the work of an unknown playwright? That makes them seem extremely insecure to me."

Maxima was startled by her remark. "They've never seemed insecure to me—but you're right! Why would they want *you* to write a play for them? Could they have been acting? Sorry—I don't mean to imply that you have no talent; but as you say, they're used to working with distinguished writers."

However, Vladimer wasn't satisfied with Pia Jo's diagnosis. "I think you got more than that from the interview—if one can call it an inter-view. I saw you looking from one to the other in a puzzled way, as if you were trying to make up your mind about something."

It took Pia Jo a while to put her other strong reaction into a cogent thought. Finally she said tentatively, "They don't seem to like each other."

"Why do you say that? I've always imagined that they adore one another." Maxima's answer was emphatic. "He plies her with jewels—she has twice as many as I have, and some of them are much more valuable."

"But does he love her, or is she a showcase for his success?" she asked. Then she added quickly, "Perhaps he does love her, but does she love him? She kept putting him down—saying his ideas were silly. He has a magnificent voice—it struck me as being truly great; yet she showed no appreciation for his golden notes."

They both looked reflective. "She's heard him sing too many times to be as impressed as you were—but you may be right," Vladimer finally conceded. "He's always trying to please her, and she never seems willing to be pleased."

Maxima regarded Pia Jo with new respect. "You know, you've put your finger on something I could never quite understand or put into words. But what does that tell you about the case? Are they suspects?"

Pia Jo shook her head forlornly. "Not really—not unless they aren't as wealthy as they pretend to be."

Vladimer was shocked by the very suggestion. "But I can easily find out for sure." While Pia Jo lunched with Maxima and gave her a cursory account of her investigation, he made some judicious calls and came back with the information she sought. Reolo was worth ten million dollars, and Sidonie's jewels had been valued at two million. Moreover, she came from a wealthy French family, and she was the primary heir. There was no doubt whatsoever about the Alligretti wealth.

- 1 7 -

Oblachnyj Dom **was lit by** tall candles and subdued lights when Pia Jo and Luisa arrived with their handsomely-garbed but self-conscious escorts and were greeted by their host and hostess in the large reception room. Beyond the imported carved doors that lead to the dining room, they could see the long table with its centerpiece of soft pink roses and white mums flanked by a mountain of fruit and a huge bowl of pink punch, and laden with platters of *hors d'oeuvres* and luxurious desserts.

"Maxima is trying to recreate our December party too authentically by using all this pink," Vladimer chuckled, displaying his puckish dimples to great advantage as he handed Pia Jo a cup of punch. "Hey, Shamus, what are you doing in a silver mesh? I was expecting you to wear a Joseph's coat to brighten up your penguin attire."

Pia Jo, who considered her own seriousness a defect, answered in kind. "Are you trying to tell me I don't sparkle? Blue said I twinkle like a million little stars!" she replied tartly. After taking a generous sip of the punch, she blinked. "Wow! It's no mystery who spiked the punch! When I've had a coupla cups of this, I'll really sparkle. By the way, I've solved the case. I've decided you planned the theft as a practical joke, Vladimer. When you get to La Scala, you'll get a belly laugh out of presenting the emerald necklace to Madame Roshnikov."

"He won't get such a belly laugh out of paying you $10,000 for finding him out," Maxima rejoined in mock-severity. "You girls look lovely. Black pendant pearls and matching eardrops, Pia Jo? I'm impressed!"

"Thank you." She didn't add, "You mean they actually passed for the real thing? Reo paid $50 for the set, and I accused him of extravagance!" Instead she lowered her voice and asked Maxima, "Was this the way the drawing room was lit on the night of the anniversary party?"

"Yes, at first. When the dancing started, we dimmed the lights."

"No wonder the thief was able to snitch the emeralds! Vladimer, may I have a private word with you?"

"Of course. But I won't put up with any of your practical jokes," he replied pontifically. Motioning the others to go inside and meet Yentl, he drew her into a library, looked at her curiously, and nodded when she made her request. In a few moments they were in the drawing room, and she too was being introduced to the guest of honor.

To Pia Jo's surprise, Yentl Androvi was a tenuous girl wearing a calf-length, white sequined gown with a white soft-lace shawl draped over her delicate shoulders. Her necklace, engagement ring, and tiara sparkled with tiny diamonds that turned her into a fairyland princess. As they moved on to make room for more guests, Gunter whispered to his companions, "Since she's Maxima's niece, I expected someone more substantial. She looks like a strong wind would blow her away."

"That's because you've gotten so fat," his sister jibed. "You must have gained thirty pounds since your divorce. Luisa, do you like fat men?"

Looking stunning in the night-blue gown, faux star sapphire beads, and matching pendant earrings, Luisa defended Gunter vigorously. "He's not fat—he's muscular."

Pia Jo regarded her brother fondly; fat or muscular, he'd always been a strong support, someone with whom she could exchange friendly insults but whose loyalty was unquestionable. In spite of his earlier complaints that he looked like a robin wearing a penguin's suit, or a Cinder Allen going to a royal ball, he did look handsome. Blue had been less graphic about his wearing apparel, his complaint having been merely one of strangulation. Since he hadn't committed a crime, why was he being forced to wear a noose?

She had shown no sympathy. "What you both need is a little culchah. Uniforms just won't do tonight, and be sure to conceal your guns. You both look as magnificent as—as emperors."

"Not Roman Emperors, I hope," Blue had disagreed. "We'd look even dopier in dinky skirts. Aren't you chilly?"

"A little—but dancing will remedy that," she'd retorted merrily. "We're going to dance so much that we'll dissolve into hot, little puddles." Then she sobered abruptly. "No, we can't do that, not tonight. We must all dance a little so as not to arouse suspicions; but while some of us are dancing, others must watch. Oh, and don't even mention your official names tonight. If anyone asks, the Roshnikovs are going to say you're here to have fun."

Pausing for a long moment in the wide doorway to the drawing room, Pia Jo noted that a number of guests had already arrived. Thelma, dressed stylishly in black lace, and Sven in a white tuxedo, were deep in conversation with the Wylies, who had also dressed elegantly. How lovely the ladies looked; how handsome the men! Sidonie Alligretti, svelte and luminous in a lambent gold evening gown adorned with a necklace of natural canary and white diamonds, was laughing with Jack and Loretta Gramm, her matching ear loops gleaming with every turn of her head. Dressed as a guest, the police chief seemed to be enjoying a date with his unexpectedly lovely wife. Horst Brenner, surprisingly well groomed in a black dinner jacket, hovered behind Sidonie impassively, while Reolo lingered nearby, his lavender cummerbund emphasizing his considerable girth.

She recognized others, too. Dag Amundson, looking almost dapper in a purple dinner jacket over a figured purple vest, lounged near the piano and chatted with the Andersons, who were less impressively-dressed; the Constantas, colorfully attired, were in conference with Madame Roshnikov, while the Dgong twins, two identical silhouettes in white, stood farther off, their dark eyes fixing in fascination on Sidonie's scintillating jewels, then moving simultaneously to Maxima's pink diamonds and pearls, which looked unbelievably authentic.

Noting that Pia Jo was lagging behind her companions, Vladimer joined her and whispered, "Come along, Ice Princess—you'll arouse suspicion if you stand here staring at the guests." Coming to life, she allowed him to steer her into the ballroom, where she joined her group and assumed the appearance of a guest. But she couldn't help observing to Vladimer and her companions *sotto voce* that they'd have to keep an eye on Sidonie's jewels or there could be two thefts tonight.

Vladimer shook his head. "Don't worry about Sidonie's jewels. She's not taking any chances."

"How come? Are they make-believe?"

"Sidonie wear make-believe jewels? Never. Haven't you wondered why our chauffeur is attending this party?"

"He blends so well with the guests that I didn't notice him right away. Did Sidonie hire him to guard her jewels?"

"Correct. He looks half asleep, but don't let that fool you—he's as alert as a prison guard. No one will steal her jewels as long as he's in her service. And here's Yentl with Nikita." As he spoke their names, the guest of honor appeared on the arm of a young man whose slender elegance complemented her gossamer appearance.

When Nikita had met Pia Jo and her party, Vladimer suggested that they join Maxima and partake of the culinary delights. Agreeing wholeheartedly, they followed him into the dining room and listened to Maxima's announcement that the party was to honor her niece, who would soon be teaching music at *Oblachnyj Dom*, after which Vladimer proposed a hearty toast to Yentyl's success. Soon the guests were helping themselves to food and accepting drinks from the trays offered by the Dgong twins. The vigorous punch was especially welcome to Gunter and Blue, who looked almost as uncomfortable as they felt; but when they'd come close to chugging their third cups, Luisa, always watchful, urged them to lay off. "You're supposed to remain alert, you two. Pia Jo needs you tonight."

Looking at her admiringly, Gunter sighed like a school boy. "I dunno which is more intoxicating'—you or the punch," he observed, while Blue appeared amused that his sedate superior could be so human.

At long last, Dag began to play soft music, someone dimmed the lights, and the romantic ambiance of the ballroom soon made the officers forget their initial complaints. The songs were all by request; and as guest of honor, Yentl was given first choice. Perhaps the sentimental surroundings influenced her, for she immediately selected "Star Dust"; and when Reolo stepped forth, unannounced, and sang the words in a melting tenor, "And I am once again with you, / When our love was new / And each kiss an inspiration," Pia Jo felt tears dim her eyes and fear lurch heavily across her heart. Was her love for Reo fast becoming a star dust melody, only a "memory of love's refrain"? But to demonstrate that her feelings for him were not to be the focus of the evening's events, she asked Blue if he'd like to dance.

Halfway through the dance Stan Anderson broke in, leaving Sandie to dance with Blue. When Stan, who danced too close and breathed down her neck, whispered that she and the dark girl who'd come in with her were the prettiest "dolls" in the room and they made Sandie look old by comparison, she despised him for his disloyalty to his wife and promptly declined a second dance on the grounds that her feet hurt.

"I'm sorry, but my shoes are killing me," she said, fracturing the truth; and when Dag announced that the Oleanders had requested that he play "Star Dust" as Hoagy Carmichael had first conceived it in 1927—as a swingy, almost ragtime piano piece—she immediately accepted George Wylie's invitation to follow the lead of the agile Afro-American couple who were already on the floor by dancing in an energetic fashion that befitted the 90's. George, it turned out, loved to dance and was willing to try practically any step, whether old or new; and Pia Jo didn't once think of pinched toes while they were on the floor; but at the end of the dance, when she saw how absorbed Gunter was in Luisa, she decided that she'd better opt for spy duty rather than enjoyment, and the sore-feet excuse again became operable.

Blue soon joined her on a couch, and they sat quietly while they watched Stan approach Dag at the piano, assume the stance of a soloist, and wait expectantly while Dag slowly and dreamily played the introductory bars of "I'm in the Mood for Love." Soon Stan was crooning, in a remarkably good voice, "Why stop to think of whether / This little dream might fade? / We've put our hearts together; / Now we are one, I'm not afraid! / ; and Pia Jo was asking Blue, "Is he singing that song to Sandie?"

"I doubt it. He hasn't looked at her once while he's been singing. She's smiling, but I'll bet she knows that her husband's a talented louse. Gunter and Luisa seem to be mesmerizing one another—doesn't she look like a princess?"

Pia Jo nodded appreciatively. "More than some princesses do. I doubt that we'll get much help from them tonight." From the corner of her eye, she saw Maxima approaching, leading Nikita like the Queen Mary towing a small, uncertain yacht. Nudging Blue, Pia Jo rose at their approach, and after a moment of hesitation, he followed suit.

"Pia Jo, Mr Wovoka, you've probably already met Nikita Morotsky, Yentl's fiancé. He's a composer, and I'll be singing one of his compositions soon. Yentl is dancing with your Uncle Sven, and Nikky's too shy to ask a girl to dance with him, so I'm asking for him. Please, Pia Jo, dance the next number with him."

"I'd be delighted!" Pia Jo said sincerely. "Blue, why don't you dance with Thelma?" Thus appealed to, Blue moved off to claim her aunt-by-marriage as his partner, and Pia Jo danced with Nikita to the rest of "I'm in the Mood for Love" and then to "Sentimental Journey." Since he responded to her comments in soft-spoken, polite monosyllables, she soon fell quiet and tried to observe the suspects, which wasn't easy to do while dancing. The dance over, they exchanged relieved pleasantries, and Nikita headed magnetically toward Yentl while Pia Jo returned to her favored couch with the thought that people who talk too little are almost as annoying as people who talk too much.

Blue soon rejoined her, but he'd scarcely seated himself beside her when the striking, handsomely-dressed Afro-American couple who'd been dancing so enthusiastically came striding in their direction. This time the two rose to greet them simultaneously.

"I'm Ebony Oleander, and this is my wife Laurel," said the tall, well-built bank employee, offering Pia Jo his hand. "Our housekeeper told us that you want to talk to us about the theft of the emerald necklace."

"How can we help you?" Laurel asked in a cultured voice when they'd shaken hands all around.

True to her decision not to talk openly about the theft while at the party, Pia Jo asked, "Could we talk in the library? Blue, please wait here for me." She hoped he'd realize that she was leaving him to watch alone.

In the library, she selected her words carefully. "I'm here to enjoy the party, not to investigate, but I'm glad you're willing to discuss the theft. I wondered if either of you had observed anything out of the ordinary on the night of the anniversary party."

"Not really," Laurel said, while Ebony merely shook his head. "Unless—."

"Unless what?"

"This is only speculation, mind you," Laurel replied after a moment of hesitation, "but Eb and I did wonder whether Stefan Constanta could have taken the necklace during his sleight of hand act. Sofia was wearing a wide black skirt which she used as a sort of screen, and he surprised us all by taking a number of objects from under it and then replacing them around the room. We were all astonished because we hadn't seen him take the objects."

"She seems to be wearing the same black skirt tonight. Did this dance occur around the time of the theft?"

"No," Ebony said, looking genuinely puzzled, "and there's the rub. The Constantas performed before Maxima sang, and we all assumed that she'd lost the emeralds when she discovered their loss. But the room was dimly lit, just as it is now—what if he took the necklace earlier and she simply didn't realize it was gone? We were, after all, focusing on Stefan's act, not on the jewels."

"But wouldn't she have felt that it was gone?"

"We wondered about that, too, but then one of Laurel's sisters told us that she'd lost a necklace of several strands of pearls one night while she was dancing and hadn't realized she'd lost it until three days later. She was feeling a little happy and concentrating on having fun, not on her jewels. The Roshnikovs drank quite a bit at their Anniversary party—she was laughing and clapping when the gypsies performed— could she have forgotten her jewels in the excitement of the evening?"

"It's worth considering, especially if the punch was as intoxicating as it is tonight," Pia Jo conceded reflectively. "I'll ask her, of course, but I'm told that her emeralds were exquisite—how could she forget them so easily? Besides, the Roshnikovs have been very good to the Constantas—they helped them escape from Rumania and provided them a home. Would the Constantas repay them by stealing their valuable property? They're well-paid for their kelims, and they have no children to worry about."

"Oh, but they do," Laurel said emphatically. "This is Sofia's second marriage—she has a son with four children still living in Rumania. She desperately wants them to come to America before she dies."

Pia Jo looked at her thoughtfully. Here was a piece of information she had not elicited during her visit to the Constantas. She was about to thank the Oleanders and leave when Laurel detained her. "By the way, we had a prowler last week. Did you see the accounts of it in both the *Miner's Lamp* and the *Courier*?"

"A prowler? No, I'm afraid I've been too busy to read the papers. Are you missing anything?"

"Not that we can determine. That's why we're so puzzled by the incident. Since our valuables weren't taken, the prowler must have been looking for the emerald necklace."

"The emerald necklace?" Pia Jo echoed, bringing all her acting ability into play. "Are you saying that you have it?"

"Of course not! "Ebony interposed hastily, "but someone may have thought we did."

"Did you—did you get a look at this prowler?"

"Not really. All we saw was a black streak going through the hall. We went outside and searched but found only the throw that was on a living room couch. He'd wrapped himself in it when he made his escape. The officer who came when we called left in a hurry when he heard that nothing was stolen."

"He probably had more pressing cases—the police department is shorthanded right now," Pia Jo explained calmly but with a quaking heart. "Cases must be investigated in the order of their importance." Then she added innocently, "Since I spoke to your housekeeper on the phone last week, I assumed that you'd left her to guard the house and the cat. That was your cat I saw on your lawn on the day I interviewed the Constantas, wasn't it? A big black cat with short hair?"

"Yes, that was Nox. Fiona said she'd received an emergency call from her daughter and had to leave for a couple of days. We can't imagine how the prowler knew the house was unattended."

"Perhaps he'd scouted the place earlier and had seen your housekeeper leave. It's odd, though, that nothing valuable was missing."

As they walked together back to the drawing room, Pia Jo asked, "Why did you name your cat 'Nox'? Is it an obNOXious cat?"

"Not at all—we adore her. We named her Nox because she loves being out at night. In Roman mythology," Laurel explained, "Nox was the goddess who personified Night. She was the daughter of Chaos and the mother of Death."

A chill went through Pia Jo at Laurel's informed explanation. Only a few days previously, Nox, the mother of Death, had crossed her path. For a moment she felt as though Night, Chaos, and Death were all accusing her of lying and trespassing, each from a different window; but when she looked at Laurel and Ebony, her fear dissolved. Like every other color, black has a positive and negative side; it can be chilling, yes, but it can also be comforting and warm.

"There's a Swedish proverb that says, 'The evening is the crown of the day,'" she mused, "and I've learned, at least partly, to deal with Chaos. And how can I fear Death when my mother looked so peaceful in her coffin?"

On their way back to the drawing room, she almost bumped into Gunter; and since his attention was so fixed on Luisa that he could scarcely see where he was going, the near-collision swiftly returned her to the reality of the theft.

"You're no help!" she snapped for his ear alone. "Are you going to stumble around like a lovesick teenager all evening, or are you going to help me catch a thief?"

"Don't be hard on me, Sis—I think I've been bewitched." He looked so apologetic, befuddled, and little like a law officer that she was immensely touched.

- 18 -

When Stan had sung the last notes of his solo, Dag Amundson rose from the piano bench and asked for quiet. "Sofia and Stefan Constanta will now sing a medley of gypsy songs and accompany themselves on violins after which our gracious hostess will sing 'Love Is a Mystery.' She will be accompanied by Nikita Morotsky, who wrote the lyrics and composed the music."

Pia Jo had taken it for granted that Dag would be at the piano all evening, so here was the unexpected, the unplanned. Because she needed to keep all the major suspects under surveillance, she'd assigned the Alligrettis to Gunter, Stan Anderson and Dag to Blue, the Wylies to Thelma ("to prove their innocence"), the Oleanders to Sven, Horst to Luisa, the Constantas to Vladimer, and the Djong twins to herself. Since the Raintrees wouldn't be mingling with the guests, she'd left them out of her plans. But now she decided that the focus should be on Maxima as well as on the suspects. Vladimer should stay fairly close to his wife, and she should signal him if anyone suspicious came close enough to grab the lustrous, though false, necklace. Since all the suspects knew that Pia Jo was investigating the case, she had to keep some distance between herself and Maxima or the thief might suspect a setup.

But if Vladimer were to watch for Maxima's signal, who would keep the Constantas under surveillance? Seeing Vladimer engaged in damage control with the police chief by the punch bowl, she maneuvered herself into a position near them. "Vlad," she said in an undertone, "I want you to keep a close eye on Maxima and have her signal you if she notices any suspicious behavior in her vicinity. I'll find someone else to watch the Constantas."

"Okay, I'll tell her." Some of his punch sloshed over when he set it down on a passing tray. "You know Chief Gramm, don't you?" Not waiting for a response, he hurried off in his wife's direction, leaving Pia Jo to wonder if he'd drunk too much spiked punch. But she merely offered her hand to the chief and said, "How are you, Chief Gramm? I'm Pia Jo Borg."

When he'd shaken hands with her and introduced his wife, he observed, "Gunter tells me you're doing a little investigating on your own. Did I hear you say you needed someone to watch someone?"

She nodded. "Did he tell you that we're trying to smoke out the thief? Yes, I need someone to keep an eye on the Constantas."

She'd heard that he and Gunter had clashed in the past, and now she wondered if he'd accuse Gunter of nepotism when he learned that he was planning to hire his sister to be his investigator. She had an answer ready, for she wouldn't allow Gunter to give her more leeway than he gave his other officers. But her respect for Chief Gramm grew when he accepted the assignment without hesitation and didn't ask for any details. After all, this should have been his case and he must have felt some humiliation over the loss of three of his officers. "The Constantas don't stay put very long," she warned. "They sing, play violins, and dance."

"I'll help him watch," Loretta Gramm offered with a reassuring smile. "We won't let them out of our sight."

Thanking them, she moved away so as not to arouse suspicion and looked around for the Cambodians; but she soon realized that she'd assigned herself more than she could handle. The Djong twins were never together and never seemed to stand in one spot, and the dimness of the large drawing room made a close watch on both of them impossible.

When the applause for the Constantas' medley of gypsy songs and their sleight-of-hand dance had died down, Nikita Morotsky replaced Dag at the piano and the diva moved to the front of the large Cupid on the tall column and readied herself for the start of her song. The pink scallops of her white lace evening gown accentuated perfectly the pink of the fabulous necklace, and in the warm glow of the flickering candles, each matched pink diamond and pearl glinted as though it were a mysterious link in a blazing circle of pink fire. As if mesmerized, all eyes flew to the tantalizing chain, and Pia Jo had a difficult time surveying the movements of the Cambodians, who were staring, fascinated, at Maxima, each from an opposite side of the room. As she watched them, she thought, "They're too young and inexperienced to plan a hoist of this magnitude—Vladimer will see them long before they reach Maxima. I'd better focus on the Cupid directly behind Maxima; its column would give the emerald thief some much-needed protection."

As romantic music filled the room and the diva sang, "Love is a sweet celebration, / a mystical concatenation, / a mellifluous destiny; / Love is a wild benediction, / a drastic and pleasurable friction, / Love is a mystery," the guests were rooted to the floor, for here was an entertainer who could hold an audience spellbound.

And then, as Pia Jo had requested, the lights came on in full force, and she momentarily caught the flutter of brown fingers reaching under the Cupid's raised arm and making contact with the clasp of the coveted necklace. But as suddenly as they came on, the lights went out and the room was plunged into Stygian darkness. Cursing herself for deciding against standing nearer the Cupid for fear the thief would note her presence there, she dived in the direction of the fingers and immediately found herself wrestling with someone who clawed her face, ripped her gown, and tore her hair. But she refused to let go, not even when she felt a pair of strong teeth sink viciously into the flesh of her bare arm and a pair of exceptionally strong legs wind themselves around her body and clench until she cried out in pain. When the lights came on, she found herself looking into a snarling face, heard herself cursed shrilly, and saw, dangling from the pocket of Dove Raintree's uniform, the glittering faux diamonds of Maxima's pink necklace.

Still dressed in their party clothes, they had all gathered around Dove in the kitchen of Oblachnyj Dom—Vladimer and Maxima Roshnikov, Sheriff Borg and Deputy Wovoka, Police Chief Gramm and his wife, Pia Jo and Luisa—and they were listening intently while she gave her account of the thefts. Pia Jo had refused to go to the

Emergency Room in Prairie du Loup until she knew what was going on, but she had allowed Luisa to wrap her burning arm in an icy towel. In the ballroom, Sven, Thelma, and the Wylies had taken charge of the party and were assuring everyone that the evening's ruckus would be explained in due time.

Vladimer was saying, "She must have doubled the amount of Vodka I told her to put in the punch—I was so groggy that I didn't catch Maxima's signal," while Maxima was holding her faux pink diamond necklace as though it were a string of prayer beads and was staring at Dove in unbelief. But unquestionably, Dove's most astonished listener was her husband, Ox-Eye, who was viewing her silently and coldly. Blue was warning her, almost gently because of their Winnebagan bond, "You have the right to remain silent—anything you say can be used against you in a court of law. You have the right to an attorney—."

But Dove cut him off with a sibilant protest. She'd been staring at the circle of eager listeners with large, hostile eyes that finally settled on Pia Jo and became triply hostile. "Why don't you mind your own business, white brat?" she spat; then, as she surveyed the swollen arm covered by the icy towel, she laughed hysterically. "I hope I poisoned you—it would serve you right."

When Blue's eyes lost their sympathy and registered disgust, she snapped, "I don't hold with attorneys; I want to tell what I know right now—before they get away."

"They? Who the hell are you talking about?" Gunter demanded, his voice at odds with the elegance of his wearing apparel. "Pia Jo caught you red-handed—take a look at the damage you did to her arm!"

"Bitch!" Dove hurled the epithet at Pia Jo, whose silver mesh gown was so badly torn that Maxima had draped a long gray bashlyk around her shoulders and had tied it at her waist. Then she turned to Gunter and spat, "I risked my neck to rip the emeralds from her neck last December," she indicated Madame Roshnikov, "but I haven't gotten a penny of the $5,000 they were to pay me. They still have the emerald necklace, an' now you've let them get away."

"Who are 'they,' Dove?" Pia Jo asked, her voice urgent. "If you don't hurry and tell us, they will get away."

Dove glared at her maliciously, then tossed two names into the air, names that made Blue turn the prisoner over to Chief Gramm while Gunter interrogated her further. "Damn! We should have kept our eyes on them after you caught Dove with the goods, Pia Jo. Where would they have headed, Dove, when they saw their plans go to pot?"

When Dove refused to answer, Pia Jo asked, "Are you sure that Dag was part of the plot? Asgard is worth a lot of money—why would he endanger it for the proceeds of a necklace that he'll have to share with three people, counting Kaito?" When Dove merely snarled that Dag was in on the theft the previous December, she went on. "If Dag was in on the plans, nine chances out of ten they stashed the necklace at Asgard last December and are planning to pick it up and Goldie, too. My talk with Horst convinced me that Goldie's in love with Stan, and he could be planning to escape with her tonight. We can't waste any more time, Gunter—we've got to get to Asgard right away."

"We? You ain't going anywhere with your arm like that! Since Jack's takin' charge of the prisoner, Blue'll come with me."

Although improperly dressed and in great pain, Pia Jo refused to be left behind. "Luisa, could you ride home with Sven and Thelma? I probably won't be gone long." Gunter protested, but he didn't have time to argue; and soon he, Blue, and Pia Jo were on their way to Asgard, the eerie wail of their siren preceding them. Upon reaching the farm, Gunter pulled up beside the house and parked hurriedly; by the dim yard light they saw at once that something had gone dreadfully wrong at the Amundson farm. A hundred feet from the house a man was lying face down on the ground with something unidentifiable protruding from his back. When they reached him, they saw that it was the worn hilt and handle of an ancient, short-bladed sword. After feeling of his carotid artery, Gunter sighed and pronounced him dead. The man was Stan Anderson.

"What kind of an old weapon is that?" Blue asked without touching it.

"It's a Viking sword, and it's recently been sharpened. Dag was showin' it to me a while back—he said it was just an ornament. What's been goin' on here anyway?" Gunter asked and then urged Blue to get a blanket from the back of his white and plum and cover the body until the coroner could examine it. "Set up a barrier and get Bert out here with the photography equipment and lights—this yard light won't give us the whole picture. I wanna look around before I call Lloyd—who knows, there might be some more bodies inside. This is a county crime, so I'll be takin' over the case. Come on, Peej—let's take a look inside."

A cursory search of the built-on shed showed that it was empty and that the sword's usual spot was empty; the kitchen and the dining room were also vacant, but they found Dag lying unconscious on the living room rug. Seeing that he was breathing and had no wounds other than a knob on his skull, Gunter roused Lloyd Lippman from his warm bed, notified him of the death, and urged him to get out to Asgard as fast as his old Chevvy van would bring him. When he got off the phone, he looked around, then called to Pia Jo, "Where are you anyway?"

"I'm looking for Goldie and her little boy," she replied from upstairs. "They have to be around here somewhere—unless the murderer took them as hostages." Not finding anyone but Dag in the house, they searched the garage but without success; they then hurried to the woodshed, and there, behind a pile of cord wood, they found Goldie huddling with her son. Keeping her back to the body as best she could, Pia Jo guided her into the house while Gunter followed with a sleepy Kaito in his arms.

Inside, Dag was sitting up with his head in his hands, groaning. "What happened?" he wanted to know.

"You tell us," Gunter said while Pia Jo settled Goldie in a chair with her son in her arms.

"Someone hit me from behind—that's all I remember." But intelligence was dawning in his eyes; clearly he was remembering more than that. "Where's Stan?" he demanded anxiously. "Have you arrested him?"

"Do you remember what happened, Goldie?" Pia Jo asked the golden girl gently. But Goldie only stared at her with unseeing eyes.

"She's in shock," Pia Jo exclaimed when Blue and an elderly man with a black bag joined them. "And here's Dr. Lippman. Thank Heaven."

When the coroner had confirmed that Goldie was in shock, he applied ice to the lump on Dag's head and cautioned him to be careful for a few days. "Is it okay if I question them?" Gunter wanted to know.

"Not her. She needs to get to the ER and talk to a crisis worker. We'll need two ambulances—one to take her to ER, the other to take the body to the hospital morgue. They can't ride together. Is there anyone who can take care of the child?"

"No, no!" Goldie cried, clutching Kaito closer.

"Okay, let her take him. You can interview Amundson while I have a look at the man on the ground." He and Blue went outside, leaving the sheriff and Pia Jo to wait for the ambulances while they questioned Dag, whose only response was that he would answer their questions after Goldie had been removed from the scene.

-19-

When a Rescue Squad had taken Goldie and her son to the Emergency Room of a Prairie du Loup hospital, Gunter and Blue examined the crime scene and consulted with the medical examiner, and Pia Jo remained with Dag.

"Please sit on the couch—you'll be more comfortable there," she suggested. When he'd moved painfully to the couch, she asked if he'd like a drink of water. He declined with a shake of his head that renewed his pain.

"You know, of course, that I'm not accusing you of anything, Mr. Amundson—this is merely an inquiry."

"Ask away," he muttered almost inaudibly, one hand gingerly investigating the lump on his head. "I want to clear my name."

"All right then." Fortunately, she'd slipped the little tape recorder and an ample supply of tapes into her handbag before she left for the party. Placing the recorder between them and switching it on, she asked, "Why didn't you want to talk in front of Goldie, Dag? Was it because she's so in love with Stan that a discussion of his death would have been too traumatic for her?" Realizing that she was leading the witness, she erased the question and began again. "Are you aware that Stan Anderson is dead?"

"Stan's dead?" he repeated mindlessly. It took him a while to register the full purport of her statement; when he did, he moaned, "Oh, no! Oh, my God, no!" Knowing how distressing this news must be, Pia Jo waited to question him further. After a long pause, he muttered hopelessly. "I told him his cockamamie plans wouldn't work. How'd he die?"

Her response was brief but graphic. "He's lying on the lawn with the blade of your Viking sword in his back."

"My God—my small sword!" Dag ran his long, white fingers through his white hair, turning it into a winter halo, then chided himself severely. "I should never have brought it from Sweden. But who threw it, and why is he lying on the lawn? Was he running away?"

"I was hoping you could tell me that, Dag. We found him on the lawn, maybe a hundred feet from the house. You were here on the floor, and Goldie was hiding behind a pile of wood in the shed, clutching Kaito."

Pia Jo had been mentally reconstructing the crime, and now she voiced her thoughts. "Judging by the condition of this room, Stan must have struggled with an assailant after he struck you on the head. He evidently got away and ran off with the emeralds, which had been hidden in that *tomte gubba*," she gestured toward the brightly-painted Swedish elf lying in front of a bookcase in a number of pieces, "and his assailant was probably close behind him. When the assailant ran through the shed, he most likely grabbed your sword from the wall; once outside, he sent it flying into Stan's back. Taking the emeralds from Stan, he fled. Does this scenario seem right to you?"

When he didn't answer, she asked, "But where does Goldie fit in? Was she running away with Stan, and did she hide when she saw him fall? Or did she conceal herself earlier? Or later?"

Dag seemed too dazed and confused to answer. After a period of intense reflection, he muttered thickly, "I only know what went on before I got hit on the head. Stan hired Dove to steal the emerald necklace at the Roshnikov party last December, but he was afraid to keep it in his house because he thought Sandie or Julie would find it. So he came here with it and offered to share the proceeds with me if I'd let him stash it here. At first I refused—I didn't want to have anything to do with the theft. But he and Goldie had been playing around for over a year, and she begged me to help them out."

He paused to consider how best to frame his words, and she waited impatiently for him to continue. "He'd asked her to run away with him—they would have left together last December but he didn't want to take Kaito, and she refused to leave him behind. Besides, he didn't know how to get rid of the necklace. When he begged for more time to convince Goldie that Kaito would be better off with his father, I said he could hide the jewels in the *tomte gubba*, but not for long."

"Horst Brenner is the boy's father, isn't he?"

He nodded. "Horst has tried to get her to marry him and not break up Stan's marriage, but she's crazy in love with Stan, and she wouldn't listen."

"Are you saying that you had nothing to do with the actual theft of the emeralds or the attempted theft of the pink diamonds and pearls?"

"That's what I'm saying."

"But you were here when we got here—why did you hightail it out here after tonight's brouhaha at Cloud House?"

Looking frightened and sullen, Dag finally managed to say, "I thought Dove would implicate me. She hates me because she comes to the Red-Eyed Bat with a Winnebago who isn't her husband, and she's sure I've told Ox-Eye on her." Since Pia Jo didn't look convinced, he added, "Besides, I didn't like the way Stan was treating Sandie at the party—he was flirting with every other woman on the floor. She's a good, loyal woman—God, if only I had a wife like that! I rushed out here to convince Goldie that she shouldn't go with him. He'd hurt Sandie and Julie terribly, and he'd never be true to her, either. That's all I know."

"Did you tell Ox-Eye on her?"

"No!"

Since he would say no more, Pia Jo accepted his testimony for the time being; whether or not he was telling the truth would have to be determined later. But she needed more than hearsay where Stan and Goldie were concerned. "If Goldie was planning to leave with Stan, where is her suitcase? She must have been here when he was getting the necklace out of the *tomte gubba*."

"Yes, she was here. He'd picked up her suitcases earlier—weren't they in his van? He and Sandie walked to the party, so he wasn't afraid she'd see them." He wrinkled his forehead in an effort to remember. "Goldie and Stan were still arguing about Kaito. Stan was saying that she'd leave the boy behind if she really loved him. The last thing I remember was seeing him clutching the emerald necklace and her saying 'I won't go without Kaito.' Is Gunter going to arrest me?"

She was taking notes to confirm the testimony on the tape. "He'll have to decide that. You acted as an accomplice when you allowed him to hide the necklace here, and you also withheld valuable evidence when you didn't report the first theft." Gunter, Blue, and Bert came inside as she was speaking; and when he'd set up his equipment, Bert began to take photos of the living area, Dag, and the shattered *tomte gubba*, which Blue, wearing plastic gloves, then sealed into a plastic bag. While Blue dusted for prints, Gunter informed Pia Jo quietly that the body had been photographed from every possible angle, the site had been carefully examined and photoed, and the body had been sent to the morgue.

"Leave Blue with Dag—I want to run his testimony by you in your car," Pia Jo said. Outside, when the coroner and Bert had driven off, she suddenly remembered what had been escaping her. "Gunter, where's Stan's van? Dag said that he and Sandie walked to the Roshnikov party."

Gunter looked puzzled. "I just assumed he rode out here with Dag. Naw, why would he? He'd have to have his car if he was planning to escape with the emeralds—and to run off with Goldie. Yeah, where is his van?" Since the only vehicles in view were Dag's farm truck and a 1995 teal Ford Taurus that Gunter knew belonged to Dag, they cruised about in his sheriff's vehicle while they searched with his headlights for the black and brown van. Taking a side road that led into an apple orchard, they were completely mystified when they located a black Toyota snuggling under a heavily-blossoming tree; but when Gunter phoned in the license plate numbers and other particulars, Windy replied that a Valerie Jones had reported the theft of a black Toyota to the police department, and the dispatcher had issued an all-points bulletin. The reason Stan's killer hadn't escaped in it became clear when Valerie Jones, a middle-aged woman with deep smoker's wrinkles above her upper lip, appeared in a cab to identify the vehicle.

"I was almost out of gas and had pulled into a gas station on Main Street," she announced forlornly. "Before I filled up, I hurried into the food mart to buy cigarettes and go to the John. When I got back out, my car was gone. I reported it stolen and took a cab home. I had to call another cab when I was notified that my car was out here."

"How close was the gas station to the Roshnikov mansion?" Gunter asked.

"Just below the hill." When she would have gotten under the wheel, Gunter held her back. "Sorry, but your car's evidence. Take the cab home, and we'll let you know when you can reclaim it."

Seated in Gunter's official car, Pia Jo went over Dag's testimony with him. When she finished, he sat for a while staring off into the distance; he'd grown up with Stan and Dag and he'd danced with them. She knew that he was regretting the criminal aspect of his job. "You got his admission that he was an accomplice on tape?"

"Sure have, but isn't the broken *tomte gubba* admission enough that he let Stan hide the emeralds here?"

Gunter had given testimony in court cases long enough to know that he couldn't afford to take chances. "A smart defense lawyer'd say that someone knocked the *tomte gubba* down an' broke it in th' hubbub. Besides, Stan could've hidden the necklace in the *tomte gubba* without tellin' Dag a thing—or so his attorney could claim. Anyway, we can't be sure Dag's tellin' th' whole truth. We're dealin' with a murder in my jurisdiction, so I can't take chances—I'm havin' Blue bring Dag in for further questionin'. You know, don't you, that I need you to investigate this crime as my detective? I can't spare you to work for the Roshnikovs any longer—I need you to work for Berger County."

"Are you saying that I can't collect the reward?" she asked dolefully.

"That's what I'm sayin'!"

At his grim words, Pia Jo felt her heart thump to her feet like a ball thumping down a flight of stairs. How could she face Reo with this disappointing development? He'd be livid with rage.

Later at Scandia, where Luisa had gone with Thelma and Sven, Sven recounted that while Dove was being questioned in the kitchen, he'd heard Stan tell Sandie to go home and take care of Julie—his boss wanted to see him about a job he'd flubbed. Then he left in a hurry, and Dag was right behind him. Since Vladimer had informed them that Stan and Dag had hired Dove to steal the pink diamonds, and since they'd all witnessed Dove's assault on Pia Jo, they'd assumed that the crime had been solved; therefore no one had stayed at Oblachnyj Dom very long. If they were needed to testify, Ebony had said, they'd be available.

Then Thelma reported on the house guests. Reolo, who was subject to migraines, had had an agonizing headache and had gone up to bed, while Sidonie had gone with Horst to lock her jewels in Vladimer's office safe, where she'd been keeping her jewel case. As soon as they'd been able to leave, Thelma and Sven had gone to the Anderson home, where they'd found Sandie in tears; she'd testified that her husband had ordered her to take Julie home; when she got there, she'd found her mother trying to phone Cloud House and Stan's clothes, all the cash in the house, and their Ford van gone. "He must have packed earlier. I can't believe he hired Dove to steal the emeralds and diamonds," she'd sobbed while Julie, pale and weak from her infection, had wrapped her arms around her neck and tried to comfort her.

"Dove testified that he did," Thelma had said. "Where do you think he's gone?"

"To the Amundson farm—where else?" the distraught woman had replied bitterly. "He's denied it, but I know he's been having an affair with Dag's sister since before the Roshnikov anniversary dance"

"How horrible for Sandie and Julie!" Pia Jo thought, then gave them a brief overview of what seemed to have taken place at Asgard.

"Since it's so late," Luisa said, glancing at a clock, "I'll drive Pia Jo to the ER first thing in the morning—that is, if you have some pills she can take now, Thelma. She'll want to interview Goldie as soon as possible." After Thelma had produced some over-the-counter pain pills, Gunter dropped the young women off at Cabin 6. "I probably won't report to work until noon," Pia Jo said as she and Luisa got out of his white and plum. "It'll be good to get out of this tattered party dress."

But the thought of losing the reward for finding the emeralds was a bitter pill for Pia Jo to accept. She was restless and wakeful during the rest of the night; and when Luisa remarked on her look of exhaustion when she got up at nine, she replied that she'd worked hard to solve the theft, and she was unhappy about giving up the reward. She didn't dare call Reo—he wouldn't be at all pleased.

"Oh, bother Reo! Life won't always give him everything he wants. Your first duty is to Gunter now," was Luisa's emphatic response."

"But I've always wanted to go to Paris myself."

"So have I, but right now that's just pie in the sky."

-20-

On the way to the Emergency Room in Prairie du Loup, with Luisa at the wheel of the Corvette, they discussed the new developments; but Pia Jo realized that she didn't have a clue as to the identity of Stan Anderson's assailant and the thief who'd relieved him of the emerald necklace. But she did have some pertinent information, and she was able to fill in some of the blanks.

"Here's what I think happened," she said to Luisa. Turning on her recorder, she speculated aloud that someone who'd attended the party at the Roshnikov mansion had lurked outside the kitchen and had heard Dove admit that Stan and Dag had hired her to steal both necklaces. He or she had seen the sheriff seal the pink diamond necklace into an evidence bag, and when Stan and Dag had hightailed it to Asgard, had realized that they'd gone to retrieve the authentic emerald necklace. Since their identities were now known, they'd have to get away fast or be jailed. The assailant had then rushed down the steps that led to the street, had stolen the black Toyota from the gas station nearby, and followed either Stan or Dag to Asgard. After eavesdropping on the occupants of Asgard, this person had seen Stan retrieve the necklace, had knocked Dag out from behind, had chased Stan outside and murdered him, and had then tried to escape in the stolen Toyota. When the assailant discovered that the Toyota was out of gas, he or she had left Asgard in Stan's van. Where the van was now was anybody's guess.

After turning off her recorder, she said, "This is all conjecture. I'm depending on Goldie's evidence—I hope she tells me the truth." But Pia Jo had to wait for the ER doctor to look at her bitterly painful arm and have a nurse put it in a temporary sling before she could talk to Goldie.

"She's still with the crisis worker," a nurse told her when she inquired at the nurses' station on the first floor. "She kept calling for someone named 'Dog,' but we didn't know who he was or where we could contact him. So we contacted her parents instead—her mother said she'd be here by eleven. We've put her and her little boy in Room 113. You can go right in."

Goldie and Kaito were having breakfast when Pia Jo and Luisa located Room 113, and Goldie looked remarkably improved. The crisis worker, a stern woman with a disapproving expression, was just leaving. "I'm the detective on the case, and I need to interview her as soon as possible," Pia Jo informed her. "Does she know there's been a murder?"

"She suspects—," the crisis worker began; but then she stopped abruptly and her tone became official. "I'd like to see some identification! What she told me is confidential."

"Oh, no!" Pia Jo fretted silently. "My badge is in my desk at the Sheriff's Headquarters." Aloud she said, "I was in a hurry to get my arm treated, so I forgot to bring my credentials along. But you can call the sheriff for verification."

When the crisis worker insisted that Pia Jo go to Lead Mines and get her credentials, Luisa joined the fray. "I'll call Sheriff Borg, Pia Jo," she said scathingly. "I don't think he'll be pleased that his detective is being held up in her investigation of a murder!"

At this implied threat, the crisis worker shrugged, muttered "Be it on your head then!" and left the room.

But the struggle wasn't over, for while Goldie allowed Luisa to take Kaito for a walk in the hall, she couldn't give Pia Jo the vital piece of information she needed. She'd thought Stan might be dead, but she didn't seem shattered when Pia Jo confirmed her suspicion.

"Will you be upset if I tape this interview?" Pia Jo asked, painfully taking her small recorder from her bag.

"I want you to tape it," Goldie said positively. "I want people to know that Stan Anderson done me wrong."

"And they should know that you 'done' Sandie and Julie Anderson wrong," Pia Jo observed silently but kept her observation to herself. Instead she said, "Then answer fully and truthfully. Your testimony might be heard by a jury." She turned the recorder on, identified herself, gave the time and place, and explained, "I'm interviewing Goldie Amundson regarding the theft of the Roshnikov emeralds and the death of Stan Anderson." Setting the recorder on the bedside table, she nodded encouragingly. "Just tell us what you know," she said.

"I was waiting for Stan at the farm," Goldie began a bit importantly. "I'd packed three bags of clothes for Kaito and me, and I expected Stan to kiss me when he came. But he didn't—he went right to the elf to get something he said he'd hidden there. When he put his hand inside the jar, it got stuck. That made him so mad that he banged the jar against the shelf and broke it. And then I saw the necklace—it was shining and sparkling, and he was in such a hurry to pick it up that he wouldn't look at Kaito or me. I asked him what was wrong, and he said we couldn't take Kaito—if a bulletin was put out on us, we'd be too easy to spot if we had a kid along."

"Did you know that he'd hired Dove to steal the emerald necklace at the Roshnikov party last December?"

"No, I didn't know Stan very well then. He'd flirted with me at the Scandinavian Dances last summer, and he told me that his wife Sandie was a drag—he loved his little girl but he didn't think he was much of a family man. I liked him, but I didn't think he was serious about me—after all, I had a little boy, and most men don't—. Well anyway, he started showing up at the farm in February—you know, Asgard, where I live with my brother Dag. They played cards a lot, and his hired man, Horst Brenner, and I played with them."

"Did your brother Dag help Stan plan the theft of either of the necklaces?"

"No way!" she said sharply. "Dag wouldn't hire anybody to steal anything—he got awfully mad at me for shoplifting when I was fifteen."

"But Dag allowed Stan to hide the emeralds in the *tomte gubba* at Asgard?"

"Yes, but I didn't know about the emeralds until two weeks ago. Stan kept them a secret for a long time. I think it was in March that he said he had a hidden treasure—I figured he'd been saving money to get away from Sandie. We'd been kissing a lot by then, and he said he wanted to leave her and marry me. I asked him how he could afford to do that if she got to keep the house they were living in, and he said their—their eq—something in the house was real small, so she could have it; but he had a—a nest egg that we could live on for a long time."

"Was the word 'equity'?" Pia Jo prompted.

"Yeah, that's it."

"What did you say when he told you that his nest egg was the emerald necklace?"

"I said it was wrong to steal other people's property and we'd go to hell if we kept the necklace, but he said that rule only applies to stealing from poor people. He said he was Robin Hood—he'd stolen from the rich Roshnikovs and was giving to the poor—himself and me.

"And Kaito?"

"He wouldn't say nothing for sure about taking Kaito at that time. When I asked him if I could take him, he said, 'We'll see.'"

Pia Jo turned the recorder off. "Let's stop for a breather. So far you've done very well, Goldie. I think you're telling the truth."

"I am telling the truth. Could I have a coke or something?"

"I don't think hospitals serve Coke," Pia Jo responded with a smile. Turning on the light above the bed, she thought, "What a child Goldie is! Way too young to rear a child all by herself." When the nurse responded, she asked for juice for Goldie and pain pills for herself. "Dr. Morrison gave me a prescription, but I haven't had it filled yet," she added. While the nurse was gone, they talked about Goldie's parents and Horst.

"Did you love Horst when you had sex with him?" Pia Jo asked sympathetically.

"I just wanted to be loved, and I didn't know that sex made babies. My parents told me that it's sin to go to bed with boys or men before marriage and if I got pregnant, they'd kick me out. I didn't know what 'pregnant' meant."

"But your mother is coming for you today?"

"She said she would—unless I'm going to be arrested. Am I?" Goldie looked frightened.

"That's not up to me," Pia Jo said, "but you knew about the theft, and you withheld evidence so you're not home free by any means. But since you're a minor and were being influenced by an adult, a jury might be easy on you."

"My mom said the devil made me have sex with Horst. Do you believe in the devil?" Goldie asked pensively.

"I believe he's a Christian symbol for temptation."

"What's a simbell?"

"Most often it's a picture that explains something at a glance. 'Temptation' is an abstract word—it can't be seen, smelled, touched, tasted, or heard; so people who weren't educated had a hard time understanding what it meant. Then someone made it easy to understand by giving it a body."

Goldie looked intensely interested. "A red body with horns and a tail with a spear on the end?"

Pia Jo smiled at the hackneyed description, which so clearly revealed the fear tactics of the ancients. "Yes, that's one depiction of the devil."

"And he's not real?"

Recalling her class in "The Bible as Literature," Pia Jo explained, "The 'devil' is another name for Satan, a character in the Book of Job who pointed out that it's easy to believe in God when life is good; but I see him as a figment of someone's imagination. But to be tempted means to be asked to do something wrong, something we'd like to do very much. You were tempted to run away with Stan, but you didn't have a right to do that because he was Sandie's husband."

Goldie's forehead wrinkled in honest puzzlement. "How could it be wrong when I loved him and wanted Kaito to have a father?"

"But he was *Julie's* father, and your wanting him contributed to his death," was all Pia Jo could think to say. For a moment or two, Goldie looked sad; she seemed to be thinking of Julie. But she was extremely immature, and her sorrow passed quickly. After a nurse had given her a small glass of juice and Pia Jo two pain pills and a glass of water, Pia Jo turned the recorder back on. "Now please tell me exactly what happened after Stan retrieved the emerald necklace from the *tomte gubba* last night."

Goldie sipped her juice, then began to tell her story. "Stan wanted me to go with him and leave Kaito with Horst, but I refused and Dag backed me up." She paused for a reaction, clearly enjoying the attention she was getting; in fact, she waited expectantly and didn't continue until Pia Jo prompted her.

"Yes, go on."

"Then a man came in the back door and hit Dag with the statue of a horse with eight legs that was standing on the piano. After Dag fell, the man and Stan wrestled for the necklace. Stan brought his knee up, and it hit the man under the chin. The man seemed dizzy, for he fell back. Then Stan ran into the kitchen and out the back door with the necklace, and the man got up and ran after him. I grabbed Kaito by the hand and followed. It was almost dark outside, but I saw the man throw something at Stan and I saw Stan fall. When I screamed and hid behind the shed with Kaito, the man grabbed the necklace from Stan and ran into the orchard. But soon he came running back and drove away in Stan's van."

"Dag was struck with Odin's eight-legged horse? I think his name was Sleipnir."

"Dag said he was a—a make-believe horse."

"Why did you follow Stan and his assailant when your brother had been knocked out and might have been dead?"

"I thought Stan might change his mind and take both Kaito and me." This response seemed cold and thoughtless to Pia Jo; but she reminded herself that Goldie hadn't learned how to empathize, and she continued with the interrogation.

"Why didn't the assailant take Dag's car? It's much newer and faster."

"He must have heard the sheriff's siren—I heard it, too—and Stan's van was closer. He stumbled and fell flat on his face—twice. He had to crawl some of the way—I guess he decided he didn't have no time to lose."

"But why did the sheriff and I miss him when we came up the road?"

"He took the road by the barn—the men take it when they work in the fields. Maybe the sheriff didn't know about the road."

It was time for Pia Jo to ask the vital question. "Who was it, Goldie? Who knocked Dag out, threw the small sword at Stan, and escaped with the emerald necklace? Had you ever seen him before?"

"I don't know who it was or if I ever seen him before."

"Are you saying he was a stranger? Think about it carefully—you may be asked to pick him out of a line-up."

But Goldie was adamant. "I'm saying I don't know who it was. He was wearing a long robe, sort of like a Wise Man wears, only he wore a hood, not a crown—I couldn't even see his face."

A robe like a Wise Man wears? The scene was clarifying in Pia Jo's mind. The assailant had been cunning enough to wear a disguise when he followed Dag and Stan to Asgard after the theft the previous evening, but he evidently hadn't considered the difficulty of escaping in a long robe. "Can you describe the robe, Goldie? Luisa will draw it—she's an artist."

"Maybe I'll try."

"I'll go get her then." Pia Jo found Luisa in the gift shop purchasing a stuffed horse for Kaito. The gift shop didn't carry drawing paper or colored art pencils, but the aide in attendance scrounged up some typing paper and a pencil from a nurse in Reception. They weren't art mediums, but they would do for the present. Back in Goldie's room, Luisa made a sketch of the robed suspect under Goldie's guidance. Her young memory soon produced a robe embellished with braid and tied with a cord around the waist. Upon completing the sketch, Luisa looked at Pia Jo questioningly. Though drawn in pencil, the robe was fanciful—was the girl being creative? She did seem to be preening for an audience.

"It's an elaborate costume," Luisa finally ventured.

"Of course! It's an opera costume! Maxima has to see this—but first I must talk to Gunter. Do you want to come with me, or shall I drop you off at the Cabin?"

Since they were in Prairie du Loup, and Lead Mines was between them and Innisfree, dropping Luisa off would entail a fifteen-mile drive to Cabin 6 and another five miles back to Lead Mines; to save time, Luisa opted to accompany her friend.

Before leaving Room 113, Pia Jo had one more question for Goldie. "Was the person you saw tall or short? Heavyset or slender?"

"Tall maybe—anyways not real short. And heavy. When the robe flared out, he seemed to take up half th' room."

"Maybe that's because the ceilings are so low at Asgard," Pia Jo said as she put her recorder in her bag. "Thank you for cooperating, Goldie. Your testimony could help solve the crime." As she and Luisa walked down the hall, they saw a gray-haired woman wearing a nervous expression go into Room 113 and heard Goldie's "Mom! Golly, Kaito—here comes your grandma."

On the way to the sheriff's headquarters, they discussed Goldie's testimony and wondered how much of it was truth and how much imagination. Obviously Stan had taken advantage of a very naïve seventeen-year-old. "But she did refuse to leave with him," Luisa pointed out. "That should count for something."

"I was waitin' for you t' come around," Gunter said when Pia Jo came flying in the door with Luisa at her heels. "Why're you runnin'? Are you tryin' to escape with the Roshnikov emeralds?"

"Don't be bizarre! I came to inform you that I'm not accepting the job of Sheriff's detective yet. My interest is not in solving the murder— it's in retrieving the emeralds for the Roshnikovs. I signed a contract to do so, and that's what I'm going to do." She was determined not to surrender the $10,000 without a fight.

Gunter had been looking at Luisa with a half hopeful, half mournful expression; but now he turned to Pia Jo and said, "You're real cute! You know bloomin' well you'll be able to identify the murderer if you retrieve the emeralds. But since you need money so bad, I'll buy into your scheme—you're not my criminal investigator, at least not yet. But I expect you to share any information you have—an' I can see by your smug look that you have plenty. Unless you want to be arrested for withholdin' evidence, you'd better start talkin'."

Thanking Heaven that he didn't know about the tape in her tote bag, Pia Jo did some quick thinking about the situation. What if he acted on her information and solved the case before she did? Then it would be "Goodbye, $10,000!"

Seeing her indecision, he urged, "You can trust me, can't you? Hell, you don't even need to trust me. With you outta the picture, I might have to put Windy on th' case—do you think he'll beat you to a solution? He can't even figure out if a car's parked illegally."

Ignoring Windy's resentful snort, Pia Jo offered a viable alternative, "No, but you might! You're a hands-on sheriff who hates doing administrative work, and I know you'd love to solve this case so Luisa'll think you're a champ. And if you don't solve it before I do, Blue might."

But Blue's headshake was emphatic. "Can't. I'm a hands-on road deputy, and administration duties are keeping me up nights."

"Okay, so I trust you both. But my first report must go to my employers—all I can tell you is that I've interviewed Goldie and I'm armed for bear, that is, if she isn't lying. You haven't heard anything about the Amundsons being pathological liars, have you?"

Her comment drew the attention of everyone in the office. Windy, who'd been looking red hot spikes at Gunter, now eyed her like a cat eyeing a bug on the wall; Melissa turned from the switchboard to regard her curiously; and Blue punched the button of a tape recorder. Even Gunter paused to review what he knew about the Amundsons. "One thing's sure," he finally decided, "Dag's more involved than he claimed to be last night. He wouldn't run off an' leave the farm—it's way too valuable; but Stan could have promised him a share when the necklace was sold—he could be lyin' without Goldie's bein' lyin'. Still, she could be 'broiderin' somethin' muddy to keep Dag out of trouble. He's been her protector, an' he's good to Kaito. Blue an' I are goin' out to Asgard to 'xamine the scene by daylight, an' then I'll have another go at Dove and Dag. I've got 'em both here in detention cells waitin' for the bail hearin'. Go ahead an' do your thing, trinket—just keep an open mind 'bout everybody's testimony. You been doin' some sketchin' of a killer, Luisa?"

His attempt to gain information from such a reliable source fell on deaf ears. "I wish I'd brought my paints—or even some sketching pencils," she said sweetly. "I'd love to do a painting of Oblachnyj Dom for the Roshnikovs."

"Hey, that's a great idea," Pia Jo agreed. "I'll bet they'd pay handsomely. Come on, then. We'll stop at the Artists' Loft for sketch pencils and colored chalk."

- 21 -

While Luisa went into the Artists' Loft on Main Street, Pia Jo stayed in the Corvette and began to outline the report she'd soon have to give the Roshnokovs, but her attention soon strayed to the activities on the street, and her interest picked up when she spotted a black and brown Ford van similar to the one she'd seen parked in the Andersons' driveway on the evening she'd interviewed them. To verify that it was Stan's van, she got out of the Vette and peered into a rear window; sure enough, there were two flowered suitcases, a child's blue bag, and two boxes of male clothing on the rear seats. The suitcases each had an attached label with "Goldie Amundson" written in big, childish letters.

Returning to the Vette, Pia Jo called the information in from her cellular phone. After Melissa assured her that Gunter or Blue would be right over to seal off the van as evidence, she waited for Luisa to return with her art supplies. Later, when Luisa was showing her a set of sketch pencils with a variety of charcoal leads and a colorful box of colored chalk, Pia Jo pointed out the car and said with a laugh, "You should have seen those childish suitcase labels. With an APB out on them, a gas station attendant could easily have spotted the labels and called them in."

"But wasn't the black and brown van itself a dead giveaway?" Luisa wanted to know. "I wonder why he didn't trade it in on a different vehicle when he planned his escape."

"He's not a practiced criminal," Pia Jo conceded. "It was easy to follow his movements. I'll bet his assailant didn't leave anything in the van that can be traced." They waited until Gunter and Blue drew up, each in a separate vehicle.

"Good work, Peejay," Gunter called when he coasted by, his eyes pealed for the van. "Blue's going to check it out and dust it for prints while I interview Dove and Dag again. Roshnikov called—he wanted to know if we found the emeralds at Asgard. I fudged—I said you were on your way up there with a report."

The Roshnikovs were impatiently waiting for the two young women at Oblachnyj Dom. "What's happened? Why didn't you bring us up to date last night?" Maxima demanded, opening the door so suddenly that they almost tumbled into the hall. "The last we heard, Dove said Stan and Dag hired her to steal the pink necklace—did they also hire her to steal the emeralds last December?"

"Stan evidently hired her—Dag claims he wasn't involved. Unfortunately, the case has now become a murder investigation."

"Murder? Why wasn't it on the morning news? Who's dead?"

"It happened in the dead of night, too late to be on the news. Stan Anderson is dead, and the emeralds are still missing. Let's sit down somewhere, and I'll bring you up to date."

When Maxima chided Pia Jo for being gone so long, Vladimer reprimanded her sternly. "Lay off, Max! She must have taken time out to have her arm looked at—it's in a sling. Come along, we'll talk in the library." He led them down a hall to a stately room lined with books and indicated the chairs around an ornate round table with three fauns, each facing a different direction, on its pedestal. While Pia Jo and Luisa seated themselves, he drew out a chair for Maxima.

"I hope the Alligrettis are still here," Pia Jo said anxiously. "I'd like to have a word with them after I've talked to you."

"They're still here," Vladimer assured her. "Last night your uncle made it clear that no one was to leave the area until the sheriff gave the all-clear sign. Reolo wants to leave—he's to appear at Ravinia in a couple of weeks and needs to rehearse; but Sidonie wants to stay here for another week. And of course they both want to know what's going on. So what's going on?"

Because she wanted to get on with the investigation quickly, Pia Jo gave them a succinct oral report on what they'd found at Asgard the previous evening, including her interview with Dag and the one with

Goldie earlier in the day, and winding up with Goldie's description of the assailant. "I have tapes you can listen to later. Luisa, show them the sketch you drew from Goldie's directions."

Luisa took the pencil sketch and her colored pencils from her bag and placed them on the table before her. "Let me finish the sketch first." The Roshnikovs watched, fascinated, while she colored the robe a royal purple and the braid an antique gold.

"Why, that's _my_ robe—the one I put in the giveaway box last week," an astonished Maxima exclaimed. "We change costumes for every opera, and I've been giving my used ones to the Hillside Players—you probably know their director, Glenda Brooks."

Pia Jo nodded briefly; because of her own involvement in theatre, she'd known Glenda for a number of years. But she kept to the point. "Where do you keep this costume box?"

"In the laundry room at the rear of the building. It opens on the hall that leads to the rear door. Vladimer, someone at our party must have rushed after Stan and Dag and grabbed the costume from the box on his way out. But who?" The Roshnikovs stared at one another in rising consternation as they considered the possibilities.

"May I see the box?" Pia Jo asked politely but firmly. Both she and Luisa were watching the Roshnikovs closely. After all, both of them were stout enough to fit Goldie's description.

"Of course. Follow me."

They all followed Maxima to the laundry room, where she quickly searched the box of giveaway costumes. Turning to look up at the others, she breathed, "It's gone. My old purple robe is missing."

Her final interview with the Alligrettis, this one openly conducted, netted Pia Jo close to nothing. After the party, Reolo had had one of his severe migraines and had gone up to their suite to take some tablets and lie down, while Sidonie, accompanied by Horst, had gone with Vladimer to his office to lock her jewels in his wall safe for safekeeping. "With jewel thieves haunting the place, I didn't dare leave them in our suite," she explained with a tart look at Maxima.

"Have you any idea when you dismissed Horst and returned to your room?" Pia Jo asked.

"It was after midnight. I heard the clock in the entranceway strike twelve when we were on our way to Vlad's office." Sidonie's response was confident.

"Okay. That's all for now," Pia Jo said, dismissing the Alligrettis and turning to the Roshnikovs. "I'd like a word with Horst if he's around."

Instead of inviting Horst into the house, Vladimer requested that Pia Jo interview him in his apartment above the garage—he and Maxima wanted to discuss the unfolding evidence in private. Considering the size of Cloud House, Pia Jo thought this was a lame excuse, but she accepted it with an inner admonition to herself, "Mine not to reason why; mine but to do or die!" And since Horst had been told not to leave the grounds, he'd no doubt be in his quarters.

The apartment above the garage, which could be reached by both an indoor and an outdoor stairway, was surprisingly large and airy. Done in oak paneling, it was even draped and carpeted, though not expensively. Horst responded to Pia Jo's knock promptly and politely invited her in, but he could add little to what she already knew. Yes, he'd served as a bodyguard to Frau Alligretti—she was concerned about her jewels. Yes, he'd gone with her to lock them away; but since Vladimer was also there, he'd been eager to leave and had hurried back to his apartment when Sidonie dismissed him.

Why was he in such a hurry? Because he'd been worried about Goldie, and his anxiety had increased when no one answered his phone call to Asgard. To make matters worse, his old car had broken down so he couldn't drive out to Asgard and check on Goldie. Before he'd left Asgard for Cloud House earlier, he'd tried to warn her that there might be another robbery—after all, there's been one at the first party, and he was half convinced that Stan and Dag had been involved. Why? Because they talked in secret sometimes and would get upset if he came too close. He'd also tried to caution Goldie not to run away with Stan; she didn't want to be a home wrecker, did she? But she'd paid him no heed. When he asked anxiously, "Vat happened at Asgard last night? No vun vill tell me vere Goldie and Kaito are," Pia Jo gave him a barebones account of the evening's events.

His response was a series of stunned questions. "Stan is dead? Dag's in yail? Goldie and Kaito vill be stayin' at her parents' farm? She knew Stan stole the necklace? Dat is not good! Wat will happen to her now?"

"She'll have to answer for her part in the crime, but since she's so young and has a child to rear, she'll probably get parole."

"I vill stand mit her," he promised loyally; but sincere as he sounded, Pia Jo wasn't entirely convinced that he was telling the truth. So what if his car was on the fritz? He could have seen Stan and Dag leave the evening before; and after Sidonie dismissed him, he could have slipped down the back corridor to the laundry room, donned the opera gown, rushed down the steps leading to Main Street, and stolen the Toyota to drive to Asgard. Besides opportunity, he also had a couple of motives: Stan was about to run off with the girl he loved, and he and Goldie would need the proceeds from the sale of the emerald necklace to get away, to live, and to rear Kaito.

Later, in the dispatch room at the Sheriff's Headaquarters, Gunter repeated some of the spiteful remarks Dove had made about Ox-Eye when, to elicit more information, he'd told her briefly what had happened at Asgard the previous evening. She'd said that Ox-Eye most likely had followed Stan or Dag to Asgard; and since he was famous for his skill with the bow and arrow, he could easily have grabbed the small sword from the wall of the shed and sent it flying into Stan's back.

Gunter hadn't been quick to swallow her baleful conjecturing. "Somethin's wrong here, Dove. You already confessed to stealing the emeralds for Anderson and Amundson; and we know, too, that they ended up at Asgard. If Ox-Eye had gone out there to get 'em, he would have driven his Comanche Jeep, not someone's Toyota." Her tart reply had been that she'd been forced to confess to something she hadn't done, and she was going to hire an attorney and sue him for false arrest. Besides, she'd given him a lead, and it was up to him to follow it up.

"She's forgotten that she doesn't 'hold with attorneys.' Poor Ox-Eye!" Pia Jo commiserated. "I asked Vladimer to have him turn up the lights when Maxima began to sing. He'd no sooner turned them up than someone turned them off. So will he stand by Dove through the trial?"

"She doesn't want him to—she claims she only agreed to help steal the emeralds because she wanted to leave Ox-Eye and invest in the casino on the reservation," Gunter denied with an emphatic shake of his head. "She's a descendant of a Winnebago princess, she insisted, her eyes flashin' like headlights. Why should she be a servant to Russians? She should have servants of her own."

Gunter's interview with Dag had netted him a confession of sorts; to avoid being accused of having master-minded the thefts, Dag had admitted that he'd turned the lights off after Ox-Eye had turned them up; he'd allowed Stan to hide the emeralds at Asgard the previous December; and he'd also promised to help him get away after the second theft. But he swore he hadn't encouraged Stan to hire Dove to steal either necklace. Dove was making that up because she had a grudge against him and wanted him to lose Asgard. Gunter hadn't been altogether convinced. "We already know that Dove was two-timin' Ox-Eye an' that Dag knew about it. He could have blackmailed her into stealin' the gems."

"But Dag wasn't exactly poor," Luisa observed. "Asgard is a valuable farm—why did he go along with Stan at all? It's obvious that he has a good IQ."

"But IQ isn't EQ," Melissa turned from the switchboard to interpose. "In case you're wondering, that stands for Emotional Quota."

Gunter nodded. "Yeah, you might say that's what Dag lacks. He went along with Stan because he needed the cash that Stan promised him, an' he wasn't willin' to wait until farmin' paid off in a big way. He'd met a small-time actress who said she'd marry him if he'd fund her theatrical career, an' he'd already borrowed heavily from the bank to pay off winter debts an' plant his crops. He was gettin' behind on Horst's wages, too. Dove had told him where to find th' switchbox so he could mingle with the crowd an' turn out th' lights when Nikita took over at th' piano."

Pia Jo sighed. "That figures. I should have realized that Stan was involved in the theft when he moved away from the piano; but I was trying to watch both of the Cambodian twins and Maxima, too; and frankly, when Maxima took her place by the Cupid, I was transfixed by the faux diamonds—they looked so real."

Gunter looked embarrassed. "I'm more to blame 'n you are. It was my duty to be on guard, but everythin' went right outta my head when th' candlelight was shinin' on her necklace an' her dress. I thought Dag was goin' to have a fit when I told him the pink diamond necklace was a fake."

Luisa had been listening quietly, and now she asked, "Why did Stan keep the emeralds in the _tomte gubba_ so long? Why didn't he fence them and elope with Goldie long ago?"

"Probly because he's—was—an amateur criminal, but also because Goldie wouldn't leave without Kaito. Dag claims that Stan got greedy when he heard about the jewels Maxima was goin' to wear tonight, an' it cost him his life."

When Gunter had finished his account of his interviews, Blue filled them in on fingerprints. Since none of the suspects' prints were on file, he'd taken Stan's from the body in the morgue, Dag's and Dove's in the booking room, and Horst's and Ox-Eye's in the garage at Cloud House. But the fingerprinting had done little to advance the investigation, for while both Stan's and Dag's prints were on the _tomte gubba_ and Dove's were on both necklaces, there were no prints on the small sword, on Sleipnir, or in the black Toyota, which had been searched, dusted, and returned to its rightful owner. Nor did anything suspicious turn up in Stan's van; the escaping assailant must have worn gloves and disposed of them after his getaway. And while he'd found plenty of Horst's prints at Asgard, this was not surprising since he lived and worked there.

"Are you saying that you inspected the prints yourself, Blue?" Pia Jo asked suspiciously. "Didn't you have to send them to the lab in Milwaukee for verification?"

Much to his sister's surprise, Gunter laughed. "Blue is now a crime scene an' latent fingerprint expert, an' he's got the equipment, too. He can even read your character by lookin' at your prints. Give her a demonstration, Blue."

But Pia Jo wasn't about to be taken in by this claim. "He's funnin' me," she said to Luisa as they left the Sheriff's Headquarters.

-22-

Back at Innisfree, while Luisa stopped off at the Lodge to pick up some lunch, Pia Jo wrote a long preliminary report; and when Luisa returned with their food, they discussed the crime at some length. "A heavy person, Luisa," Pia Jo reflected. "Who would fit into the costume of a heavy person like Maxima?"

"Maxima herself," Luisa responded thoughtfully. "Vladimer. But they were both sitting by the kitchen table listening to Dove confess when Stan went home to get his van and money and Dag took off for Asgard. Horst is heavy, and so is Reolo. Ebony's a little on the heavy side. Who would have the skill as well as the strength to throw a small sword so it would kill a man? Horst? Reolo? Ebony?"

"Ox-Eye of course, but he's skinny as a rail. Horst's probably the only rather heavyset man with a skill like that. If I were to choose among the three you named, my vote would go to Horst. Ebony has his good name at the bank to consider and Reolo's filthy rich—why would they pull a stunt like that?" Pia Jo sipped her coffee as she considered the suspects in the light of Goldie's evidence. She doodled the three names on her notes, then turned her thoughts to Sandie Anderson. "Mom would want me to visit her and offer my condolences. It must be awful being a young widow who's just learned that her husband and her child's father loved someone else and was a thief besides."

"Do you *want* to visit her?" Luisa asked.

"Not much, but I know I'd be devastated if Reo were killed and

I suddenly learned that he didn't love me. I'll ask Thelma to go with me."

Thelma was agreeable and suggested that they bring Sandie a bouquet of flowers. Their lunches eaten, Pia Jo left Luisa sketching the three heavy men she'd named and dressing them in purple robes with gold cords while she stopped to pick up Thelma, whose arms were filled with white, pink, and red peonies from the bushes on her lawn, then drove into Lead Mines and took the road up to High Street.

Sandie, whose eyes were red from weeping, seemed grateful for the showy flowers and for their thoughtfulness. While she found a large vase and put the flowers in water, the two visitors talked to Julie and to Sally Borg, Pia Jo's niece, who were playing theatre and wearing old clothes as costumes.

"Julie was crying so hard that I thought she'd be ill—I had to think of something for her to do," Sandie explained when the two girls had departed for a bedroom to deck themselves anew. "So I called Lena, and she said she'd send Sally over with some old clothes so they could play grownups. You know how kids love to do that." She paused, then went on in a rush, "I've known for a long time that Stan was weak where women were concerned, but he always gave Julie her way—I'm the one who has had to discipline her. So of course she's been thinking only of her loss."

While Sandie was remarking that Goldie was just a child, only seven years older than Julie and poorly brought up, and that she couldn't blame her for what had happened, a knock sounded on the kitchen door. It was Ox-Eye, and he was holding a round, thickly-frosted cake with a bouquet of sweet peas in a small crystal vase in its center hole. "For you, ma'am, from the Roshnikovs. If you need anything, you're to let them know."

"Did you make it, Ox-Eye?" Pia Jo asked.

He nodded but gave the credit to Maxima. "Madame asked me to, and she picked the flowers. The Cambodians made the icing."

"How nice of Maxima!" Pia Jo mused as she watched Sandie put the cake on the table, remove the vase of flowers, and cut generous slices for the little girls and the guests. "She's just learned that Sandie's husband stole her $100,000 necklace and tried to steal another one worth $180,000, and yet she's among the first to express sympathy. Well, why not? Sandie and Julie had nothing to do with the theft."

And then the girls came out of the bedroom each wearing several dresses, one on top of another, in an obvious attempt to play Lena; and everyone laughed and clapped. As Pia Jo watched the two girls do a clumsy version of a folk dance, her eyes suddenly grew large and she muttered, "Why didn't I think of that before?" When the other women looked at her questioningly, she said quickly, "I just remembered I have something I must do for Gunter. Please excuse me! I'll pick you up later, Thelma."

But Thelma was ready to accompany her. "Please excuse me, too, Sandie. I promised Sven I'd do some of his business this afternoon. We'll come around for the visitation—it's to be at the funeral home, isn't it?"

"Yes, tonight. The medical examiner is releasing the body this afternoon." The thought was so terrible that Sandie began to weep all over again; but then realizing that the girls had stopped dancing and were looking troubled, she dried her tears and showed her guests out.

"This isn't the way to Gunter's office," Thelma observed when they were back in the Corvette and headed for Cloud House.

"I need to ask Maxima if she put more than one costume in the giveaway box. When I saw Julie and Sally wearing all those layers of clothing, I suddenly realized that the assailant could have been a thin person wearing more than one costume."

"Why another costume? Why not ordinary clothes?" Thelma asked, perplexed.

"Because whoever it was would have had to dress in a hurry, and the giveaway box was near the back door."

"So now you don't know whether the prime suspect in the murder was a slender person wearing two cloaks or a stout person wearing one," Thelma surmised.

"It could depend on a second robe having disappeared from Maxima's giveaway box," Pia Jo decided. "For starters, let's go see if there were two opera robes in the box."

When they questioned Maxima at Cloud House, she agreed that it was entirely possible that the man who'd assaulted Dag, killed Stan, and escaped with the emerald necklace had been wearing two robes.

The giveaway box had indeed held two discarded costumes, one of which had been a black velvet gown padded to give her a stouter and more self-indulgent dowager presence; unfortunately, in their haste to identify the suspect, they'd only considered the purple and gold robe because that was the one Goldie had described.

A further search of the box revealed that the black velvet robe was also missing. "So your primary suspects have changed?" Vladimer observed. "Your stout suspect has become a thin suspect. We were expecting to be arrested any day now, but that lets us out, Max."

"Actually, he could have been either slim or stout," Pia Jo said after she'd pondered the new clue. "A stout suspect could have taken them both to see which one fit best." While doing a cursory search of the laundry room, she caught a glimpse of Ox-Eye hovering in the background. "His making a cake doesn't eliminate him as a suspect," she decided, then said aloud, "I'd rather not discuss the case until I've done a little thinking. May Thelma and I use your study for an hour or so?" She'd settled on the study because it was almost completely soundproofed by books.

"Of course! Come with me." Maxima led them to the study, asked if she couldn't send in some tea, and closed the door behind her when Pia Jo said they were fine. Alone with Thelma, she suggested that they sit on a couch far enough from the two doors to allow them to converse without being heard. The last thing they needed at this point was an eavesdropper.

"So what are you thinking?" Thelma asked when they'd sunk into the overstuffed couch.

"If the suspect is either a stout person who wore only the robe that fit best or a thin person who was wearing two robes, I'm thinking I have way too many people to investigate. But it would have taken a quick-change artist to try on both robes and discard one in the time allowed, and if the black one was discarded, where is it? So let's first consider slender people who might have hurriedly donned two robes. Try to remember what slender people were at the party. Ox-Eye was one—he was watching and listening closely when we were going through the discard box, and he's a skilled bow-and-arrow hunter. Blue once told me how he got a deer when those who were using rifles missed. Throwing the small sword couldn't have been that different from shooting with a bow and arrow."

Thelma shook her head. "But wasn't it dark, and wasn't he with you when Gunter questioned Dove?" she cross-examined.

"It wasn't entirely dark—the yard light was somewhat revealing—and he didn't stay long at the interrogation in the kitchen here. When he hurried off, I thought it was because he was upset with Dove, but what if they were in it together and merely pretended that they were on the outs? Or what if he decided to play a lone game after she confessed to stealing the emeralds for Stan and Dag? I can't cross him from my list—not yet."

Thelma had to agree that she had a point, then made a reluctant suggestion. "Both Bess and George are slender; and though wealthy donors may provide funds for the Home, they can't use those funds for private travel." But it wasn't long before she was defending her close friends. "We all belonged to an archery club once, and they were so unskilled that they withdrew in embarrassment—their arrows either fell short or overshot the mark. What about Laurel? She and Ebony belong to a health club and often take part in athletic events. Either one of them could have knocked Dag out with Odin's horse and sent that small sword hurling into Stan's back."

"Yes, and Laurel loves jewelry," Pia Jo conceded unenthusiastically. She admired Laurel, who was bright and had style. "We'll keep her in mind, but being slender and athletic and loving jewels doesn't give her probable cause. Yentl and Nikita are slender, but they're also petite—the costumes would have been way too long for them. The same goes for the Cambodian twins. What about Sidonie?"

Thelma laughed. "The Alligrettis are filthy rich, and Sidonie has a large case of jewels. Why would she need any more? And she looks positively frail—how could she have thrown the sword with such force?"

Retrieving her notebook from her tote bag, Pia Jo made some jottings disappointedly, a sudden darkening of the sky and a clap of thunder accentuating her dark mood. She was getting nowhere—how could she urge Gunter to arrest anyone without probable cause? And how could he get a warrant to search any of their private domiciles for the emeralds if he had no convincing reason for doing so?

When they went to take their leave of the Roshnikovs, they found the place in an uproar, a storm that matched the one that was brewing outside. The four—Maxima and Vladimer, Sidonie and Reolo—had dined and played bridge with friends of the Roshnikovs the evening before; and upon returning, Sidonie had slipped off her earrings, placed them on a sideboard in a dining alcove, and had promptly forgotten them. She'd just remembered them, and when she'd gone to the alcove and looked on the sideboard, the earrings were gone. Now, with the help of Reolo, Ox-Eye, the Cambodians, and the Roshnikovs, she was searching frantically for the missing earrings.

Upon hearing about the missing jewelry, Pia Jo's spirits deflated even further. Surely she wasn't going to have to investigate another jewel theft before the first one was solved! But when Thelma asked if they should stay and join in the search, Reolo answered in the negative.

"Sidonie's absent-minded," he insisted. "She's always mislaying things—she can't be sure she left the earrings on the sideboard. No one was here last night except us four. Ox-Eye had the night off, and he took the Cambodians with him in that old jeep when he left—they only returned an hour ago. You ladies go on home and don't worry about the earrings. We're leaving in the morning—Maxima can send them to Sidonie if we don't find them before then."

On their way back to Lead Mines, Pia Jo asked skeptically, "Why would Sidonie mislay her earrings? She has nothing to do but keep track of her jewels."

Thelma didn't agree. "Perhaps she forgot she wasn't in her own home. I have to admit that I've taken off my jewels when I got home from a party and put them down somewhere. I'm so careless with my jewelry that Sven's glad it isn't costly."

Grateful that the missing earrings weren't a top priority but disturbed by the sudden ominous clouds, stabbing flashes of lightning, and peals of thunder, Pia Jo stopped briefly at the Sheriff's Headquarters before she returned Thelma to Scandia. There she reminded Gunter of Goldie's testimony, of the two missing robes, and of Laurel's slender, athletic body and fondness for jewels. "What more would you need to obtain a warrant to search the Oleander home on High Street?"

Her own secret and illegal search had been too hurried to turn up the emerald necklace.

"You gotta give me more'n that," he said with a decisive shake of his head. "Ox-Eye's slender, athletic, and fond o' money, ain't he? And he works at Cloud House—he would have known about th' giveaway box. He may even have known that it held two opera costumes. But you sure as hell did a good thing when you called on Sandie—Emeline woulda been proud of you. If you hadn'ta gone and seen Julie an' Sally playin' at bein' Lena, you wouldn'ta made th' two-robe connection; an' makin' connections is what Law Enforcement's all about."

She was grateful for the praise, but since she was no nearer solving the case, she could only smile disconsolately. Seeing her discouragement, Thelma urged her to return to Cabin 6 and turn her attention elsewhere. "Answers often come when we least expect them," was her wise counsel.

The evening weather news was also disheartening. Alarmed at the speed with which the storm had quickened, Pia Jo flipped on the TV switch only to have a local announcer deepen her dismay. The storm would be intense, she said, but it would perhaps move on to Richton by morning; however, anyone traveling in the direction of Richton should be especially careful as the main road was undergoing repairs and the detour was none too safe. The bridge over Stony River, which skirted Richton, had been hastily repaired after a semi truck had fallen through it into the river a couple of weeks ago; but the repairs were only temporary and no heavy vehicles could pass that way.

"I wonder if the Alligrettis are listening to this forecast. They'll have to take that road tomorrow when they return to Evanston," Pia Jo mused.

"Tonight's storm will make things worse," Luisa predicted as the wind whistled eerily around the corner of Cabin 6. "Oh, by the way, Reo called while you were gone. He's thinking about driving up to see what progress you're making on the case. You'd better call him and tell him to map out a different route if he decides to come."

But when the answering machine announced that Reo wasn't in, Pia Jo left a message for him about the road and joined Luisa in front of the television set. Thelma had been right about changing focus when a solution to a problem can't be found, for when she and Luisa were watching a special on British mysteries, her superconscious (that repository of delectable bits of constructive but unrelated information) slipped her an idea. Or perhaps the idea came from a clip of Sherlock Holmes peering from the bushes in the disguise of a beggar.

"Since we found Stan's van parked on Main Street not far from the steps that lead up to High Street, whoever stole it probably lives on High Street. I need to go up there and search the grounds for the discarded robes," she suddenly decided. "And I need to wear a disguise."

Luisa wasn't convinced. "The Roshnikovs are your employers—why would you need to wear a disguise to search their grounds?" she wanted to know.

"Because the perp could have hidden the robes somewhere on the place. Besides, Gunter said I need specific evidence before he can get a search warrant, so I'll have to search the Wylie, Oleander, and Anderson grounds—."

"The Anderson grounds? You're joking."

"No, I'm not. Sandie seems to be grieving, but she may be gifted at pretense—she's probably had a lot of practice since she married Stan. She's slender—two costumes would have made her look heavier, and the low ceilings at Asgard may have made her look taller. Besides, Goldie might not be an observing person—who knows exactly what she saw? And Sandie had the strongest motive of them all. It was obvious that she wasn't happy on the day I first interviewed them, and this morning she said she's known about Stan's philandering for a long time. She may have even suspected him of stealing the emerald necklace last December. I found it very curious that Dag went so far as to wrangle them an invitation by refusing to play unless Stan could sing. Did he do it because of a preconceived plot? It was obvious that they didn't belong to the Roshnikov crowd."

Finding the scenario plausible, Luisa added to it eagerly. "And if she's a housewife with no education or training, she'll need money to live on and support her daughter." Then she paused in her speculation. "But how skilled is she at throwing a sword? You're right—when she's at the visitation tonight, you can safely search her grounds for the costumes; and since she and Julie might come home early, you should wear a disguise. If you're discovered, you can say you're out looking for your dog."

"Come with me, Luisa!" Pia Jo pleaded. "The weather's settled down, at least for a while." When Luisa promptly refused, Pia Jo charged, "You fight too hard to repress your jaunty Italian spirit."

Something in Luisa rose to the challenge. "Okay, you've convinced me! It was sort of fun going to the Red-Eyed Bat. But we'd better take our umbrellas—we can leave them in the car if the weather stays calm. What disguises do you have in your theatre trunk?"

-23-

Wearing excessively curly wigs and the clashing clothes and heavy-soled shoes of teenage girls, the two young women armed themselves with umbrellas, flashlights with new batteries, disposable gloves, zip bags in various sizes, whistles to call their imaginary dog in case they were discovered, and boxes of dog biscuits left over from Boffo's recent sitting. Getting into the little Corvette, they drove to Lead Mines, where Pia Jo parked in an inconspicuous spot on Main Street; then, carrying their tote bags and struggling mightily against the whipping wind, they battled their way up the steep steps to High Street.

They would have begun their search with the Home for Exceptional Children, but its grounds and garage were ablaze with lights. "We'll have to come back to the Wylies when we're through with the others," Pia Jo decided. So starting with the Anderson home, which was dark, they began their search with the zeal of sleuths bent on solving a case in the face of extreme odds. The Anderson garage was empty; evidently Stan's van was still impounded as evidence and Sandie had ridden to the visitation with someone else. After searching the garage meticulously, they turned their attention to a large, red metal chest with several drawers. Finding it locked, Pia Jo pried it open; inside were expensive tools, girlie magazines, and posters of nude women that Stan had evidently been hiding from Sandie and Julie; but neither the garage nor the chest held anything that seemed relevant to the investigation.

The other small building on the grounds turned out to be Julie's playhouse; and as she lifted the hook that held the door shut, Pia Jo wondered if Stan hadn't loved Julie very much after all. Who else would build a good-sized playhouse for his child? But when she shone her light around, she saw the name "Olig Anderson" and the date "May 1990" painted on a board above the door. Evidently Julie's grandfather, or a carpenter uncle, had built the little house. Here they found the box of used clothing that Lena Borg had sent over with Sally; turning its contents out on a homemade bench, they went through them diligently but found no opera gowns hidden among them.

"Holy Gana!" Luisa muttered when she tripped over a row of Sandie's discarded shoes, some with high heels. Empty cocoa and spice boxes filled with sand, cereal boxes crammed with confetti, sand-colored plastic eggs, and milk cartons of water were stored on small shelves; these and the faded paintings hanging on the walls reminded Pia Jo of her own childhood and her playhouse on the farm. She chuckled when she saw the little dressing table with its swinging mirror, its used make-up, and its pegged rack that held a beribboned bonnet, a veiled toque, and a straw garden hat.

Wondering who Gana was, she remarked to Luisa, "Childhood is such a fun time. I just hope Julie's life won't be ruined by the scandal of her father's thievery and defection."

"It'll be even worse if Sandie's the guilty one! Julie'll have to be in counseling for years," Luisa observed bleakly. "We've looked at everything—the robes aren't here."

"Do we dare to break into the house?" Pia Jo whispered when they were on the grounds again.

"Not on your life! I'm still quaking from your breaking into the Oleander house," Luisa returned, her voice braced with steel girders. "Gunter would never forgive me if I joined his sister in a life of crime."

"Okay, okay! Stay cool. We'll just sneak onto the Oleander grounds and see what we can turn up there."

The Anderson lawn and the Oleander lawn were separated by a brick wall covered with ivy and rambling roses; the two sleuths had no sooner found a passageway through it than they were challenged by a stern female voice. "Stop right there or I'll spray you with cold water!" Shining their flashlights in the direction of the voice, they saw a stout, middle-aged woman with pepper and salt hair; she was wearing a severe white apron over a severe black uniform, and she was wielding a garden hose threateningly.

When the light over the back door illumined them, Pia Jo said, "We ain't here to steal nothin'—we're just lookin' for our dog, Calypso." At the same time, Luisa began flashing her light around and calling, "Here, Calypso! That's a good dog. We got biscuits for you." They both made use of the whistles suspended from their necks and then called again, "Here, Caly! Come on, old girl!"

Seeing their abundant curls and their heavy shoes, the woman sniffed, "What're you yunguns doing out in this kind of weather? Your parents don't have the sense they were born with. All right, be on your way! And after this, keep your dog penned up. We don't want no doggy pooh on this here lawn." But just then a boxer, a border collie, a cocker spaniel, and two small terriers responded to their whistles, all barking ferociously; and to escape their curious onslaught, the two miscreants scrambled up a ladder that was leaning against the Oleanders' garage. Flattening themselves over the peak of the porch and looking down, they could see the woman turning the hose on the five nocturnal canines and hear her chiding them in an incomprehensible dialect as they evaded her wrath.

"They're gone!" Pia Jo breathed jaggedly. "Do we dare to climb down?"

"Let's wait a bit," Luisa cautioned. "She went inside and slammed the door, but she could come back out. She must work for the Oleanders."

"It was Fiona, their housekeeper and cook. She was probably 'commenting' in Gaelic. She answered the phone when I called for an appointment; and before I escaped from their house, I heard Laurel say that Fiona must have left a basement window open for the cat. Okay, I'm going down. It's beginning to rain, and we still have a lot of places to search."

Deciding not to use the umbrellas, which didn't allow them freedom of movement, they sought cover first in the Oleander garage and then in the little potting shed by the newly-planted garden; but these buildings netted them nothing. They were no luckier at the Carriage House. "The Constantas need money to bring some relatives to America," Pia Jo observed, "But aren't they too old to scramble down all those steps in opera robes?"

"They're strong for their ages," Luisa objected, remembering their performance at the Roshnikov party; but then she revised her opinion abruptly. "Neither of them could knock Dag out and throw that small sword so far," she agreed. When they'd gone over a small garage where a 1932 Ford with a rumble seat was stored, she added, "Every hear of a carriage house with a garage? We're wasting time, Pia Jo."

But once outside and headed in the direction of Cloud House, Pia Jo almost fell over a receptacle of some sort; flashing her light on it, she saw a square cement-block incinerator without a grate. It was filled with rich soil and looked as if it were going to be used as a planter; near it on the ground, a flat of petunias in assorted colors confirmed this assumption. They were about to move on when Pia Jo paused and said, "Wait, Lu—we have only the Roshnikov garage left, and that's not in line with this path. The suspect would have had to go the long way around to reach it. Let's search this thing—it's in line with this path and the back door, and it's much closer to the mansion, too."

Luisa joined her, and donning thin plastic gloves, they poked through a thick layer of packed topsoil. "What's this?" Luisa asked, tugging at a black piece of material. Pia Jo joined in the tugging, and their efforts soon revealed a large black garment. Shaking it, Pia Jo held it up and exclaimed, "It's the black opera robe." One glance set Luisa to digging further under the soil, and it wasn't long before she unearthed the purple and gold cloak. "Gin!" she said in a loud stage whisper as she shook out the soil. "Your thin-suspect theory must have been correct—whoever killed Stan must have been wearing both costumes."

While she bagged the evidence, Pia Jo's mind mounted a roller coaster and began to take curious twists and turns. "But whose grounds are we on? Incinerators are illegal in Lead Mines, so who's doing the planting here?" Since the Roshnikovs owned the Carriage House grounds, the petunia gardener could be the Constantas or someone who lived at Cloud House. A few more mental ups and downs of reflection led nowhere and caused her to focus on the suspects. "We've ruled out the Constantas as the killer, and I think we can rule them out where disposing of the robes is concerned. The incinerator is deep and nearly filled with soil—one of them could have been planning to plant the petunias in it without knowing that the robes were hidden there."

Luisa agreed and pursued her reasoning further. "Right. Besides, there are openings in all the walls, fences, or hedges that separate the residents of High Street, so any of the suspects would have had access to the incinerator."

Rustling in the bushes drew their quick attention, and this was soon followed by the sound of feet thumping off on a path that led away from Oblachnyj Dom. They gave chase, but the darkness hid the intruder's movements and they soon realized that further pursuit would be useless; hurrying back to the incinerator, they examined the ground for the intruder's tracks. But rain was now bucketing down; and the prints, almost formless, were rapidly disappearing into the soil.

Pia Jo's mind stopped its gyrations with a bump. "This arbor has a roof and benches," she observed, directing her flashlight at a structure enshrined with sleeping morning glories. "Let's sit here and rest a bit." She didn't add that she was cold and wet and that her arm was excruciatingly painful. "That must have been the killer coming to retrieve the robes—we're probably lucky to be alive, Lu. And since we're dealing with a clever criminal, we'd better speculate on the thin suspects' movements from the time Dove tried to steal the pink necklace. Almost anyone at the party could have overheard her confession; and since the guests left hurriedly, Sven and Thelma couldn't give any of them an alibi."

"They all needed money except Sidonie, and she's too frail to have driven that sword into Stan's back," Luisa surmised. "So that leaves us with five major suspects: the Wylies, Sandie, Laurel, and Ox-Eye."

Pia Jo shuddered as she pulled off the curly wig and stuffed it into a plastic bag. When Luisa had followed suit, Pia Jo added, "Let's go back to the cabin and get out of these heavy shoes. They weigh a ton. But first I'll have to turn this evidence over to Gunter, and tomorrow I'll have to interview the thin suspects all over again." She was beginning to think that $10,000 was far too small a sum for all the agony she'd endured. And the end was not yet.

- 24 -

Nancy Hogan, the night dispatcher, was on duty when the two dripping shamuses brought the robes in and locked them in an evidence locker in the booking room until they could be examined further. "Did Gunter and Blue go home?" a disappointed Pia Jo wanted to know. "I need to report on the progress we made today, which is considerable."

"You can drive to Rendezvous to see the sheriff or report to him in the morning. Bert's around somewhere, and Windy's on desk duty. Do you want him to see the evidence?"

"Heaven forbid! I'll report to Gunter in the morning." She wasn't ready to go to Rendezvous of the Four Winds, where the memory of her mother lingered everywhere—the very idea brought her a stab of pain. Instead she'd go to Cabin 6 and write a long report on the day's events; it was the best way for her to remember details and stay focused on the case.

The storm raged until well after midnight; the wind kept the two sleuths awake by battering the shingles and slapping the branches against the windows in incomprehensible hostility; but by morning it had abated considerably. Luisa still had touch-up work to do on Pia Jo's portrait so begged off going to Lead Mines with her friend. It was just as well; Gunter had a tendency to get rattled and forget the case he was discussing if Luisa were present. Keeping copies for herself and the Roshnikovs, Pia Jo gave him her written report, recounted its contents orally, and received his commendation.

"You've made progress, trink. I've looked the op'ra robes over an' sent 'em to the lab for further examination. They're musty an' smell like dirt, an' I doubt that there'll be any clear prints on 'em; but they do suggest, as you say, that a thin person wore both of 'em to throw us off the scent. So what's your game plan?"

"I want to talk to Blue about Ox-Eye right now," she said, glancing at the chief deputy out of the corner of her eye. "I know he's Blue's friend, but he's inscrutable, he's thin, and I'm sure he could use some extra money." She turned to face Blue directly. "Since Ox-Eye's too bright to hide the emeralds in his quarters, there's no point in getting a warrant and searching them; so I'd like a psychological profile of him, Blue. How was he reared? Were his parents good to him? How honest is he? Is he a religious man?"

Blue doodled a sketch of Ox-Eye on a paper in front of him as he considered her questions. "His parents were good to him, but they were very poor; their poverty and Dove's greed have been his downfall. He met her at a dance when they were in their teens, and he fell head over heels—she was pretty and fun-loving then. They went to different high schools, and he got into trouble at the Settlement School for her sake—he stole a necklace and several pairs of earrings from other girls' lockers to give to her."

"He did what?" Pia Jo demanded in shocked tones while Gunter looked at Blue with new interest.

"Yeah, I knew you'd get excited if I told you about that. Then some girl caught him making off with her beaded boots and reported him to the principle, who in turn reported him to the current sheriff. Ox-Eye admitted his guilt and spent three months in a correctional institution and six months on parole. Later he married Dove, but living with her's been hell for him—she's tried to corrupt him in more ways than one. Believe me, she's earned the face she has now!"

"She wanted him to steal?"

"Yeah, that and other things."

"Did he steal for her?"

"Not again! He learned his lesson and tried to teach it to her; but she was raped by the son of a wealthy white man when she was twelve or so, and she's bitter because nothing was ever done about it. Ox-Eye thought she'd learn to like sex during their honeymoon, but she didn't. She would shudder when he touched her."

Blue's testimony put Dove in an entirely new light and made his listeners wish they could get their hands on her molester. As Pia Jo taped his remarks, however, she decided that Dove's bitterness, though perhaps warranted, hadn't solved anything. In fact, her desire for revenge had only gotten her into more trouble, and surely Ox-Eye would not have jeopardized his freedom to get the emerald necklace for her! A sudden suspicion made her turn on Blue. "Was it Stan who raped her, Blue? Did Ox-Eye kill him because he made Dove lose her tenderness?"

But Blue was firm in his denial. "I doubt it! Would she have consented to steal both necklaces for him if he'd been the one? Besides, she's mostly bitter against rich people like the Roshnikovs. Stan was poor."

With a new platter of food for thought, Pia Jo called Thelma and set up an appointment with her and Sven. "I'm sorry, Thel, but I have to know more about the Wylies; and I might not have to bother them if you can give me some background. This morning at ten? Yes, I'd love to come for an early lunch—I had a cold bagel three hours ago."

Over a chilled vegetable salad, sandwiches, and fruit, Thelma and Sven told Pia Jo what they knew about the Wylies; and none of their testimony was in the least bit damaging. Sven had met George at the University they both attended, and their interest in Irish literature had been an instant bond. Both were single, but Sven had just met Thelma, and he'd asked George to invite a girl and double date with them. George had hemmed and hawed a little and had then asked if he might bring his sister, who was majoring in Special Education in a nearby school, and Sven had said "Fine!" They'd gone to a movie—had it been *The Sound and the Fury?*— and then to a four-star restaurant; there, in the ladies' room, Elizabeth had asked Thelma whether they'd mind if they knew that George was gay.

Since the struggle for gay rights had not yet gained momentum, Thelma might have had to think twice before replying; but she was not a judgmental person, and her response had been instantaneous. "Why should we mind? Our Code is 'live and let live.'" From then on, the two couples had been close. A brief marriage to a bigamist, which had been annulled, had soured Bess on love; and she'd found contentment in keeping house for herself and George and in working with exceptional children. When a legacy from an aunt and uncle-in-law gave them possession of their house on High Street, they'd been able to pursue both their common and their individual goals.

Not being a homophobe, Pia Jo took this information in stride. She merely nodded and made a few notes in her ubiquitous notebook. "Doesn't he have a personal life?" she asked, then added quickly, "Not that it matters to the case."

"George is very private," Sven replied. "He and his lover have a cabin somewhere, and they also travel together. We've entertained him and his male friend, who is as intelligent and well-mannered as George is."

Pia Jo nodded. "I met gays while at the university, and I felt secure with them. They didn't come on to me as though I were a hound in heat. It was great not to have to worry about being raped. One other question: we've established that wealthy donors take care of most of the children's needs, but what about their personal expenses?"

Thelma looked a bit exasperated when she responded to this query. "They have a right to salaries, don't they? George does his share—he keeps the accounts and other records, and he launches fund drives. In addition, Bess tutors high school students who've fallen behind their class, and George writes literary criticism. They don't get rich on what they do, but they don't have to steal to augment their income."

"Don't get huffy, Thel!" Sven counseled. "Pia Jo has to ask pertinent questions whether or not she offends people."

Thelma was instantly contrite. "I know that, and I'm proud of her for her thoroughness. But George doesn't flaunt his sexuality, he's not a child molester, and they're both angels to those kids. I hate to have their integrity doubted."

Pia Jo rose to go. "I wasn't doubting their sexual or social integrity, Aunt Thel," she said firmly. "I have a Code, too. If they'd stolen the necklace from a wealthy woman to get cash for needy children, I would probably have looked the other way. But if they'd stolen it for personal reasons, I would have had to give Gunter the evidence." Popping the last bite of a cheese-spread cracker into her mouth, she thanked them and left with the conviction that the Wylies were innocent and that George had not raped Dove.

Regretting that Ox-Eye remained a suspect but relieved that she could cross the Wylies off her list, Pia Jo drove along High Street until she came to the Oleanders' approach. Reflecting that she'd already searched their house and grounds, she parked and headed for the front door. But the same voice that had challenged her and Luisa the night before challenged her a second time. "You want something, Miss?"

Turning in the direction of the voice, she saw Fiona emerging from the thorny shrubbery with an unhappy Nox in her arms. Although Pia Jo didn't question her about the cat's behavior, she seemed compelled to provide the information. "He hates to be brushed when he's full of tangles."

"I'm Pia Jo Borg, and I'm investigating the theft of the emerald necklace for the Roshnikovs. I'd like to ask you some questions."

"You the sheriff's sister?"

"Yes, I am, but the Roshnikovs are employing me at present."

"You're talking to the wrong person, Miss. I wasn't asked to attend either party."

Pia Jo smiled and clarified the purpose of her call. "The questions aren't about you, Fiona—they're about your employers."

"How'd you know my name?"

"It's on the pin you're wearing."

Fiona fingered the pin. "I guess it is. Come into the kitchen then."

Pia Jo followed her into a neat and cheerfully-decorated kitchen, watched the cat scamper away when she set it down, and asked conversationally, "Fiona? Isn't that an Irish name?"

"My parents were born in Ireland but came to America when I was a little girl. Have a chair. Would you like something? Coffee, tea, or milk? Or I could make you some lemonade."

"Thank you, a glass of water will be fine—I just ate with my uncle and aunt. Are the Oleanders good employers?"

Fiona took a purifying pitcher from the refrigerator and poured her a glass of water. "The best. They treat me better than most white folk do."

"Were you here on the night of the recent Roshnikov party?" If she'd been around, she could either alibi the Oleanders or cast doubt on the time of their return.

"I was here, but I was in bed."

"You didn't hear them come in?"

"No. I was asleep."

Blast! Why is nothing ever easy? "So they could have gone out again after they returned from the party?"

Fiona looked at her appraisingly. "I suppose so—I don't keep track of their movements. But I did read about the case in the *Courier*—at least I read what the sheriff gave out."

"What did he give out?" Pia Jo had been too busy to read newspapers and hadn't realized that Gunter had talked to the press.

"He said that Dove Raintree had been arrested for attempting to steal a pink diamond and pearl necklace from Madame Roshnikov. She'd also confessed to stealing the emerald necklace as the party last December and had accused Dag Amundson and Stan Anderson of hiring her to steal it. Stan Anderson had later been killed at the Amundson farm by an unknown assailant, and Dag had declared his innocence. That's about all he'd say to the press."

"Haven't you also heard the Oleanders discuss the case?"

"I suppose I have, but hearsay can't be used as evidence, can it?" The loyal servant seemed to know something about the law.

"So you can't give either of the Oleanders an alibi?"

"No, and I can't say that one of them went to the Amundson farm and killed Stan Anderson, either." Fiona was losing her patience and would clearly be a hostile witness if questioned about her employers.

Pia Jo sipped her water, then asked, "Laurel has a lot of jewelry, hasn't she?"

Fiona grunted, "I expect so."

"Would you say she has an abnormal love for jewelry?"

"No, I wouldn't. I'm not a psychiatrist."

"Sorry! 'Abnormal' was the wrong word. Does she wear different jewels every time she goes to work or to a social occasion?"

Fiona didn't answer until Pia Jo prompted her. "Well?"

"She has jewelry to go with every outfit if that's what you want to know. Who doesn't?"

Realizing that Fiona would say nothing that would implicate the Oleanders, Pia Jo thanked her for the interview and the water and was on the point of departing when she caught sight of a pile of mail on the hall table; Colombo-fashion, she turned back to say, "There's one more thing, Fiona. Would you say that the Oleanders live beyond their means?"

Fiona followed her glance, but even her body language was non-committal. "I don't pry into my employers' business affairs," she said coldly. Then she asked a question of her own. "Don't you have jewelry to go with all your outfits?"

But back in the Corvette, Pia Jo jotted down the date, place, situation, and a brief record of the interview, then added, "Large stack of letters on hall table strongly suggested that the Oleanders live beyond their means. Since they both work and don't have much time to write personal letters, my gut feelings is that most of them were bills. One had the gold-border logo of a credit card used by wealthy people."

As she drove to Oblochnyj Dom to bring the Roshnikovs up to date and to give them a copy of her most recent report, Pia Jo felt her frustration mount; she'd just interviewed three reliable sources about the prime suspects, and she'd eliminated only the Wylies. Ox-Eye had stolen jewelry once, and who could say he'd never do it again; and the Oleanders were probably in credit-card debt.

At Oblochnyj Dom, Ox-Eye admitted her with his usual aloof dignity, informed her that the Roshnikovs were on the terrace, and suggested that she find her own way there. The Cambodian twins had been given the day off and were celebrating their birthday somewhere, and he had to do all the work alone. Wondering if he missed Dove's companionship or merely her help, she made her way to the rear of the house and entered the huge terrace through elaborate French doors embellished with gold scrolls. The theme of cherubs had been extended to the out-of-doors; and as she glanced about at the expensive statuary, she thought of Emeline and the two little white cherubs she'd been able to afford. Yet the garden at Rendezvous of the Four Winds appealed to her more than this stylized place.

The Roshnikovs and the Alligrettis were seated around a large, white patio table that matched the French doors; and when Pia Jo took her written report from her tote bag, handed it to the diva, and asked for a private interview, Maxima said firmly, "Of course, but not now. You must help us find Sidonie's earrings, Pia Jo. Reolo wants to get back to Evanston, and Sidonie won't leave without them."

It was on the tip of Pia Jo's tongue to reply acidly that she'd been hired as a detective, not a flunky; but then she remembered that detectives are often required to conduct searches, and setting her bag on a chair, she asked cooperatively, "Where have you looked?"

"Everywhere!" Sidonie said in despair.

"Let's concentrate on the rooms you've been in since you took them off," Pia Jo suggested.

"I've only worn them in the main rooms," Sidonie assured her.

"Then you go over the dining and living areas again, and I'll do the den, the study, and the library."

When they'd agreed to her proposal, she left them to their tasks and went down to the den, but a careful scrutiny revealed nothing beyond its usual furnishings. An intense search of the library was equally fruitless; even the area where Sidonie's greatest interest lie—the stage— yielded nothing. As she progressed to the study, Pia Jo wondered why a home had to have both a library and a study—couldn't people study in the library? But since this thought didn't help find the missing earrings, she removed pillows and poked under cushions, meanwhile thinking fancifully that Sidonie would probably be at Oblochnyj Dom for the rest of her life if she wouldn't leave without the earrings.

Ultimately her diligence paid off, for under the cushion of a chair Sidonie favored because it set off her frail sophistication, she found a gleaming pair of earrings. "Eureka!" she yelled in the hall so the others could hear; then, fearing that a stone may have come loose, she closely inspected the dark blue glassy stones in their attenuated white gold settings.

When Vladimer joined her, she searched his face curiously and remarked, "These seem cheap compared to Sidonie's other jewels. Have you any idea why she values them so highly?"

For a second or two his expression became pained, but then its joviality returned. "Who knows why women treasure what they do?" he asked carelessly. "Why don't you bring them up to her? She's helping him pack his bags. He has a role waiting for him in Evanston; now she'll probably go with him." He sounded strangely relieved by the idea.

"When I get back, I'd like to talk to you and Maxima—if that's okay with you," Pia Jo said as she turned to comply with his request. "I brought a written report, and I want to discuss some further developments."

"Of course! We'll be on the terrace—the breezes are refreshing today."

The suite of rooms that the Alligrettis occupied while at Cloud House was on the second floor; and as she hurried up the sweeping staircase, Pia Jo could hear the couple arguing heatedly. When she came into hearing distance, she realized that they didn't yet know that she'd found the earrings, for Sidonie was saying haughtily, "I've told you ten times I won't leave without the earrings!"

"You've got such a grand passion for Vladimer that you'll use any excuse to stay at Cloud House," was his astonishing reply. Stopping in her tracks, Pia Jo tried to digest this new information as question after question raced through her mind. Was Sidonie really in love with Vladimer, or was that merely the ranting of a jealous husband? Was Vladimer also in love with Sidonie? Could this new development have a bearing on the case? Backtracking, she approached their suite more slowly and called ahead excitedly, "I found your earrings, Madame Alligretti. They were under a cushion in the study."

The double doors to the suite parted, and Sidonie stood framed in the opening. Behind her, a pile of expensive luggage, packed and strapped, waited to be carried downstairs; and leaning against one of the suitcases was a flat red box wrapped in opaque plastic. It must be a painting, Pia Jo surmised as she made out the word "ART" through the wrapper.

"Thank you so much, Pia Jo," Sidonie said graciously as she reached for the earrings with her long, gold-tipped fingers. "They aren't terribly valuable, but someone I love deeply gave them to me." She seemed exhilarated over the return of the jewels, while behind her Reolo's face resembled the stark mask of tragedy.

-25-

When she was about to return to the first floor, Pia Jo realized that she'd been ignoring Nature's call all morning; pausing abruptly, she looked for a half bath on the second floor and found one at the end of the corridor, several doors down from the Alligretti suite. The call answered, she lathered her hands with rich, subtly-scented soap, rinsed them, and dried them on the corner of a towel that seemed too elegant for ordinary use. Wondering, as she did so, if she'd overlooked an important aspect of the Alligretti/Roshnikov relationship, she hurried to the steps and, glancing down, saw that Ox-Eye was carrying the last of the luggage out the door while the Alligrettis were saying a fond good-bye to their host and hostess. It didn't take a bright sleuth to realize that Sidonie's arms remained around Vladimer's neck longer than was necessary or that he looked extremely embarrassed as he pried them off.

"Ask them not to leave yet!" she called ahead as she took the steps two at a time to the hall below. "I want to interview them again." But she'd descended only a third of the way when her feet flew out from under her and she crashed headlong down the rest of the steps. After seeing an entire galaxy of stars, she was able to focus on the Roshnikovs, Ox-Eye, and the Cambodian twins, who were all leaning over her with concerned faces.

"Pia Jo! Are you all right?" Maxima was demanding shrilly, while Vladimer was adding, "Have you broken anything?"

"She come too fast!" one of the twins was saying, while the other was nodding his head in emphatic agreement. Ox-Eye remained silent and impassive, but the indignation in his dark eyes astonished the young investigator.

As Pia Jo grasped the balustrade, pulled herself up, and tested her limbs gingerly, pain followed a lightning path from her battered arm to her bruised ribs and down to a foot that had twisted under her and felt as though it could never be untwisted. "No, I'm not all right," she said crossly, "but never mind that now. You mustn't let the Alligrettis go yet. I need to question them again."

"We can't stop them from leaving," Vladimer rebutted firmly. "Haven't you questioned them enough, for Heaven's sake?"

"Take a good look at the sixth step," Pia Jo countered grimly.

Vladimer immediately mounted to the sixth step, examined it closely, and said, "It's been smeared with some kind of grease." He bent closer, sniffed the grease, and said, "Face cream! But how did it get there?" Then he made the necessary connection. "But that's impossible!" he exclaimed. "They wouldn't—good God, Pia Jo, you could have been killed!"

Realizing that Ox-Eye and the Cambodian twins were listening in wide-eyed curiosity and unwilling to believe that her friends greased the step, Maxima said diplomatically. "Come along to the terrace, dear—we'll talk there. Is it safe for you to walk, Pia Jo, or shall we take you to a doctor?"

"We'll talk here," Pia Jo said aggressively as she gingerly tried her legs. "I wasn't kidding when I told you to stop the Alligrettis. When I went to return the earrings, I heard Reolo accuse Sidonie of being so in love with you that she'd use any ruse to stay on at Oblachnyj Dom, Vladimer. Is that true? Did she hide the earrings herself?"

At her searching question, Vladimer's face lost its ruddy glow. When Maxima's eyes flew to his face, he looked at her gravely and answered without hesitation. "She thinks she's in love with me, and she's tried to lure me into an affair for years. That's why I've protested when you invited them to be our guests so often."

Clearly Maxima was shocked by this revelation. "But she's my closest friend!"

"You just thought so!" Vladimer said firmly. "She's a jealous vulture with only two things on her mind where you're concerned: jealousy and revenge."

Maxima's confusion deepened. "Jealousy and revenge? Why should she be jealous of me, and what reason does she have for revenge? Surely you've never been personally involved with her."

"Don't you remember, dear, that she introduced me to you? We'd met at various elite functions, and since we were both single, I sometimes saw her home. At one of these functions, we celebrated her success in a stage role; and I gave her the earrings. Believe me, I wasn't the only one who bought her a gift—she got huge bouquets of flowers and truly expensive jewelry from her other fans."

He paused to scan his wife's face keenly, and seeing only curiosity there, he went on. "My grandfather had just left me the emeralds, and Sidonie heard me tell a friend that I planned to design an elaborate necklace for my ladylove. I hadn't met you yet, and I certainly didn't mean her; but she evidently thought I was designing the necklace for her."

"So when you met Maxima and fell in love with her, Sidonie felt betrayed?" Pia Jo quizzed.

Vladimer nodded unhappily. "When she heard I'd given Max the emerald necklace, she raged at me for breaking my promise to her. When I asked, 'What promise?' she said I hadn't promised her the emeralds in so many words, but I'd given her the earrings! 'You wouldn't have done that if you hadn't loved me,' she said. When I pointed out that others had given her greater gifts, she cried and insisted that the earrings and the necklace were tokens of my love for her; and she swore that some day the emerald necklace would be hers. I tell you, she was obsessed with that necklace!"

Maxima was so affected by her closest friend's treachery that tears flowed down her cheeks. "And she's been accosting you whenever she found you alone? She mislaid the earrings so she'd have a reason to stay on here? Did Reolo know this?"

"Yes, Reolo knew. He's tried to win her love, but she's always withheld a part of herself. We talked about it once. When I told him I'd never intentionally tried to deceive her, he said he didn't blame me for her obsession."

"I can believe that she overheard Dove's confession and followed either Stan or Dag to Asgard," Pia Jo said grimly. "And since she's an actress, I can see that it would have been natural for her to put on the opera gowns to disguise her appearance. I can also see her rushing down to Main Street, stealing the Toyota, and making it to Asgard in time to knock Dag out with the statue of Sleipnir. But she's a frail woman—I can't believe that she had the skill and strength to hurl the small sword into Stan's back and kill him on the spot."

Maxima, who had been listening keenly, was quick to dispel her disbelief. "The pirate production, Vlad! You remember it, don't you?"

"Yes, of course. How could I forget it?"

"What pirate production?" Pia Jo demanded.

Maxima supplied the details. "It was a panoramic production put on in a park by Lake Michigan. She played a beautiful wife who was bored with her rich husband. When she met a romantic, swashbuckling pirate, she promptly fell in love with him, and he taught her to use the crossbow. It was a heavy thing, but she handled it skillfully. She looks frail but she's really very strong."

"That was a few years ago—she must have kept on practicing," Vladimer surmised. "But I'm no prize. How could I inspire such passion in anyone?"

Maxima looked at him affectionately. "She had an excessive desire for a prize that belonged to me! I guess we can say that she lusted for your love, Vlad." Then she looked at him reprovingly. "If you had warned me about her, I never would have invited them here so often!"

Pia Jo came down to earth and reached into her tote bag for her phone. "While we're gabbing, they're getting away—I have to call Gunter right away." But Melissa's riveting response shattered her hope for help in stopping the Alligrettis. Blue and Windy had gone to the Winnebago Settlement to prevent trouble between two inebriated Winnebagos; and Gunter had rushed off to help the Richton police, who were on a desperate rescue mission and needed his expertise. The bridge over Stony River, which bordered Richton, had collapsed in the storm, and a car holding a family of five had gone headlong into the water and was trapped under a heavy tree limb in the swift, cold-water river. Should the family escape from their car, they would either suffer from hypothermia or drown if they remained for long in the wildly turbulent water.

Turning from the phone, Pia Jo briefly explained the tense situation to the Roshnikovs, then added, "Where would the Alligrettis go if they feared capture?" She could see the reward for her labors disappearing into thin air.

"They have a private plane on an Evanston airstrip and a yacht on Lake Michigan—my guess is that they'd head for the plane," was Vladimer's hurried reply. "But you aren't planning to go after them by yourself, are you? You can hardly walk."

"I have to. I can't bother Gunter now—he's had training in helicopter rescues; and Blue and Windy consider trouble at the Settlement a top priority." She didn't wait to hear their dire arguments against her going alone; instead she returned the phone to its case; slipped it into her tote bag, which already held her pain pills and bottled water; and hobbled around the building to her car.

But Lady Fortune was not in a cooperative mood; try as she might, she could not get Sven's old Vette to start. At her first attempt, the motor groaned and died; and after three more attempts, her groan matched the motor's.

Ox-Eye, who had followed her outside and had heard her groan, lifted the hood and examined the engine. Now he called excitedly, "Here's your problem, Miz—Alligretti yanked out your main distributor wire and took it with him. He meant to slow you up all right. I'm surprised that he knew anything about cars—he hates to drive." Barely registering that he had addressed her humanely, she got out, limped around to the front, and looked where he pointed.

"Now what am I going to do?" she wailed. "They must be half way to Richton already." Then catching sight of his old Comanche Jeep, she asked, "Can you take me in your jeep, Ox-Eye?"

His response sent a chill of defeat through the young sleuth. "I can't find my glasses and I can't drive without 'em," he said firmly. He was looking at her meditatively, and he finally asked, "You ever driven a Jeep?"

"Yes, Gunter drove one for a while before he got to be sheriff, and he let me drive it. He got rid of it after it tipped over and almost killed him. Trust me, Ox-Eye—I'm a good driver."

Since time was passing too swiftly, he didn't wait long before he nodded. "But I'm going with you. The man is big as a grizzly, and I can see good enough to fight. With all those bruises, you might not even be able to handle the snake woman."

Although she felt intensely grateful that he was trusting her with one of his most valuable possessions, she merely said "We have to hurry" as she took the keys he handed her and hopscotched to the Comanche. He kept pace with her, and soon they were climbing into the Jeep's front seat; but she'd barely settled herself under the wheel when she realized that his Siberian Husky, Chukchi, had installed himself in the rear seat, his expression frozen in dignified canine determination.

"Tell him to get out!" Pia Jo yelled over the roar of the motor.

"No time! He won't hurt nothing," was Ox-Eye's laconic reply.

"Wait! Wait!" Vladimer was yelling from the step. "You said you own a gun—where is it?"

"It's at Innisfree, and I don't have time to get it!" She suddenly realized that "ART" didn't stand for a painting. "She might have darts—I saw a dartboard set in her room. But don't worry—we know how to duck," she flung back as she backed up sharply, straightened the wheels, and bounced down the driveway. But her bravado quickly diminished as she turned into Low Street. The memory of Sidonie's skill with a crossbows and a small sword was more than a little daunting, and she wished with all her heart that she'd brought her gun.

-26-

The twenty-five miles between Lead Mines and Richton were enough to discourage a mountain climber; and Pia Jo and Ox-Eye hadn't covered ten miles before "Road Under Construction" signs announced that the main-traveled road was closed to the public. The detour was also in poor condition, and it had been further eroded by the ferocious storm that had lashed the area in the night. "Did the Alligrettis know that the highway is closed and the bridge is out over the detour?" Pia Jo asked as she swung the wheel to avoid a huge rock that had rolled down into the road.

"Can't say," was her companion's laconic reply.

"I wonder if brevity is really the soul of wit," Pia Jo mused as she maneuvered the Jeep through a pool of muddy water that was covering the road and felt it splash her arm. Aloud she asked, "Why did you call Sidonie 'the snake woman'?"

"I saw her parade in front of Mr. Roshnikov in her slip, and when she moved her body this way and that, she reminded me of a snake."

"Aren't you being unjust to snakes?"

He chuckled dryly but didn't answer. "With Dove in jail he can chuckle?" she marveled. Then recalling Dove's difficult personality, she added, "He probably feels like Dr. King—free at last, free at last."

If the first ten miles were disastrous, they were child's play compared to the next five miles. They were in high country now, and the storm had recommenced; the Jeep's top was off and they'd run into cold rain that clouded the windshield and penetrated to their bones.

Catching a glimpse in the mirror of the dog in the rear, Pia Jo felt a thrill of admiration, for he was facing the storm stoically, scarcely heeding the cold water that cascaded down his snout. But if huskies weren't like that, they'd be useless on the Iditarod Trail.

"Washout ahead!" Ox-Eye warned abruptly.

Staring through the rain that slid down the glass, she saw that the road was now a deep ravine; and in the middle of the ravine stood a bright red Corvette, its low-slung chassis mired in thick mud. Its youthful owner was standing beside it on the left, his feet also mired in mud—at the speed Pia Jo was going, she'd crash into him and the car in a matter of moments. Having no time to think of the outcome, she turned the wheel to the right and drove almost perpendicularly up the embankment on the right side of the road; the Jeep, tipping precariously, roared down on the other side of the washout.

Beside her Ox-Eye let out a deep breath, but his thoughts were on the Caddy—not on the Corvette. "Something must have slowed them down," he said, peering ahead owlishly. "That looks like them—maybe a quarter of a mile ahead."

Straining to see through the mud-spattered windshield, Pia Jo made out a black car, now gray with mud, plowing up a distant hill. After observing its progress for a few minutes, she said, not without admiration, "Whoever's driving has plenty of chutzpah."

"The woman was in the driver's seat when I took the luggage out. She thinks her husband drives like a drunken baglady."

"A drunken baglady?"

"That's what she said."

"When did she say that?"

"When I drove them to the French restaurant in Prairie du Loup. Horst wasn't available, and their regular driver stayed in Evanston—he was getting married."

"Didn't they like your driving?"

"No! She insisted on taking over—said I drove like a mule trainer."

As the Jeep slid around in an attempt to find the tracks of the narrow detour, the rain stopped and the sun flashed a brilliant smile. "They've slowed down!" Ox-Eye announced authoritatively as the Jeep's wheels found the grooves they'd been seeking. His pronouncement brought a yelp of agreement from the watchful Chukchi, who seemed fully aware that they were in pursuit of criminals.

Still on high ground, they could see the Alligretti Cadillac, covered with mud and debris, skillfully rounding some hairpin curves now an eighth mile below them. Sidonie was driving like a movie stunt person.

As the Jeep lumbered down into the valley, its occupants saw signs advertising an International Arts and Crafts Fair that was being held in tents, rain or shine, on the main street of Cranshaw, a hamlet not far from Richton. "The main street will be closed to traffic," Pia Jo observed as she reflected on the possible effects of the Art Fair. "Start looking for signs detouring the villagers around the Fair, Ox-Eye. I'd better slow down and follow the Alligrettis—they'll be aware of the detour before we are. Have you any idea how far it is from Cranshaw to Richton and Stony River?"

Ox-Eye consulted a map and said, "Maybe five miles."

Since her arm bruises and the bruises she'd sustained in her plunge down the stairs were becoming unbearable, Pia Jo toyed with the idea of letting Ox-Eye drive, glasses or no glasses; but her desire for relief from agony fled when she remembered one of Emeline's favorite Swedish proverbs, "She who would harvest honey must endure the sting of the bees." Forgetting her desire to be rescued, she said, "Hand me the bottle of pain pills and the water in my tote bag, will you, Ox-Eye?"

He looked at her curiously but complied; twisting off the cap, he shook two pills into his brown palm and handed them to her along with the water bottle. Maneuvering the Jeep with one hand, she popped the pills into her mouth, took a long swig of water, thanked him, and prayed that the pills would take effect immediately. While her endurance was rapidly descending the scale of her fortitude, her determination was rising to a fever pitch. She'd damn well recover that necklace and earn the reward, or she'd die trying. "Could you use some of that water to clean off the windshield, Ox-Eye? I can barely see the road."

Removing a navy and white handkerchief from his pocket, Ox-Eye soaked one end of it and reached over the glass to swipe some of the mud off the windshield.

"Thanks—that's better!" she acknowledged and then fixed her gaze on the Alligretti brake light. But if she had thought that Sidonie would heed an unincorporated village's traffic laws when she'd already ignored the far greater laws of humanity, she was soon to discover her error; for the brazen woman merely leaned on her horn and headed straight for the orange sawhorses that were blocking Cranshaw's traffic. Seeing her intention, people scattered in every direction, and Pia Jo found herself praying again, this time desperately, that the aisle between the tents on the left and right sides of the street would be wide enough for the Cadillac and the Jeep to squeeze through, and that mothers would restrain their children from running into the street.

A careful driver would have done little damage once the people had fled for safety; but Sidonie was now concentrating on saving that precious commodity, her own neck. As she increased her speed and barreled through the small space, hats, clothes, arts, crafts, and food flew in every direction. While a string of red chili peppers from a Hispanic display draped itself around Chukchi's neck, a black lace mantilla settled over Pia Jo's head and shoulders, and a black Charro sombrero with silver ornaments landed jauntily in Ox-Eye's lap, a colorful man-shaped straw piñata leaped to the hood of the Jeep and clung there with goatlike tenacity.

When the Cranshaw crowd became aware that a chase was in progress, some of them clapped their hands, some screamed, and some hooted as Ox-Eye clamped the sombrero on his head uncharacteristically and shouted "Olé!" and Pia Jo guided the Jeep through the Fair. But the chase did not abate, and soon the tempestuous wind dislodged a hot-purple balloon in the shape and size of a man from its moorings and attached it to the Caddy's antenna, where it whipped and gyrated in eccentric synch with Cranshaw's rock 'n' roll band.

As she gained the village's limits and the Jeep bounded after the Alligretti vehicle, Pia Jo half feared that a State Trooper would come roaring after them in a high-speed chase, but such was not the case. Evidently Cranshaw's dilemma could not be compared to the dramatic collapse of the bridge over Stony River.

Judging from the speed with which the new Cadillac and the old Jeep covered the distance between Cranshaw and Richton, it seemed far less than five miles between the village and the small town. And there, an eighth mile ahead of the Cadillac, the river's wild waves shimmered in the sunlight, its bridge hanging precariously; below it the submerged vehicle could barely be discerned, its doors and windows closed against the power of the river. High above the vehicle the helicopter hovered, its pilot holding it steady while a man (most likely Gunter) extended a long rope from its open door to a man who seemed glued to the top of the sunken car. Instinctively stopping the Jeep to watch the maneuvering of the man as he tried to get a car door open, Pia Jo momentarily lost sight of the Cadillac and the fleeing criminals.

"Look—they're all in the water," she yelled to Ox-Eye. "Sweet Dias, it looks like they can't swim!" The car door had swung open, the family had escaped the confines of the car and were being submerged by the busy waves. Squad members and officers were plunging into the river; but its tremendous and indifferent power was impeding their progress, and for a horrible moment Pia Jo feared they'd all drown right before her eyes.

But then two of the children were clinging to a stout rope, and Gunter was slowly pulling them into the hovering helicopter; Squad members were towing the parents toward shore; and the third child seemed to be in the safe hands of an officer. But then the officer yelled, "I'm cramping—I need help," and both he and the boy, who was perhaps ten years old, went under. Fear engulfed Pia Jo, and she was about to jump from the Jeep and swim to the child herself; but Ox-Eye detained her with a hand on her arm and gave an order. "Chukchi, go get the child." In a second, the Siberian Husky was out of the Jeep and in the water; Pia Jo watched in astonishment as, still wearing the string of red chili peppers, he swam out to where the boy had gone down, dived beneath the water, and came up with the boy's shirt gripped tightly in his teeth. Retaining his hold on the child, he swam toward shore, leaving a Squad member to rescue the helpless officer. Seeing Chukchi's bravery and skill, the assembled crowd began to clap and shout words of praise.

When Chukchi had dragged his burden safely to dry land, he let go of his shirt and jumped back into the Jeep, sending sprays of water over Pia Jo and Ox-Eye; not until then did Pia Jo's thoughts return to the chase. She'd caught a glimpse of the Alligrettis, indifferent to the drama being played out in the turgid water, going up a road that bordered the river. But where did that lead? How much of an advantage did they have? Had her brief lack of attention allowed them to escape with the emerald necklace?

She'd been sitting like a grieving Spanish senorita, the black lace mantilla still shrouding her fair hair; but when Ox-Eye urged, "We'd better get going," she came to with a start and looked around her Much to the amusement of some of the children who had gathered to watch the rescue, he still wore the ornate, silver-decorated sombrero; and the varicolored straw man was still splayed across the hood. Leaving it there, she started the Jeep and followed the barely passable river road in the direction the Alligrettis had taken; once they got beyond the woods, she connected with a rocky part of the river's shore, which was under two feet of water. Sensing rather than seeing her way, she mounted huge stones that rocked the old Jeep as it see-sawed over them, slipped into dips that seemed to have no bottom, and climbed under fallen trees whose branches almost scratched their faces. As she abruptly emerged from another small woods where the wet treetops were swarming with a colony of raucous crows, she caught sight of the Alligrettis' Cadillac. It was stuck on a muddy portion of the road, the hot-purple plastic man still attached to the antenna and still dancing wildly in the wind; Sidonie was still behind the wheel, and Reolo was pushing with all the strength in his ungainly body in a vain attempt to get it unstuck.

It didn't take Reolo long to spot their rapid advance and to alert his wife that the Cadillac was of no further use to them; in seconds they saw Sidonie emerge from the front seat; reach into the back for her purse, binoculars, a good-sized case, and the red box that held the fearsome darts; together, they scanned the rocky incline to the left of the car for a place to conceal themselves. Locating an empty space, she scrambled up an incline with Reolo lumbering after her; but when she indicated, through inaudible speech but also through body language, that the rock she'd found wasn't large enough to conceal both of them, he hurriedly searched for another.

"What are they up to?" Ox-Eye demanded. "Do they think we haven't seen where they're hiding?"

"They must be digging in," Pia Jo surmised, stopping the Jeep to consider their next move. "She knows we can't get around the Caddy because the river's to our right and the rocks on the left are too huge to maneuver. If we move any closer, we'll be easy targets in this open Jeep. She'll wound or kill us with the darts. Get the binoculars from my tote bag, will you, please?""

Retrieving the binoculars, Ox-Eye surveyed the situation and then observed, "He's talking to someone on a phone! Could he be calling for a tow truck? No, that would be too risky. Here, have a look!"

Pia Jo had a look. "Maybe he's trying to get help from a servant—or a hit man!"

"You should've brought your gun," he reproved hopelessly. "Now what can we do?"

But Pia Jo was in no mood to give up; in fact, she felt dangerously in control. "It must be seventy-five miles to Evanston and not ten back to Richton—we can get help before they can. Hand me my phone!" she ordered.

"It'll be soaking wet," he surmised glumly, but drawing it out of her bag, he actually smiled when he saw that she kept it in a case. "Smart lady," he approved as he handed it to her. But after dialing several numbers, she almost burst into tears. "Damn! Gunter must still be at the rescue scene, and I can't reach anybody else."

Ox-Eye surveyed the territory in Indian-scout fashion, then said, "The rocks aren't big enough to stop us here, and those tall bushes will screen us from the Alligrettis. Drive the Jeep up on this side of the bushes and let me slip out—they won't be able to see me from where they are. Then turn around and drive down to the road again. Go back to the woods and keep trying to reach the sheriff. The rescue's over—he'll probably be back in his car soon."

She saw at once what he planned to do but wasn't pleased that he was trying to take over. "You plan to circle round and descend on Reolo from behind? That might work if you take him by surprise. But there are two of them—what if they hear you and turn? Is your skin impervious to darts as sharp as medical needles?"

"You think they'll hear a Winnebago?" he demanded, stung by the very idea. "He's above her—I'll reach him first and take him out. Then only the woman will be left."

"But she'll hear you wrestling with him, and she's the dangerous one—she's got the darts. We need to think of a ruse of some sort." She stared through the windshield for a long moment, then said, "I've got it! When you get out, give me that Charro hat and your shirt—it doesn't matter if they're wet."

When she'd driven the Jeep part way up on their side of the incline and stopped in the protection of the tall bushes, he handed her the Charro sombrero, stripped off his olive khaki shirt, slipped from the Jeep, and watched while she dressed the straw man in his shirt and the huge hat and stood him beside her on the seat. Looking amused at the misfit, he asked, "What's on your mind?"

"You circle round and wait for me behind one of the big rocks above Reolo. I want them to think we've gone for help, so I'll drive back down and head in the other direction. But when I get back in the woods with all the crows, I'll look for an open space that will take me over the hill and back this way. I'll leave the Jeep hidden somewhere and join you on foot."

He looked doubtful. "What if you can't find any open space on the other side of the hill? It looks rocky to me."

"Then I'll walk. It'll take longer, but they aren't going any place—unless they walk." She made a difficult turn between rocks and headed back down the incline. Once on the road again, she drove back into the woods from which they'd recently emerged.

"They saw me turn back, and they must have seen I'm not alone," Once in the woods, she tried again to reach Gunter but got only a disturbing silence; but just when she was about to hang up, he identified himself, and she explained the situation. "I'm through here," he assured her, "an' I'll be there in two shakes of a dog's tail. Tell Ox-Eye to hold off until I get there; and Pia Jo, don't for Heaven's sake do anything foolish."

But when she thought of the reward, his wise counsel vanished like a dream. She'd have to make her own road, but wasn't that what Jeeps were for? She located the incline that held only a few well-spaced trees; and putting the Jeep into four-wheel-drive and low gear, she stepped on the gas and began the tough ascent.

"It's risky, yes—if she sees me, she'll let fly with one of her darts, and I'll be a dead duck. But she's got her jewel case with her, and the emerald necklace must be in it. I can't let Ox-Eye or Blue retrieve the emeralds—that's my job, and by all that's holy, I'm going to do it."

But when she reached the top of the incline, she suddenly discovered that the open space that led to the hill where the Alligrettis were concealing themselves was covered with trees that were less than a yard apart; and she had to waste precious time by forging straight ahead over terrain that was so ridged and grooved that the Jeep seemed more like an ancient wagon traveling on a trunk highway than a vehicle of relatively contemporary vintage. Time was running out, and her goal seemed as unattainable as King Arthur's Avalon or Hilton's Shangri La. If Gunter arrived before she'd reclaimed the necklace, she'd be out $10,000!

Lines from an old song prodded her on. "To dream the impossible dream, / To fight the unbeatable foe!" If she didn't try her damnedest to stop the Alligrettis before they got to their plane, Sidonie would not only get away with Maxima's symbol of love; she'd also get away with murder. With a determined look, Pia Jo checked the gauges, surveyed the territory anew, stepped on the gas, felt the land level out, sighted open space leading almost directly to the top of the next hill, shouted "Hallelujah" when she plowed through it and reached her goal, and conceded, "I guess the impossible does take a little longer."

- 27 -

Having reached the crown of the hill, Pia Jo slowed down and searched for a place to conceal the Jeep. Spying a little grove of evergreens, she swung into it, shut off the motor, removed the keys, and got out, hoping against hope that Ox-Eye's plans had not gone awry or that the Alligrettis had not escaped by following some old Indian trail—after all, Winnebagos once roamed these woods. But she had no time to worry—she had to find such a trail herself, one that would take her over the crest of the hill and down to the hiding places of the escaping killer and her love-struck mate.

She must have encircled trees, ducked branches, and threshed through bushes for at least five minutes before she found a path that, though faint and soggy from the recent rain, was still discernible. Moving with caution, she gave thanks for having worn thin athletic shoes, for they made no sound on the softly- packed soil of the trail. Abruptly emerging from a stand of linden trees, she suddenly felt exposed, for there was no cover and the sun was shining directly in her face. Bending low and gumshoeing to the hill's summit, she ducked behind a rock and peered around it so she'd have a clear view of the scene below.

It was a panoramic view; she could see Ox-Eye and Chukchi clearly, and directly below them, concealed by an enormous rock, his attention focused on the road below and the stalled Cadillac, Reolo crouched like a scruffy bear. Ten feet farther down but to his right, Sidonie aimed a small pair of binoculars in every direction, her ears tuned to the indifferent wind.

Anxious not to wait until Gunter's official car approached and robbed them of their advantage, Pia Jo slipped slowly from large rock to large rock until she was only a few feet behind the Winnebagan. Some instinct must have told him that she was there, for he turned slowly and held up a warning hand; still and unobtrusive as a windless night, he signaled her to precede him and tackle Sidonie from behind while he and Chukchi moved in on Reolo. It was sound thinking; she knew now why Ox-Eye had allowed Chukchi to accompany them; the dog was to be their back-up in the absence of official help.

But what if Chukchi didn't understand what he was to do? And now that the rocks were becoming progressively smaller and less reliable as cover, how was she to get by Reolo without alerting him of her presence? As she stood there hesitating, a striking image appeared before her eyes, the image of a cougar leaping on its prey from above. Feeling nothing like a cougar but recalling the diving lessons she'd taken in camp one summer, she pantomimed her intention to Ox-Eye. Perceiving his hesitant nod, she selected a spot directly above Sidonie; mounting a small rock, she gathered her courage and launched herself in a dive that landed her directly on top of her enemy, sending the binoculars and red box of darts in one direction and the purse and jewel case in another.

Pain seared through her as she and Sidonie rolled over and over, each attempting violently to gain the upper hand. Where once she'd considered Sidonie frail, she was now forced to revise that opinion, for the elegant woman was like pliant steel, the product of years of exercise at an advanced health club. As they rolled, she could hear the horrific struggle that was going on between Ox-Eye and Reolo; and a sudden threatening growl informed her that Chukchi had joined in the fray.

In the end it was the mud that saved Pia Jo, for when Sidonie grabbed her head and pounded it against the ground, the mud cushioned it and prevented a concussion; and when Sidonie would have pulled her hair out by the roots, Pia Jo reached for a handful of mud and ground it into her opponent's eyes. Screaming, swearing, and rubbing her eyes, Sidonie could battle no longer; as Pia Jo tied her hands and feet with strips of cloth torn from the socialite's long, stylish dress, she looked upward and caught a glimpse of Reolo lying flat on his back with Chukchi triumphantly astride his stomach and Ox-Eye placidly giving her the victory sign.

When, a few minutes later, Gunter stopped his official vehicle on a dry strip of road behind the stalled Cadillac and got out to evaluate the situation, he saw Pia Jo standing on a rock above him waving something that scintillated in the bright sunlight and threw sparks in every direction. It was the diamond and emerald necklace.

Back in the booking room at the sheriff's headquarters, after Melissa had forced Sidonie to stand under the shower until the mud rolled off her eyes and hair and had dressed the stylish socialite in orange coveralls, she confessed that she'd killed Stan and stolen the emerald necklace because she loved Vladimer and believed with all her heart that he'd designed it for her and Maxima had cheated her out of it. Reolo was arrested as an accomplice, charged with concealing evidence, obstructing justice (he admitted to smearing face cream on the step), and helping a criminal elude justice. He confessed that he was so madly in love with Sidonie and so insanely jealous of Vladimer that he'd considered killing him more than once. They had both lacked restraint in their lust for love.

When Pia Jo returned the diamond and emerald necklace to Maxima along with a complete report of her investigation, Vladimer handed her a check for $10,000 and said, "Be sensible, Pia Jo. Don't spend it all on fancy jewels."

"But what about your advance?" she asked. "I owe you $500." He shook his head firmly. "You owe us nothing. The $500 is your bonus for a job well done." When Maxima thanked her with a hug, she asked, "How was I to know, Pia Jo, that a woman I trusted could be so dangerous?" Then it was Vladimer's turn to envelope her in a bear hug and to say ruefully, "I should have trusted Max to understand my predicament." And in that instant Pia Jo knew that trust was the most important ingredient in a relationship.

Back at Cabin 6, with her arm turning several shades of purple and with pain pills easing the discomfort of her various other bruises, Pia Jo realized that she'd missed lunch and was ravenous. While Lousa fixed her a bowl of three-bean soup and a plump egg salad sandwich, she related the day's events and proudly showed her the check Vladimer had given her.

"Reo called. I told him you were out investigating," Luisa finally remembered. "He's probably pacing the floor waiting for you to call him." When Pia Jo had eaten the last crumb, she dialed the number of the apartment in Chicago that she'd shared with Reo for some three years.

"Did you solve the case?" he asked eagerly when he heard her voice.

"Yes, it's finally solved," she responded in a strangely subdued way.

"And they paid you $10,000?"

"Yes, and I earned every penny of it."

"You did it! I knew you would." He was exuberant. "I'm coming right up to get you—we have to brush up on our French before we leave for Paris. *Je vous adore!*"

"Wait, Reo," she urged, raising her voice. "I have something important to say to you."

"You've already told me what I wanted to hear!" he insisted ecstatically.

"We have to talk, Reo! The main road is under construction by Richton and the bridge is out," she hurried to inform him. "But that's not all—."

"Of course we have to talk, darling dodo! I'll take the scenic route along the Mississippi, and we'll talk when I get there." He replaced the receiver with an emphatic bang.

While they waited for Reo to drive to Lead Mines from Chicago, Uncle Sven called to congratulate Pia Jo on solving the case and to announce that Rex Tremaine planned to visit Scandia in a few weeks. "How do you cure a matchmaker, Lu? If I never meet Rex Tremaine, it'll be too soon!" she groaned as she replaced the receiver; but it was a rhetorical question that needed no response.

During the long wait, Luisa put some finishing touches on her portrait and they discussed the case. "I saw Horst when I returned the necklace to Maxima." Pia Jo related. "He said that Dag has asked him to farm Asgard if he has to go to jail. Goldie's living at home for the present, and her parents are letting them see each other now and then.

He hopes she'll marry him when she's earned her high school diploma and he's learned the English language. He was very pleased."

"Hey, that's great! He'll help her grow up, and Kaito will have his father's companionship," Luisa approved as she deepened a shaded area.

Pia Jo was quiet for a while; then she said pensively, "I certainly misjudged Ox-Eye. I wanted to give him and Chukchi a reward for helping me capture the Alligrettis; but he said the excitement had taken his mind off Dove, and that was help enough." She changed the subject abruptly. "Something's been puzzling me ever since I visited the Constantas, Lu—would you be offended if I asked you a personal question? I wouldn't ask, but it would help me understand Reo's art."

"Ask away! There's nothing I can't confide in you."

"Are you and Reo part gypsy?"

Luisa put down her brush and smiled at her friend. "I wondered when you'd tumble to that fact. Yes, we are, on our father's side. My grandfather Romano was a full-blooded gypsy and Reo and I are one-fourth. What made you think of that?"

"It was when I did some research on Rumania and gypsies. I knew that 'romano' is an Italian cheese; but it's also close to 'Romany,' which is the Indic language of gypsies. And then you said 'Holy Gana' when you tripped in Julie's playhouse. One of the articles I read said that some gypsies revere Diana, the Moon Goddess, and that she's called 'Gana' in some regions. Since you're generally so conventional, I didn't think anything of it until I remembered the paintings I saw in the Constantas' home. Their colors were so much like Reo's that I began to wonder if he had gypsy blood."

"Conventional? Me? Only on the outside. My family's only loosely Catholic, and I've always been fascinated by the moon goddess. Reo's gypsy blood shows in his art, but mine doesn't—I guess my Italian blood is paramount in that direction. Does it matter?"

"Does it matter that my ancestors were Vikings? If anything, it makes you and Reo more interesting. I'd love to get some gypsy costumes together for disguises—let's make that one of our goals. But," she added cryptically, thinking of Reo, "I do care about some things."

Luisa nodded presciently. "Whatever happens, I'll back you all the way."

When Reo arrived some three hours later, he glanced at Luisa's painting of Pia Jo and said, "Not bad for an amateur"; then he turned his attention to Pia Jo, "I thought you'd be ready to go back to Chicago with me. We've got to get tickets and travelers' checks, and we have to wash clothes before we pack—."

Facing him squarely, Pia Jo said, "I tried to tell you on the phone, Reo, but you wouldn't listen. I'm not going back with you."

"You're not going? Whadda you mean, you're not going? It's all settled—you said you'd pay for our trip to Paris if you won the reward!" Standing by Luisa's portrait of Pia Jo, he turned on her, his handsome face freezing in indignation.

"I didn't say that, Reo—*you* did."

"I did what?"

"*You* said I'd pay for a trip to Paris—*I* didn't promise."

He looked at her in amazement, his temper rising. "Of course you did!" he contradicted. "We talked about it in bed for hours."

"No, *you* talked about it for hours. I just listened. I'm sorry to disappoint you, Reo, but I went through hell to win that money, and I don't plan to spend it on a trip to Paris to check out the Fauves. I'm going to put the money down on Rendezvous of the Four Winds."

"Your mother's place!" he shrilled. "You'd rather buy an old shack near a two-bit town than go to Paris with me? You can't be serious."

"It's not an old shack—it's a good house with a wonderful garden, and I love every one of its sixty acres. My brother Soren wants us to sell it to developers with dollar signs for eyes. They'll turn it into a play park or a strip mall where the winds will never want to rendezvous, and I'd rather die than let that happen. It would be an insult to my mother's memory."

He looked at her coldly. "I knew your mother was trying to turn you against me—!"

Remembering his selfishness when Emeline died, she said sadly, "No, Reo, she didn't turn me against you—you did that all by yourself. You didn't tell me that Gunter called and said that Mom was dying. Your career was more important to you than my being with her during that crucial time. While you were finishing a painting for your exhibit, she died!"

Realizing that he was getting nowhere, he changed his tactics. "Aw, come on, *Amore*. That's all water over the dam—."

She had risen from the chair and was facing him bravely. "I can't love a man who has feelings only for himself, and I've decided to spend the money I earned on something *I want*. You and I are history!"

Angry to the core and totally ignoring her battered condition, he lunged at her and shoved her so violently that she went flying into the stone fireplace; in a second series of furious movements, he ripped up Luisa's portrait of her, swept her painting supplies off the table, and sent everything on the mantel—all her favorite Native American jugs, bowls, and figurines—crashing to the floor, where they lay, a heap of broken images.

"There, you lying bitch! You promise-breaker. Don't ever come back to the apartment—I'm going to burn everything you own." With these harsh words, he glared at his sister, who had rushed to see if Pia Jo had broken any bones, and slammed out of the cabin. They heard him gunning Le Car's little motor all the way to the highway.

"My God, my own brother's a monster! Are you all right?" Luisa asked anxiously as she helped Pia Jo to a comfortable chair.

Pia Jo ached all over, but her heart ached even more. "I'll never trust another man!" she burst out in hopeless fury. "My father was a deserter, and the man I trusted is a sadistic brute."

Luisa wasn't so sure. "Then there's Gunter," she reposted. "And your Uncle Sven. And what about the mysterious man who had a love sonnet carved on your mother's gravestone? He must be capable of a great love."

"Perhaps he is," Pia Jo reflected wistfully. "Perhaps he is."